Prospect Heights Public Library
3 1530 00317 5360
W9-BCQ-951

The Haunting of
SPRINGETT
HALL

E. B. WHEELER

SWEETWATER
BOOKS
an imprint of Cedar Fort, Inc.
Springville, Utah

ISBN 13: 978-1-4621-1672-0

Published by Sweetwater Books, an imprint of Cedar Fort, Inc.
2373 W. 700 S., Springville, UT, 84663
Distributed by Cedar Fort, Inc., www.cedarfort.com

Library of Congress Cataloging-in-Publication Data

Wheeler, E. B., 1978- author.
The haunting of Springett Hall / by E.B. Wheeler.
pages cm
Although eighteen-year-old Lucy does not remember how she died or why she is haunting Springett Hall, she does remember one thing: she was trying to fix a terrible mistake.
ISBN 978-1-4621-1672-0 (perfect : alk. paper)
1. Ghost stories. 2. Historical fiction. [1. Ghosts--Fiction. 2. Household employees--Fiction. 3. Haunted houses--Fiction. 4. Magic--Fiction. 5. Great Britain--History--19th century--Fiction.] I. Title.

PZ7.1.W438Hau 2015
[Fic]--dc23

2015008588

Cover design by Angela R. Decker
Cover design © 2015 by Lyle Mortimer
Edited and typeset by Justin Greer

Printed in the United States of America

10 9 8 7 6 5 4 3 2 1

Printed on acid-free paper

To Dan, who dared me to do it.

Chapter One

Light drew me back from oblivion. The sun's rays pooled around me through a crack in red velvet curtains and spilled across the floor. Shimmering flecks of dust hovered in the air. I waved to stir them. They floated through my palm.

I gasped and jerked my hand back, staring at it. Through it, really. Even when I covered my eyes, I could see the furniture on the other side of the room: a grandfather clock with its hands stopped, a side table and sofa, and a framed painting draped in black.

Someone had died.

I turned my translucent hand back and forth. Yes. Someone had.

My eyes tingled, but no tears came. I raced to the curtains to fling them open. My fingers passed through their thick folds. Trembling, I wrapped my arms around myself and paced. It was a nightmare. I would wake up. Everything looked solid and real, though. Everything except me.

I fled the room. My skirts swayed but didn't rustle, nor did my corset squeeze my ribs. The memory of them clung to me, but I'd moved beyond their pressures.

A housemaid dressed in black for mourning strolled down the wide hallway, dusting delicate side tables. She didn't glance in my direction even when I hurried closer.

"Hello?" my voice rasped out.

The girl shook her dust rag and walked through me.

I didn't feel anything. No pressure, no chill. Just the mental discomfort of having someone much too close. Then she was gone to her next chore.

What had happened to me? I ran shaky fingers over my face, my hair, my bustled dress. No injuries marred my body, but did ghosts remain as they were when they died, or did they return to some earlier state? How was I supposed to know? I straightened slowly. I couldn't even remember my name.

"Help!" I tried to push my faint voice past my isolation. "Can anyone hear me?"

Nothing.

A black smudge stained my right index finger. I rubbed it and turned my hands over to find another mark on my left palm. Not a blotch, but traces of writing, difficult to read on my translucent skin. I squinted at the word: *Limes.*

What on earth did that mean? Was I a cook? At least it was likely just the remnants of ink and not some supernatural warning. If God wanted to send me a message in the afterlife, I was certain He'd have something more important to talk about than citrus.

I traced the phantom word, and a memory of writing it flashed through my mind. I'd been glancing over my shoulder, fingers trembling. The steel nib of the fountain pen had pricked my skin. My fingers twitched at the recollection of pain. I blinked several times and flexed my hand.

The rest of the memory hung just out of reach. There was something I needed to do, some important task left unfinished. That fit my notion of ghosts. Didn't they—*we*—always have a purpose binding us to this world?

Not that it did me much good if I couldn't recall my task. Perhaps I was an incompetent ghost. That word rang in my memory: a sneering male voice chiding, "Silly, incompetent girl." Heavy disappointment settled over me. I had failed.

No, I'd prove him wrong. Whoever *he* was. I'd finish my task. If I was dead, failure wasn't going to be my legacy.

I squeezed my eyes shut. It made no sense that I could see through my hand and not my eyelids, but I was grateful for it.

It might be easier to remember what I was supposed to do if I knew who I was. Who I'd been. Drat. I shook my head. I thought death was supposed to be peaceful, not confusing.

I studied my dress. It was blue silk with a pleated ruffle around the bottom. I touched one of the brass buttons on the bodice. My clothes seemed solid enough under my fingertips, as did the rest of me, but when I turned, my skirt twirled through the side table. The dress was not especially fancy, but too fine for a servant or cook. Had

I been the mistress of this grand house, possibly, or the daughter of its master? It seemed like an easy question to answer. The shrouded painting likely showed the deceased.

I glided back into the room and pinched the black fabric, imagining the cool touch of silk against my skin. My fingers met without catching a fiber. I pursed my lips and tried again. Nothing. Not as easy as I thought, then. I drifted out of the room.

Unsympathetic paintings lined the long hallway. The women in the pictures cradled books or fans or tiny dogs. Drapes of pearls, lace, and intricate beading enriched their gowns. Even the lady in the freshest portrait, with her tiny waist, blonde curls, and huge bell-shaped skirt, looked dreadfully old-fashioned compared to me. My straight, dark hair and unadorned dress didn't belong in this distinguished company.

I didn't know who I was, but I was learning who I wasn't.

If I wasn't a member of the family, then the servants weren't in mourning for me. Someone else had died. Perhaps I wasn't the only ghost. I quickened my pace.

My hand slid through the first doorknob I grabbed. The solution was obvious, but I hated it. With a sigh, I stuck my head through the door. The rooms along the corridor were like the one where I woke: neat, silent, and in need of dusting.

Then I came to the library near the end of the hall. When I stepped through the door, peace enveloped me in imagined warmth and my worries slipped behind me: the feeling of returning home.

Glass boxes displayed scientific collections, and colorful maps decorated the walls, their edges swimming with sea serpents and mythical beasts. Books in many languages filled the oak shelves, grouped roughly by topic. I gave a start. I understood the titles: German, French, even a little Latin and Greek. How many young ladies read Latin and Greek? Certainly not silly, incompetent ones.

I bit my fingernail and frowned. My frown deepened to a scowl as I studied my ugly-looking fingers. My skin was smooth, but the nails were ragged and chewed down. It seemed I had some bad habits. I turned my attention back to the books.

They covered every topic I could imagine and some that seemed preposterous. An entire bookcase at one end of the room was devoted to alchemy and magic, many of the titles in Greek, difficult for me to decipher. I shuddered and glided back to the novels, itching to get lost in one. Daylight slipped past as I perused the shelves and studied the displays.

A rustle whispered through the room, like a breeze brushing past dry leaves. I blinked and looked around. The sound came again, though nothing stirred in the stillness.

"Hello?" I asked faintly.

An answer rasped through the library like the last breath of a dying man. The voice was too faint to hear clearly, but one word resonated in the room and pierced my mind with cold determination.

Return.

I whirled, looking for the source of the otherworldly message, but I was alone. Or perhaps not. My back crawled with the feeling of being watched.

"Return?" I called. "Where? What am I supposed to be doing?"

Echoes of despair stirred in my chest, bringing vague memories of the cold oblivion I'd just escaped. Wherever I'd come from, I didn't think it was heaven, and I didn't want to go back. Hovering on the edge of the living world, at least there was light and hope.

A sigh rippled through the library, followed by an oppressive, watchful silence.

"Well, that wasn't at all helpful," I muttered.

The lingering force of the voice's command tugged at me. I took a step against my will. Toward what, I couldn't guess. It might be easier to obey than to stumble along blindly on my own.

The haughtiness of the voice reminded me of the man who had called me incompetent. It roused fear and anger beneath the surface of my hidden memories. Whatever I might be, I was no one's puppet. I grasped that conviction and forced myself to be still, my legs trembling against the need to obey.

The distant whinnying of horses and rattle of carriage wheels pierced the quiet. The pressure on me dissipated, but my hands still shook. Was something pursuing me, even beyond the grave? I shuddered and drifted to a window, scowling at the heavy curtains before sticking my head past them.

A coach stood far below in the curved drive of the house, black crêpe hiding the coat of arms on its side. From my vantage, I could see little of the men crowded around except their hats. Two silk top hats stood out from the workers' caps. They all moved together and apart like dancers at a country ball as the men unloaded the carriage.

I gathered my skirts out of habit and rushed to the sweeping staircase at the end of the corridor, gliding down two flights to the entrance hall below. Servants scurried through the house in a bustle of efficiency, carrying trunks upstairs and sweeping the white cloths from furniture. I shied from their paths, avoiding further proof that I had all the substance of starlight.

The front doors stood open. I stumbled to a halt and stared out at the sunshine. If I stepped beyond the limits of the house, would the tendrils of supernatural power binding me to the earth whisk me back inside? Might I disappear forever? I shrank from the door. It wasn't death that was frightening, but the looming specter of oblivion. That was all I could see beyond the doorway.

I scuttled back into the tiled entrance hall where a butler oversaw the servants' activity. His long, wrinkled face triggered no recognition in me. Either he and the gentlemen arriving were new occupants, or I possessed no memories of the people who inhabited this place.

I fidgeted with the dark locks hanging loose around my shoulders. That seemed wrong. All the other women wore their hair pinned up. What was different about me? Perhaps I'd been insane. I straightened. That sounded familiar. Insane, locked in an attic by a disgusted husband, and then the house had burned around me. A hazy image of thick black smoke and crackling bursts of flame made me cringe.

This house hadn't burned, though. What was I remembering? A story, *Jane Eyre*. I'd read it so many times, it lived in my imagination, as vivid as real events. I grinned. My memories were still there, waiting to be unlocked. I bit my fingernail, watching every person who passed for some glimmer of familiarity.

A pair of gentlemen sauntered into the hall. They had a fraternal resemblance, both young, elegantly dressed, and fair-haired, but the similarity ended there. The shorter man had a flat face, like a bulldog, with neatly trimmed hair and mustache. The tall one had long, wild hair framing a face made exceptional by his blue eyes and long eyelashes.

Both men wore suits of black bombazine for mourning, though elaborate black stitching enlivened the taller one's waistcoat. They had to be close relatives of the deceased. The *other* deceased.

The bulldog-faced man clasped his hands behind his back, frowning at a white marble statue of a man wrestling a strangling serpent. The handsome dandy stared, open-mouthed, at the grand entrance hall, with its cut-glass chandelier and mahogany staircase.

"Baronet Springett," the butler said, his slow words drooping like his wrinkles.

The dandy jumped and glanced over his shoulder. The bulldog-faced man gave him a reproachful look.

"Yes, George." The dandy laughed nervously. "You had me thinking there was a ghost about." I stepped forward, but he went on: "What is it?"

"We've readied the late baronet's chambers for you, sir."

The late baronet. That explained the mourning household.

"Oh." The new baronet swallowed and looked at his short companion. "That will be fine. Of course. Uh, John will require a room as well. He'll be staying on, um…"

"As long as you need me, Edmund," John said. "Mother asked me to put my studies on hold until you've adjusted to your new circumstances."

"Of course, of course. Thank you. As always, I'll rely on your steady head to guide us through this period of tragedy. Good old John."

John's frown deepened, and his chest rose in a quiet sigh. He was probably relied upon often, good old John.

"Very well," the butler said. "If you will follow me?"

Sir Edmund and John made their way up the first flight of stairs.

I drifted behind, hoping to learn more about the late baronet. Had he been fond of limes? From the landing, the house branched into an L, the short leg facing north and the longer one west. The men strolled down the north hallway and through an antechamber into a lofty bedroom. I peeked in after them.

An enormous four-poster bed with embroidered curtains dominated the room. A single needlework tree filled the entire panel at the foot of the bed. Its branches curled and twisted to cover the wide space, with red fruit stitched so realistically I imagined plucking it from the picture. As Sir Edmund inspected his closet, I drew nearer to the garden scenes decorating the cream-colored bed-curtains.

My fingers slipped through the neat, smooth threads on the underside of a bluebird's open wings. I lowered my hand and leaned in to study the embroidery. It must have been the work of a lifetime. My gaze flicked further through the scene, and I gasped and turned away in embarrassed understanding. It was the Garden of Eden, and of course Adam and Eve belonged there, but fig leaves were hardly my idea of proper attire.

Sir Edmund and John stood beside the bed, showing no reaction to Adam and Eve's innocent state. I backed toward the doorway. Even dead, it would be shocking for me to linger in a man's bedchamber. Still, I was too curious to stop eavesdropping.

"Bed curtains are unhealthy," John said. "You should take them down."

"Perhaps." Sir Edmund trailed his fingers over the stitches of the velvety red roses, and I ached to do the same. "They're beautiful, though. A work of art. If I do remove them, I'll have to hang them on display."

Now John looked at Adam and Eve and gave a short, barking laugh. "Not where Miss Ridgewell can see them."

Sir Edmund sniffed. "She appreciates art."

John bared his teeth in a grin. "I'm sure she'll learn to appreciate just about anything when she sees Springett Hall."

"John! Miss Ridgewell and I have been fond of each other for years. I'm certain the idea of my inheriting Uncle's estate never occurred to her. He wasn't that old, anyway. I assumed he'd remarry someday."

"This was always a possibility," John mumbled, though Sir Edmund seemed not to hear.

"Well," said Sir Edmund, circling the rug covering the spacious wood floor. "Is it right for me to take this room?"

"Of course. It's your estate now."

"It was Uncle's, though. Didn't he used to frighten you?"

"When I was quite small, possibly. Really, Edmund, what are you afraid of?"

Sir Edmund shrugged and paced past me into the antechamber. "Father should be here instead of me." His gaze turned distant. "It's almost poetic that two men who hated each other so much would pass on within weeks of each other. Maybe he and Uncle are at peace now."

He stopped in front of a portrait and pulled down its black veil. I drifted to his side, mesmerized by the figures in the painting. The man shared Sir Edmund and John's fair hair, but his expression was all hard lines, his mouth a thin dash across his face, and his nose as sharp as chiseled wood. Even his eyes seemed to cut through the painting to stare into the room.

The woman seated by his side was the same one I'd seen in the portrait hall with the elegant, bell-shaped dress. The harsh-looking man redeemed himself, and the whole picture, by the way he touched her shoulder, his gentleness conveyed across the years by the skill of the painter's brush.

"I'd forgotten how beautiful Aunt Henrietta was," Sir Edmund mumbled. "What a tragedy. She might have saved him."

"You sound as if he were a terrible sinner," John said.

Sir Edmund waved grandly at the painting. "Well, I'll have to move it. I can't work with him staring at me."

John rolled his eyes. Sir Edmund ambled across the room and whisked the cover from one of the mirrors. The light glinting off its surface caught my eye. I tiptoed to stand behind Sir Edmund, then peered around him at the silvery image.

The mirror showed only Sir Edmund. I stumbled forward, heedless of passing through the new baronet, and tried to touch the surface of the looking glass, my hand trembling. A sob caught in my throat. I was really gone. Even if I did remember who I was and finish my forgotten task, I might be trapped like this, alone, forever.

"Do you feel a chill?" Sir Edmund whispered, glancing around.

"It's probably just a draft," John said.

Dusk dimmed the room. A vibration rang through me. I turned and caught the eye of the late baronet in his portrait. His glare pierced me from the canvas. Terror crept down my limbs, fixing me in place. Did his spirit linger too, stalking these halls? That was not the company I wanted.

The walls quivered, and the painting of the sharp-faced man and his lady crashed to the floor. I stumbled back. This was not my doing, I was fairly certain.

Sir Edmund rushed to the fallen image.

Hazy darkness seeped from the floor. I screamed. The men didn't hear, didn't see. I tried to flee, but my feet wouldn't obey. Black mist swirled around me, dragging me into the dark.

Chapter Two

Sunlight cast shadows over the floor, but they slept at my feet. I stood in the room with the shrouded painting and silent clock, possessing no memories of the night. I bit my fingernail. Perhaps my existence stuttered to a stop when the darkness took me, like a flame flickering in a draft.

No, I wouldn't let oblivion claim me. I was here for a reason. Something must have drawn me back to the room. Maybe it was where I died. A worn rug sprawled over the hardwood floor. No stains hinted at a bloody murder. Of course, I might have died less violently: choked on something or had a terrible fright. I wrinkled my nose. Those were silly ways to die.

Might I have been ill? Limes were used to treat scurvy, but I was no sailor. I wasn't so thin to make me believe I'd wasted away, and I couldn't see my reflection to know if I had horrible dark circles under my eyes or pale skin. Wouldn't I be pale anyway? Did ghosts ever look healthy?

I paced, brushing past the sofa. A vision struck me like a physical blow: agony cracking through my bones, my throat raw from screaming, a dark figure closing in on me as I huddled by the sofa. A torrent of fear rushed through the memory—terror at the pain, but even more at the realization of failure.

I gasped and staggered back. The vision faded, but its truth hummed through me. I scrambled for the safety of the corridor, where I rocked back and forth, my hands over my face.

"I can't do this," I whispered.

There was no other option, though, if I didn't want to spend eternity alone in the empty darkness, or cease to exist altogether. That dreadful glimpse of the past might help me fight my extinction. I forced myself to pick through the memory.

Someone had been chasing me. Male. I couldn't actually see

him, but I knew he wasn't far behind. Had he killed me?

The sense of defeat lingered. This was my forgotten task. I still didn't know what it was, but I'd glimpsed the moment of my failure.

No matter how many times I forced myself to relive the scene, I couldn't see anything more. I groaned. I had to keep exploring, finding places that stirred my memories, however terrible.

Recalling *Jane Eyre*, I wondered if the attic might hold any secrets, but I saw no way to reach it. The room where I awakened was on the top floor, an area reserved for less important guests, or perhaps a governess. I crept down the corridor to the library.

The door stood ajar. I peered in.

The library was truly enormous, stretching back across the shorter northern wing of the L-shaped house, above the family's bedrooms. It was in a dreadfully inconvenient location, though, up all those stairs.

John Springett lounged at one of the desks, smoking a pipe. In my library! Stinking the place up with his foul smoke. Actually, I couldn't smell anything, but it was bad for the books.

John bent his blond head over a stack of ledgers. I strode over and swept my hands across the desk. They passed through the books and papers without so much as a rustle. I yelled in John's face, swung at his pipe, and slammed my fists through the desk. He rubbed his nose and yawned. What a useless ghost I was.

He cleared his throat and turned a page, comparing it to something in one of the other books. Then he snorted and sat back, putting his pipe down to rub his eyes. "This makes no sense."

"What doesn't?" I glanced over the ledgers. The numbers meant nothing to me.

He leaned forward, his head passing into mine. I recoiled. He ran his finger along a word. "What the devil is that?"

I squinted at the spidery, masculine handwriting cramping the page. "It says 'tallow.' It seems clear enough to me. I don't know why you find it such an odd expense. Baronets need soap and candles too, after all."

John still scowled at the ledgers. I looked objectively at the messy handwriting. Only someone with a great deal of practice would be able to make sense of it. It was clear the late baronet and I weren't strangers, then. I wasn't his servant. I wasn't his wife. The idea of being his mistress was too repulsive to be true. What had I been doing at Springett Hall?

I wrinkled my nose at John's pipe and retreated from the desk. Curious about my incorporeal abilities, I returned to the corridor by pushing through the wall. It was stuffy and uncomfortable, with the darkness pressing around me, so I decided not to try it again. I drifted down the curving main staircase to the landing below.

Sir Edmund came up the stairs, whistling to himself. I froze, but he walked past without a glance at me. I considered following him, but he continued down the north corridor toward his chambers. Nothing had triggered any memories the last time I'd been there, and I was not anxious to encounter the sharp gaze of the late baronet in his portrait again, so I turned to the west wing.

It housed a long gallery filled with art: a place for the family of the house to walk and amuse themselves on rainy days. Some of the lightly clad sculptures made me look away, but I admired the tasteful paintings of landscapes and portraits of past baronets. With such a long history, it wouldn't be surprising if the house had other ghosts. I tried to imagine meeting some of those stern faces and fancied they were looking down on me as an interloper.

Something clicked behind me, and I jumped. The wood-paneled wall at the back of the long gallery opened to reveal a dim staircase that allowed servants to move about unseen. A pair of footmen walked through, their even steps echoing off the high ceiling.

"This place is filthy," one said, running a white-gloved finger over a statue of Pandora opening her fateful box. "Were the old baronet's maids that lazy?"

"He was eccentric, from what I hear. Died alone in this place, deserted by all his servants."

"What a sorrowful way to go."

They continued past me toward the family's chambers. If the old baronet had died alone, where did I fit in? The memory of an ache tightened in my chest. Was there anyone out there missing me, looking for me?

I hurried down the curving stairs to the entrance hall with its glass chandelier. The double doors, centered in the short leg of the L, were open for the servants bringing in more of their master's belongings. I forced myself to peek out. The house faced into the morning sun and looked over an oval-shaped lake that was too symmetrical to be natural. I strained to see farther, but something deep in my core pulled me back. I retreated from the doors.

Directly opposite them was a grand salon with hardwood floors for dancing. I closed my eyes and imagined violins playing and people twirling around the floor in gowns and black suits. With a few tentative steps, I joined them. I knew how to waltz. I couldn't remember doing it, though.

I sighed and left the grand salon. To the north of the entrance hall was a vast room lined with bookcases. A few cases displayed dusty knickknacks, but most were empty. From the look of the place, it had once been the library. It would be lovely to curl up with a book by one of its huge windows. With the bright sunlight streaming through the glass, I could almost imagine being warm. Why would anyone abandon this library for the space two floors above? I drifted the length of the room, but nothing about it looked familiar.

I wandered back through the entrance hall, past the grand salon and the main stairs. A corridor led to a drawing room with a piano, then took a sharp turn to the right, into the west wing. Doors opened to other spaces for entertaining: a morning room, a small sitting room decorated almost entirely in blue, a dining room, and a billiards room. Servants laughed and gossiped as they aired the chambers and shuffled furniture.

The house had awakened with the arrival of its new master. That may have woken me as well and set me about my unfinished task. Perhaps I was supposed to protect everyone in the house from the figure in my vision. I paused and fidgeted with my hair. I'd already failed once at my task. Could all these people be in danger because of me?

" 'Ave you seen the ghost, then?" asked one of the housemaids, a broad girl with mousy brown hair crammed under her cap.

I gave a start and stepped closer, longing to see her gaze on me. But she spoke to another maid, a blonde with permanent dimples. Feeling more insubstantial than ever, I drifted behind them.

"No, but I 'eard murmurin' and thumpin' on the walls, like someone tryin' to break through," said the dimpled girl in a quiet voice.

I bit my fingernail. I couldn't recall pounding on the walls, but who knew what happened when I faded?

"Oy, Susan, that could 'ave been somethin' else." The broad girl gave a dismissive wave. "It's not a ghost every time you 'ear strange noises in an old 'ouse."

"Maybe not, Nellie, but Mr. Parker said 'e 'eard a wailin' out in the woods, like the lament of some cursed soul."

Nellie put her hands on her wide hips. "If it's out in the woods, then it's them what's 'aunted, not the 'ouse. I won't believe in somethin' unless I see it for myself."

"I 'ope I never see it," Susan said, her eyes wide and her voice a little too loud, as if addressing the shadows in the corner. "I believe right enough as it is. I've been 'earin' strange stories about the old master of this place. People say 'e sold 'is soul to the devil, tryin' to bring back 'is wife what died. They say the whole place is cursed."

"If you believe that, why don't you find a position somewhere else? What a bunch of nonsense."

I fell behind. Was all this possible, about curses and the devil? The late baronet could have worked some dark magic over me. On the other hand, I might have done something wicked, and this was my punishment. Drat. What a mess to untangle, like a jumble of knitting yarns.

I hurried to catch the maids as they entered the servants' area at the end of the west wing. We crossed into the kitchen. The shelves and tables were free of limes. Not certain if I was relieved or disappointed, I ventured forward. Some of the servants gathered around a long wooden table, laughing and talking as they dipped thick slices of bread into steaming soup. No familiar faces turned my way, no savory scents made my mouth water, but I longed to join them. It was like being trapped outside, watching a feast through a window.

One of the servants, a young man with dark bushy hair and a slightly crooked nose, sat apart from the others. Instead of the black suit of a footman or page, he wore a tailored brown coat and slacks. Traces of mud clung to his boots. He looked too well-dressed for a stablehand, but I couldn't guess what else he might be. I didn't know if stablehands even ate with the other servants.

The dark-haired young man scowled at his soup as he picked through it. I walked closer.

"What's wrong with you?" I asked. "Do you know how lucky you are to be able to eat anything at all? To taste and feel and smell?"

His dark eyebrows drew together, and he raised a spoonful of soup. "I don't think they gave us even a little meat. This is just broth and a few soggy vegetables."

My eyes widened. "Did you hear me? Were you talking to me?"

He glanced up, but his gaze swept through me. Watching his face for any flicker of acknowledgment, I didn't notice the maid until she stopped halfway through me. I scrambled away.

"'Ello, Mr. Ketley," the girl said.

"Good evening, Miss . . . Matthews, isn't it?" The dark-haired young man gave her a bright grin that would have made my heart flutter, if I still had one. "You're looking well today."

She blushed and giggled, scurrying off to sit with her friends. Mr. Ketley smiled and raised his glass to them before turning back to poke at his supper.

I drew back. Of course he couldn't see me; he'd just been mumbling aloud, like John. Still, his gestures—his smile—struck a chord of familiarity for the first time. It seemed too much to hope that I'd known him, but maybe he reminded me of someone. I hovered near, enjoying the imaginary companionship.

Susan plied her dimpled smiles on a footman—probably her Mr. Parker—who gave her a condescending smirk. She picked up the teapot to refill his cup but got distracted when he turned to talk to a pretty brunette parlor maid.

"Watch out!" I jumped forward, but Susan dumped the steaming tea over Mr. Parker's hand.

He shouted and scrambled back, glaring as he put the burned fingers in his mouth. Susan gasped, and a few other girls snickered.

"Leave her alone!" I said, standing between the red-faced maid and the others.

"Stupid wench!" Mr. Parker wiped his hand dry, glaring at Susan.

"Watch your tongue!" snapped Mr. Ketley.

"Watch your own." Mr. Parker sneered, turning toward him. "You think because you've been here longer than the rest of us, you own the place?"

I gave a start. If he wasn't new like the others, then perhaps I *had* known him.

"No, I'll leave that to Baronet Fop," he said.

I scowled at his tone. Sir Edmund might be a dandy, but he deserved deference from his employees. I was a dreadful protector, though, not even able to speak in his defense.

Mr. Parker folded his arms. "You ought to talk of our master with respect."

"When he earns it, I will."

"People shouldn't eat with their betters until they're ready to act civilized." Mr. Parker settled back on his chair and shook out his tea-stained napkin.

"I agree." Mr. Ketley smiled. "I'm afraid that means you won't be dining in the presence of these ladies for quite some time."

The girls giggled, and he winked at them. I rolled my eyes but wondered at Mr. Ketley. His accent had rough edges, but his language showed the polish of education.

"I'm going to teach you some manners." Mr. Parker tossed his napkin on the table and pushed back his chair.

Mr. Ketley stood, towering almost a head above the footman. Mr. Parker paled, but after a glance at the girls, he set his jaw.

"Well?" Mr. Ketley raised an eyebrow. "How shall we settle this? We could box, Marquess of Queensbury rules."

Mr. Parker sat and braced his elbow on the table.

"Arm wrestling?" Mr. Ketley laughed and took the place opposite, grasping the footman's hand. One of the other footmen counted off, and Mr. Parker tensed. Mr. Ketley slammed his arm to the table.

I laughed along with the other girls as Mr. Parker slunk back to his supper. When they settled down to their meals, loneliness pushed me back to wandering the corridors. I had no place among the living, and I wasn't certain I wanted anything to do with the dead.

The sun sank behind the estate's gardens, its golden rays glancing off the rippling lake in front of the house. I hadn't lasted long past sunset the previous evening, but ghosts belonged to the night. I might be stronger after dusk, if I managed not to disappear. Darkness embraced the house, and faint ribbons of moonlight shone through the lacy curtains.

I turned away, coming face to face with another woman.

She stared at me. Moonlight fell through her airy form. I screamed. She covered her mouth and shrank back. Not the actions I expected from a hostile spirit. I collected myself and smiled, trying not to scare the poor woman again.

"Hello," I said.

Eyes wide, she backed away.

"I didn't mean to startle you."

She hunched her shoulders and retreated another step, avoiding my gaze.

I swallowed and glanced around. "What are you frightened of?"

The woman winced and pointed at me.

I almost laughed, but the terror in her eyes sobered me. "I'm not going to hurt you. We can help each other."

She shook her head violently and mouthed something.

"I can't hear you. Can you speak louder?"

Her lips moved silently.

"I still don't understand." She looked more faded than I, but perhaps she'd been dead longer. Her dress was soft-shouldered and wide-skirted, and neat blonde curls fell from beneath her bonnet. I gasped. "You're Aunt Henrietta . . . er, Lady Springett. The late baronet's wife!" What was the proper etiquette for addressing the deceased spouse of a recently departed baronet?

Her eyes widened, and she mouthed, *Late?*

"You didn't know?"

She shook her head and shuddered, looking over her shoulder.

"Is something chasing you?"

Covering her face, she fled.

"Wait! Please! I just want to understand."

I pursued her up the stairs, but she vanished outside the library. The gaslights flickered, and the library door banged open. When I ventured closer, the rest of the doors along the hall creaked ajar. I pivoted, looking for anyone, living or dead.

"Lady Henrietta?" I asked.

The doors slammed shut with an echoing boom. Shadows bled from the walls. I gasped and whirled away, but my movement jerked to a stop. A cold laugh echoed from a great distance, and darkness rushed over me.

Chapter Three

Daylight. The hands on the grandfather clock stood frozen at twelve. The pendulum hung quiet in its casing. No breath of air stirred the black silk over the portrait. Not again! I needed an anchor to keep the dark tides from washing me into the abyss.

I rushed from the silent room with its reminders of death and glided down to the bedrooms on the second floor—the only part of the house I hadn't explored thoroughly.

Sir Edmund sat at the desk in his antechamber, staring at the ceiling, his mouth moving silently. Finally, he bent his head and scribbled a few lines, smiled, and gazed up again. I cast a wary glance at the portrait of the late baronet and Lady Henrietta before tiptoe-ing to peek over Sir Edmund's shoulder. His paper read:

Oh, gentle flower of lovely hue
blooming in the morning dew

Not terrible, but nothing like Blake or Tennyson. I smiled at this new bit of knowledge. It wasn't just that they were great poets. An image flashed in my mind of sitting under a tree, the sun heating my dress as I pored over a well-worn book of poems. The memory of warmth and peace settled through me, giving me a flicker of hope. I could still find myself, and the pieces weren't all frightening.

I may have been a poet myself. That would explain the ink stains on my finger. Maybe I'd written "limes" because it would complete a composition. What went with limes? Times. Crimes. Rhymes. All silly. Certainly nothing to inspire the fear I remembered.

Sir Edmund's eyes kept their distant look, and he wrote nothing else. Uneasy under the stare of his uncle, I drifted out of the room and wandered downstairs. The housemaids, Susan and Nellie, pol-ished the long table in the dining room.

" 'Ow could you sleep?" Susan asked. "Didn't you 'ear the voice?"

"I grew up sharin' a room with three sisters," Nellie said. "There's nothin' what can wake me. Did anyone else 'ear it?"

"No." Susan's lip trembled, and she flicked her rag over the gleaming wood. "Everyone says it was just a nightmare."

Nellie shrugged, but her expression was sympathetic. "You'll 'ave to finish up in 'ere. I'd better get to cleanin' out the fireplaces in the empty rooms. That old baronet, 'is staff left things a mess."

"I 'eard they all left on account of the ghosts," Susan whispered.

Nellie rolled her eyes and hefted her buckets to lumber out of the room.

"I believe you," I told Susan, but the dimpled maid was lost in scraping a disk of wax off the table. "Don't listen to the voice. I'm going to find a way to protect everyone."

Susan finished the table and wandered to a wide mirror hanging on the wall. She rubbed at a dark spot clouding the surface. The spot spread like spilled ink, blotting more of the reflection. Susan pursed her lips and glanced at the white cloth in her hand.

The inky spot pulsed like a heartbeat. Thick darkness covered more of the mirror with each throb.

"Get back!" I reached for Susan's arm.

Dark fog roiled beneath the surface of the mirror. A deep laugh echoed off the high ceiling.

Susan screamed.

The mirror exploded, blasting shards of glass over the room. Susan clutched her cheek, blood seeping between her fingers. With a sob, she raced from the room. I glared at the broken mirror and ran after her.

Incompetent. I had failed before, I was failing again, and innocent victims would pay.

I darted back upstairs and stumbled to a stop. Mr. Ketley ambled around the long gallery, looking down his crooked nose at the lords and ladies in the portraits. Dried mud still clung to his boots. I clenched my teeth. Haunted mirrors, pipe smoke in the library, dirt on the oriental carpets. Whatever the problem, I was helpless to do anything.

"What on earth are you doing wandering in the house?" I stormed up to Mr. Ketley. "Shouldn't stablehands keep their dirty boots outside?"

His gaze focused on me, and he raised an eyebrow. "I'm not a stablehand. I'm the assistant gamekeeper. What gives you the right to be so rude?"

I gaped at him.

"Is something wrong? You seemed capable of speech a moment ago." He folded his arms. "Maybe I was too brusque, but you ought to expect it when you talk to people like that."

"Y-you can see me?" Hope shimmered around me, as bright and insubstantial as moonbeams.

"Of course," he said. Then his expression softened. "Oh, maybe you're . . . not well? Should you be lying down somewhere?"

He reached for my arm. I jerked away, afraid the spell would break when his hand passed through me.

"Uh." He rubbed his chin. "Look, I really am sorry. Do you need some kind of help?"

"Yes, please!" I clasped my hands. "I can't touch anything, but you can! We could find clues—"

"Oooh. Clues." His face wore the forced politeness some people assumed when talking to small children. "You're trying to solve a mystery."

I managed not to roll my eyes. I couldn't offend the only living person able to hear me. "Listen carefully, in case I fade again. I'm a ghost. I think there's something I'm supposed to do, but I don't remember it, except something about limes."

"What's that supposed to mean?" He shook his head. "I don't have time for this."

"Wait!" I reached for him, my hope scattering. "I can prove it." I swung my arm into the portrait-lined wall. The plaster slowed my momentum as if I were pushing through water.

He gasped and stumbled back, bumping into a pillared bust of Shakespeare. The display rocked precariously, and he flung his arms around the great bard's shoulders.

"Do you believe me now?" I asked, withdrawing my hand from a painting of a dour-faced man in armor.

I wasn't certain if Mr. Ketley was supporting Shakespeare or vice versa. The assistant gamekeeper's face was as white as the statue's, but the bard wasn't staring, open-mouthed, with his eyes bulging. Finally, Mr. Ketley blinked rapidly and righted the display.

"All right, Philip," he mumbled. "Insanity can be temporary. A good night's sleep will set everything right."

"It also might help if you didn't talk to yourself," I said.

"I think talking to myself is the least of my problems." He glowered and rubbed his face. "I don't suppose you could just disappear? I'd really appreciate it, especially after the week I'm having."

"Sorry, I can't. I'm not very good at being a ghost." I was getting used to the idea, though. Hopefully it wouldn't be difficult for him to do the same. "How can I show you I'm real? Unless you want me to keep haunting you until you're ready to listen?"

He groaned. "All right, I'll play along. Umm, you'd have to tell me something I couldn't possibly know myself."

That was fair. Philip tapped his foot as I paced the gallery, searching for inspiration. I peered down the corridor leading to the bedrooms. Nellie strolled toward us with a dustbin of ashes. Perfect!

"A housemaid's about to come around this corner. Her name's Nellie, and she doesn't believe in ghosts either." I glanced at his boots. "Also, she's going to get angry at you."

Philip cocked an eyebrow. "That's very specific. Nellie?"

"It's Miss Brown to you, Mr. Ketley," she said rounding the turn.

He jumped, and I wondered if Shakespeare was in danger again, but Philip caught himself. I laughed, and his gaze darted between the maid and me.

"What's a matter with you?" Nellie asked. "Spooked about ghosts like everyone else in this 'ouse?"

"Uh . . ."

I gave him a little wave and passed my hand through the maid's shoulder. He paled.

Nellie shook her head , stopping when she noticed the carpet. "We just cleaned those! Who's got 'em all muddy?" She glared at Philip.

"I'd best let you get back to work, Miss Brown." Philip hurried back to the servants' staircase. I was laughing so hard I could hardly keep up.

"You're a ghost?" he asked after shutting the door behind us.

"I am. Can't you see through me?"

"No. You look normal. There's a bit of a glow about you, but I thought it was just the light."

I turned my hands over. *I* could still see through them, and I didn't notice any glow. "This makes no sense."

"What would happen if I touched you?"

I shrugged and held out my hand. If I had breath, I would've held it. His fingers passed through mine.

"Did you feel anything?" I asked.

"Nothing at all." He stared at his hand and wiggled his fingers. "Am I the only one who can see you?"

"As far as I can tell. Yesterday, in the kitchen, I asked you about your soup, and you just looked through me."

"In the kitchen? I thought I heard something . . ." He folded his arms. "Are you saying you've been watching me?"

"What? No!" The memory of a blush tingled over my cheeks. "I was trying to figure out what happened to me."

He scuffed his boot on the carpet. "Do you think it has something to do with me, and that's why I can see you?"

"I *did* think you looked familiar. Do you recognize me?"

"No, but that's the problem. Two days ago I woke up in the woods, and I couldn't remember who I was or what I was doing there."

A shiver raced across my shoulders. "It was two mornings ago when I woke up too. How did you remember who you were?"

"I still don't remember much. I have a lump on my head, like I knocked it against something pretty hard. The new gamekeeper found me wandering around and questioned me. Answers kept jumping into my head—things about the estate, anyway. He assumed I worked for the former gamekeeper, and I decided it was as good an answer as any." He smiled, but his voice was tight.

I studied him. Something dark had happened in this house, and he was likely involved. "You don't know for certain?"

"No." His shoulders slumped. "I was in here looking at the portraits, hoping they'd trigger some recollection. I've been worrying that my memories are gone for good, or that I've lost my mind."

"At least you're still alive!" I rubbed my forehead. "Sorry. It's just...I think something's stalking me, trying to control me. I vanish sometimes, and I always reappear in the same room. I don't understand why or what I'm supposed to be doing."

"Could it be where you . . ." He turned his hands up in a helpless gesture. "You know?"

"Died?" I sighed. "I'm not certain, but something dreadful happened there. I remember being in pain, knowing I'd failed at something important and someone was chasing me."

He pressed his lips together. "All right, I'll help you. As best I can remember, I'm Philip Ketley." He bowed, and a trace of humor brightened his blue eyes. "Since there's no one to make a proper introduction, may I take the liberty of asking your name?"

"Lucy Tregarrick," I said, and as soon as my mouth formed the words, I knew it was true, a habit ingrained from an early age. "I remember my name! It feels so . . ." I grinned. All it took was someone asking to restore a huge part of me, a weapon I could wield against the darkness.

"I know." Philip's smile matched mine. "It was the same for me. Shall we see what else we can find out?"

"Yes, please!"

I directed him up the narrow servants' staircase and toward my room. On the way, I showed him the word written on my hand and told him about Lady Henrietta and the darkness in the mirror. He listened with a deep frown. We reached the room, and he stood in the doorway, scanning the furniture.

"What sort of room is this?" Philip asked.

"A sitting room, I suppose."

"Not very convenient way up here." He tugged his tailored coat closer. "It's drafty too."

"Does it look familiar?" I asked.

"Just a moment."

He closed his eyes and stepped into the room. Blindly turning his head from side to side, he paced past the clock, the shrouded painting, the sofa, and the side table with its paraffin lamp. I watched the performance with a sinking concern that his mind might be even less intact than my own. He crossed in front of the window and wandered to the empty wall on the left-hand side of the room. There he stopped, opening his eyes to stare at the wood panels.

A rat scurried along the floorboard in front of him. I yelped, and he jumped and swung his foot at the fat creature as it fled the room.

"Doesn't this house have a cat?" Philip wrinkled his nose.

I cleared my throat and gestured at the wall. "What was that all about?"

He blushed faintly and tousled his dark hair into a disarming mess. "I've found, sometimes, that my feet know things my mind doesn't. When the gamekeeper asks me where something is, if I try to remember, I come up blank, but if I just start walking, I find it."

"And this room?"

"Looks like any other to me, but I thought I'd see if my feet remembered something. I guess not. I still haven't given up the notion that I may be insane." He gave me a boyish grin, and I couldn't help smiling back.

"Maybe there used to be something there." I studied the wall. "No, the wood isn't faded."

"The rug isn't indented or wrinkled, either. There's still more to investigate, though." He strode over to the veiled portrait. "Shall I uncover it?"

"Yes." I stepped back, clutching my hands. If this room had something to do with me, I might see my face beneath that cloth.

He swished the black silk aside. I shrank away, chills racing over my intangible skin. Philip backed up too, his eyes wide.

"The late baronet," I said.

"Sir Jason," Philip replied, his teeth clenched.

I nodded at the familiar name. The painting showed a man much altered from the portrait in Sir Edmund's room. Jason Springett was alone now, the sharp lines of his face cold and hard. Gray touched his hair in places, but few wrinkles marred his skin. His eyes penetrated me, and I felt the cruelty and mockery of his gaze. Philip leapt forward and threw the shroud back over the image, his teeth bared.

"We knew him," I said.

"I hate him." Philip glared at the draped portrait. "If he weren't dead I would kill him myself."

Chapter Four

I backed away from Philip's dark expression. Maybe I'd been too quick to trust him. Of course, it wasn't as if he could hurt me now.

"Blast it!" He wiped his hands on his brown coat. "You don't think I *did* kill him, do you?"

I doubted a murderer would look as horrified as Philip did by the idea. "I haven't heard anyone mention how he died. I think if it had been violent there would be rumors." I cleared my throat. "Do *you* think you killed him?"

He rubbed his face. "No, I guess not. I think I hate him because I'm afraid of him. Even knowing he's dead, I felt sure he was going to hurt me as soon as I saw his eyes."

"I know." I met his gaze. "What do you think he did to us?"

"I can't even guess. Someone that wealthy and powerful, there are too many options." He tugged at his cravat and paced between the window and the sofa. "Could he have been the one chasing you?"

"I didn't see, but it would make sense." I shuddered. "I wonder if he's still trying to stop me."

"You said something's stalking you?"

"Darkness and shadows, and there's a voice."

"A voice?"

"I've heard it laughing. Once, it said 'return,' and I had to fight to keep from following."

"Where?"

"I don't know." I cocked an eyebrow. "It didn't seem wise to obey. But you know what you were saying about your feet knowing things? The library was like that for me. I could read the titles of most of the books, even the foreign ones. And the handwriting in the account books looked familiar to me. I assume it was Sir Jason's."

"If you're willing to go back, we may find some answers there."

I nodded and led him down the corridor, motioning for him to wait while I put my head through the door. The room was empty. When I turned around, Philip looked queasy.

He slipped inside and shut the door before whispering, "Doesn't it feel odd, putting yourself through solid objects like that?"

"I can't feel it at all. I wish I could." I gestured at the rows of shelves. "If I could turn pages, I'd lose myself in these books for the rest of eternity."

"You think that's why you're stuck here? You didn't finish your reading?" Philip grinned and ran his fingers along the books. My fingers twitched with the urge to do the same. "Is it normal for libraries to be this big?" he asked.

"I don't think so. The library used to be downstairs. Maybe they moved it to have more space."

Philip wandered from the books to examine the glass cases displayed throughout the library. Each had different scientific specimens, neatly labeled: samples of glinting semi-precious stones; the white, hollow-eyed skulls of various mammals; hairy spiders preserved with lifelike integrity.

"What do you make of these?" he asked.

"Someone liked collecting things. Probably Sir Jason."

"I suppose that doesn't help us much."

"Try not to overlook anything. We don't know what's important."

Philip nodded and went back to the books. He circled around with a bored expression until he reached a bookcase on the far wall, where he stopped to read off the titles.

"*On the Making of the Philosopher's Stone. On Discourses with Spirits Helpful and Hostile. A Small Book of Summoning Spells.* These don't sound like the kinds of things a proper gentleman reads." He poked the spine of one of the books with careful curiosity, like a boy prodding a sleeping snake.

"Do you realize you just read Latin and Greek?" I asked quietly.

"I did? Oh, yes, I see. Do I seem like the sort of person who ought to know Latin and Greek?"

"No, and neither do I, for that matter."

"Interesting. So, why would we know all these languages?" Philip's expression fell. "Oh."

"What?"

"Oh, blast it. We'd need to know them to read these books. Everyone says Sir Jason dabbled in the dark arts, trying to summon his wife from the dead." I willed him not to say it, but he gestured at the bookcase. "Maybe we helped him."

"No, you must be wrong." I backed away. I couldn't atone for using black magic, and if I didn't fix my mistakes, I'd never be free from the darkness. "There has to be another explanation."

"Possibly, but why does the idea upset you?"

"Why do you think? I'm stuck haunting this house, and I don't know why. I heard the maids talking about curses . . ." My eyes widened. "About the wailing of a cursed soul in the woods. That's where you woke up."

"Oh, now you think I'm cursed?" Philip snapped, but his face paled. "We would know if we were, right? That would only be fair. Besides, I'm not dead yet. There should still be time for me to fix it."

His words stung like a slap to the face. Was redemption only for the living? "What a horrid thing to say!"

"Quiet!" Philip hissed. "Someone will hear you!"

"Not likely! I can scream forever, and no one will hear me except some wretched assistant gamekeeper. I really am cursed."

I sank to the rug and buried my face in my hands, my eyes aching with unshed tears. Philip knelt beside me.

"I'm sorry, Miss Tregarrick. It was a horrible thing to say. I wasn't thinking. I'm sure, whatever happened, there's hope for both of us. We just have to figure it out."

I met his eyes. He reached to pat my arm but yanked his hand back and ran it through his hair. I winced. Not exactly reassuring, but at least he tried.

"Let's see what else we can find," he said. "We'll look outside too, where I woke up."

Outside, beyond the protection of the walls. I shivered. "I don't think I can leave the house."

"Oh?"

"I stood on the threshold and had this terrible fear . . ."

"Like a warning?"

"No, I was just afraid." It sounded silly, saying it aloud.

"I can search out there myself. I suppose since we don't even know what we're looking for, it's just luck if we find anything."

"No." I shook off my brooding. "We can't leave it to luck. We need a system to help us find out everything we can about what Sir Jason might have been trying to do here."

"You sound very organized. Where do you propose we start, then?"

I sighed and gestured to the books about magic. "I guess with those." My voice dropped. "I'm not certain I want to, though."

"Aren't you a little curious?" Philip stared at the books, his expression hungry.

Darkness huddled in the nooks between the leather-bound tomes. The last lingering hint of dusk faded, and the shadows lengthened, wrapping around the shelves like jealous fingers. I drew back. It was a dangerous appetite, to want whatever those books held.

"Do you think it's safe to read them?" I asked.

"We're not planning on using them."

Shadows deepened in the corners as he scanned the shelves. I'd never lasted this far into the night. Perhaps having someone to talk to kept me here. I glanced at the clock, but no one had bothered restarting it. Its hands were stuck at eight.

The bottom of the velvet curtains rippled, and I caught a glimpse of a wormy tail, too long for a mouse. A pair of tiny eyes glinted at me from the darkness. I shivered.

"That looks interesting." Philip reached for a book, but Lady Henrietta materialized in front of him, frantically waving her hands.

"Stop!" I cried.

He recoiled. "What?"

"Can't you see her?"

"Who?" He scrambled away. "What are you talking about?"

"Lady Henrietta. She's here." I turned to her. "What's wrong?"

She pointed at the books and shook her head.

"We have to look at them, find out what happened." I tilted my head. "Unless you can tell us. You don't want to be stuck like this, do you?"

She shook her head and covered her face, shoulders trembling.

I reached to comfort her, but my movements froze.

"Miss Tregarrick?" Philip's voice was full of concern.

I couldn't answer. The room went dim. Darkness swirled around me, filled with a chorus of taunting, bitter voices.

Lucy. We're waiting for you, Lucy.

Oblivion swallowed me.

Chapter Five

"That was unnerving," Philip said from the sofa.

I gasped. Morning light washed over the veiled portrait of Sir Jason and highlighted Philip's dark hair. "What are you doing here?"

He cleared his throat. "You told me you always reappear in this room, and I was disconcerted. It was astonishing to see someone flash out of existence. I'd almost forgotten you weren't, you know..."

"Alive?"

"Well, yes."

Shadows and the dreadful voices lingered at the edges of my awareness. "What happened when I vanished? Did you see the darkness take me?"

"No, but apparently I don't see everything you do. You just froze and then flashed away, like a soap bubble popping."

But when a soap bubble popped, it was gone forever. I shivered. "And when I reappeared?"

"Oh, well . . ." He pushed up from the sofa and strolled to the window.

"Was it terrible?" I asked.

"Rather beautiful, actually, like light shooting together from all different directions. You stood there for a moment like a statue, then blinked and looked around."

"Where do you think I go?"

"I don't know. Everywhere? Nowhere?" He caught his reflection in the glass and straightened his lopsided cravat.

"You weren't here all night, were you?" I glanced at the rumpled sofa.

"I needed to see for myself that you were all right." He brushed back his tousled hair. "I think I heard the voice you mentioned, except there was more than one. I didn't understand what they said, but they sounded angry, rumbling and hissing. I'm not the only one, either. Miss Matthews fell down the stairs, nearly broke her neck. She felt someone push her and heard a laugh, though she didn't see anyone. I'll admit I was a bit frightened. I rather hoped you'd reappear and remind me that not all spirits are hostile."

I groaned. I could barely resist the call of one voice. What was I supposed to do against an army of ghosts? Maybe I could enlist Lady Henrietta's aid, though she didn't seem able to do much herself. "I'd wondered if the voice was Sir Jason, but I suppose not if there are more than one. Though, there was that time in his room—"

"You found his room?" Philip glared at the shrouded painting.

"It's Sir Edmund's room now."

"Oh." He folded his arms. "You're haunting that fop, are you?"

"You shouldn't talk about him like that, just because he has good taste in clothing. And art. And poetry."

Philip smirked and cocked an eyebrow.

My cheeks tingled. "The point is, while I was there, Sir Edmund spoke with his brother about removing the painting of Sir Jason and Lady Henrietta, and it crashed from the wall. No one was touching it, and I thought . . ." I looked down. "It felt like Sir Jason was watching me."

"I'm tempted to say it's a coincidence—" I opened my mouth to protest, but he held up a hand. "After last night, though, I'm willing to believe this is the most haunted house in the British Empire. I think it's time to look through those books."

Lady Henrietta had warned us away, though. I put my hands behind my back. "I don't want to touch them."

"It doesn't seem like that'll be a problem for you." Philip flashed a grin.

My jaw dropped. "What a horrid—"

"I know, I'm sorry," he said, but his eyes shone with laughter.

Wind whipped past the house, and the draperies rustled. Shadows shifted on the wall. We both jumped, and I shivered. I couldn't guess how long I had until the darkness came for me again.

"You're right," I said. "We have to find out what's in those books."

We snuck down the hall to the library, but we had it to ourselves.

No one was likely to climb all those stairs to come up here unless they had to. It made me feel lonely and insignificant, knowing that life was going on without me downstairs. Philip strode to the bookcase on the far wall. I lingered over the shelves of poetry.

"Did you find something?" He trotted back to my side.

"No, I suppose I'd just rather spend my time with the poems."

"You really are a romantic, aren't you?" He chuckled.

"What's wrong with looking for beautiful things in the world?"

"Oh, I believe the world's full of beautiful things, but I don't feel the need to write sappy verses about it. Besides"—he frowned at the neat rows of books—"poetry's so morbid."

"I've always liked it. Maybe I had a premonition I was fated for a tragic end."

"A romantic notion, I suppose." A teasing glint brightened his eyes. "Unless you died in some embarrassing way."

"What! I'm certain I didn't." I couldn't admit now that I'd worried about the same thing.

"You might have choked on a chicken bone because you were eating too fast."

"I don't even like chicken. Meat isn't good for one's constitution."

"All right." He leaned against the bookshelf with a cocky smile. "Maybe you forgot to tie your boot laces and tripped when you glanced up to watch the peaceful flight of a dove overhead."

I folded my arms, trying not to smile at the image. "My boots have buttons, not laces."

"Or you were reading a book while you walked and got run over by a carriage."

"In the house, I suppose?" I rolled my eyes. "Why do you insist on being so mean-spirited?"

"You make the most amusing expressions when you're angry."

I huffed. "You can flirt with the maids all you like, but I'm not here to amuse you. You think just because you're clever and handsome—"

He smirked, and I gritted my teeth.

"Go on," he said. "I like it when you scold me. I could listen to it all day."

I was certain he could, when I said foolish things like that. "I'm glad my death is providing you so much entertainment."

His grin faded. "I'm not entertained that you're dead. It makes me want to hit someone, but I don't even know who to blame. If I did . . ."

I imagined his broad shoulders standing between me and the vague figure from my memory. Philip would make a valiant protector, but he could do nothing against shadows.

"Let's look at those books," I whispered.

Tomes on magic crammed the far bookcase. We skimmed each title. Philip pulled out the ones that had anything to do with spirits. The pile grew so tall it leaned, so he divided it in two, hiding the stacks behind a chair so John wouldn't notice them if he came back. When we were done, the afternoon was spent and the shelves leered at us like an old man with half his teeth missing.

"Sir Jason was definitely obsessed with spirits." Philip ran his fingers over the gold-embossed cover of *The Death of the Soul*. "Do these books mean anything to you?"

"No," I said, though a couple of the titles gave me pause: *Summoning and Binding of Spirits* and *Mastery of the Spirit Realm*. I didn't want those lying around where anyone could use them against me.

Philip followed my gaze and picked up *Mastery of the Spirit Realm*, flipping through the pages. His expression hardened and he tossed it aside, grabbing *Summoning and Binding of Spirits*. He turned slowly through the pages then showed me the book, his face pale.

"Is this the handwriting you saw before?"

Cryptic words and numbers marked the edges of the page, the letters neat and precise. I shook my head no.

Philip snapped the book shut and slammed it onto the table. "It's mine, in both of them. Blast it!" He leafed through several other books. His notes also marked *A Treasury of Necromancy*.

Philip dropped into a chair. "So I *was* helping him."

"Did the notes make sense to you?" I asked quietly.

"No." He buried his face in his hands and whispered, "I'm so sorry if I had anything to do with . . . I can't even think it."

I looked away. As valiant a protector as Philip might be, he would also make a formidable foe.

"I don't like the idea that we helped Sir Jason," I said softly, "but this is just one part of the picture."

"*I* helped him." Philip scowled at the books. "We don't know what you had to do with it."

I couldn't disagree, but after the camaraderie of searching together, my throat tightened at the thought that we might have been enemies. He slowly gathered the tomes into their stacks. Orange light bathed the library as the sun slipped below the horizon.

Philip straightened, dropping a book. "What was that?"

"What? Where?" I scooted closer to him.

"The voices. Don't you hear?"

I shook my head, but then the murmuring rose and flowed past me. He was right. There were more now, a flood of restless anger. One voice, deeper than the rest, rumbled past the others.

Return it.

It faded into the river of hisses and moans, but the command beat against my ears until they ached.

"Let's get out." Philip grabbed an armful of books.

My legs trembled. "I can't. Didn't you hear? We have to return it."

"What? Return what?"

"I... I don't know. But I have to." No! I might have lost everything else, but I would not give up my free will.

"Blast it! Is this some sort of magic?"

"Maybe it's what I'm supposed to do." I didn't believe my own words. I still wanted to flee. I mouthed the word *help*.

"Fight it!"

Philip pushed at me, tumbling through. The surprise broke the pressure weaving around my thoughts, and I raced from the library with his footsteps just behind.

Chapter Six

We fled for my room, the voices fading in the corridor behind us. Philip glanced back and slammed the door. He tossed the books on the sofa and flopped down next to them, panting.

"I don't think anything followed us. Just a bit of excitement to liven up our evening." He forced a smile and leaned forward. "Are you all right?"

"No." My voice shook. "I don't think I'll ever be all right. There's nothing but darkness everywhere. I can't fight something that's inside my head."

"You've already fought it." His deep, steady voice calmed my nerves. "You can do it again. What are you supposed to return?"

"If I knew that, don't you think I would have mentioned it?"

I paced past the sofa, careful not to brush close to it again. The memory of kneeling there was so vivid, I didn't need a reminder. "I thought the voice meant *I* was supposed to return, but perhaps I had something before I died, something that had to do with Sir Jason or the ghosts." I paused. "What if it's in this room? Maybe that's why I keep coming back."

"That makes sense. Does anything in here seem important to you?"

"I don't think so." The room was bare except the few pieces of furniture.

Philip lifted the rug and sofa cushions and peered behind the draperies, but came away empty handed. "We need to know what the ghosts are after." He nudged the books heaped on the floor. "These might tell us more. I can turn pages, but you may be the only one who'll recognize what we're looking for."

He flipped open *Mastery of the Spirit Realm* and settled on the faded rug. I sank next to him and tried to make sense of the ramblings about planes of existence.

"Do you understand any of this?" I asked after several minutes of wading through the dense text.

Philip's head lolled back against the sofa, with his eyes closed and his chest rising in a slow, steady cadence.

"Mr. Ketley? Oh, drat."

I hated to wake him, even if I could; he probably hadn't slept the previous night. His brow furrowed at some troubled dream.

"Shh." I reached to brush a lock of dark hair from his forehead but pulled my hand back.

Philip's expression relaxed. I rose to glide around the room. I didn't want to leave him, for his sake or mine, yet it seemed wrong to hover around while he slept. If I did my ghostly duty and haunted the house, I might recover more of my memories, but that could also mean encountering the voices and shadows alone.

As a compromise, I searched out the other members of the household downstairs. John huddled in a dressing gown in his antechamber, leaning into a book, his bulldog jaw working his pipe as he scanned each line. Was he devouring some Gothic romance or bloody mystery? I snickered. Perhaps his taste ran more to poetry, and I could read over his shoulder. Grinning, I crept up to peek at the title, but the words *History of Common Law* smothered my interest.

"At least it should help you fall asleep."

I drifted down the hall. Sir Edmund sat at the desk in his antechamber, his head bent over the papers so I couldn't see what he wrote. Bright gaslights chased away the darkness, though I still imagined shadows around the portrait of Sir Jason and Lady Henrietta.

"What are you working on?" I asked.

He paused and wrinkled his forehead then resumed writing. My eyes widened. Was it happening again? Did he hear me? I tiptoed forward.

"Hello?" I asked close to his ear.

His pen scratched on without pause. I slunk away in defeat.

Coughs, rustles, and chatter—the sounds of life—drew me downstairs. Susan and Nellie straightened up the cavernous drawing room. A giant gold-framed mirror hung over the fireplace, reflecting polished tables, plush sofas, the harp and piano: everything but me. I kept my gaze fixed on it as I crept into the room.

"Did you talk to Mr. Parker today?" asked Nellie.

" 'Oo cares about Mr. Parker?" Susan sighed. A red welt from the mirror marred her dimpled cheek. "I saw Mr. Ketley earlier, and 'e's looking well."

"Aye, 'e would be." Nellie whisked her rag over a dark, polished table. "Watch out for 'im."

"Why do you say that?" I pressed closer.

"What do you mean?" Susan asked.

" 'E's a flirt, the type to break a girl's 'eart, maybe get 'er into trouble. Cook thinks 'e's a good-for-nothing rake, and she's got a keen eye."

I bit my lip. Philip did like to flirt, but he wasn't completely unprincipled. Was he?

Susan hefted her sloshing bucket to a dirty spot on the floor. "Cook doesn't trust anyone. A person's got to take a chance or she'll end up alone, and that's not for me."

"Suit yourself, but don't say you wasn't warned." Nellie lifted her mop. "I'm goin' to finish the entrance hall."

I frowned at her retreating back. Susan scrubbed the floor in wide circles, her eyes distant. She probably spent most of her time daydreaming, her only escape from long days of drudgery. Was she thinking of Philip? I pushed aside a twinge of jealousy and sat by her as she worked.

"You shouldn't listen to rumors," I said. "I don't think Mr. Ketley's all that bad." Except that he'd studied black magic, but that was in the past. I hoped. I picked at my ugly, chewed-up fingernails and sighed. "Habits are hard things to shake. Even being dead doesn't do much to cure them."

Susan wiped her forehead and dragged the bucket closer to the fireplace. I paced a circuit around the drawing room. The clock struck midnight. With each gong, a carved, leaping deer spun through a small door above the clock's golden face. Wolves fashioned from the black walnut case snarled at the fleeing creature, while the mythical Diana presided over the chase from her lunar chariot. I shivered at the wolves' fierce strength and the goddess's impassive expression.

"Which do you think is worse?" I asked Susan. "Being alone, or being around someone you aren't certain you can trust?" I studied the other girl, trying to guess her age and how far she was from home. "You're afraid of being alone, aren't you? So am I. I wish we could be friends."

She shrieked and knocked over her bucket.

I recoiled. "Do you see me? I didn't mean to frighten you."

But her gaze fixed on a huge brown rat wiggling out from under the sofa. I leapt next to her. My skin crawled as the creature's black eyes turned toward us. Susan whimpered and swung her broom. Heedless of the prodding bristles, the rat edged closer.

Ghostly voices murmured at the edge of hearing. My revulsion at the rat froze into a lump of dread. A single voice groaned above the clamor.

Bring it back.

Not again. The need to obey burned through me, scorching away my resistance. Maybe if I gave in, the ghosts would leave the house alone. Leave me alone.

No, the voices knew me, and they were waiting. A stubborn core of anger rose up to replace everything else. I might have failed at my task, but that didn't mean I had to quit. Death hadn't stopped me, so why should the voices?

"Bring what back?" I yelled into the corners. "I don't remember! Do you understand? I don't remember anything."

Nellie raced into the room. The rat scampered in confused circles before squeezing back under a sofa.

"Susan!" Nellie embraced her. "Was that a rat?"

Susan nodded and choked out a sob, dropping her broom.

Nellie's face contorted in disgust. "I didn't think the 'ouse was closed up that long. We'd best tell the 'ousekeeper in the mornin'."

I fled back to my room. Philip slept curled up on the floor. I was glad for the comfort of his presence, but he couldn't help me with this. I needed to remember. It was the only way to stop the voices, protect everyone in the house. Hands trembling, I knelt by the sofa and prepared to be pounded by fresh waves of dreadful memories.

No visions came. I relaxed and shut my eyes. In the earlier one, I'd been clutching the sofa. My hands were empty. Had I been holding something before that moment? My spine tingled as the edges of my memory stretched. Yes, at one point I had. Something so important, everything else hinged on it. The need to protect it poured through me with renewed urgency.

I straightened, and my movements froze. No! I had to find it. I would find it. As darkness poured over me, I screamed it in my mind, drowning out the call of the voices.

Chapter Seven

Philip sprawled on the sofa, reading a book in the daylight. His forehead wrinkled in concentration.

"Mr. Ketley!" I choked out, stepping toward him.

He jumped and dropped the book. "Miss Tregarrick! What's happened?"

I quickly told him about the events of the previous night. His frown deepened as I spoke, and he paced when I reached the end.

I lowered my head. "I think the hauntings are my fault for failing at my task. If anyone gets hurt—"

He jolted to a stop. "I'm sure you didn't cause this problem by yourself, and you don't have to fix it alone either. You're forgetting I had some role in this, and whatever it was, I want to make up for it. Do you think I'm some kind of scoundrel?"

I gave a guilty start, remembering the maids' conversation. "No, of course not."

"We'll find this thing, whatever it is. Then we'll decide what to do with it. I assume you don't want to hand it over to the spirits?"

"No. I'm certain I was trying to protect it. I think I needed it for something."

"We'll figure that out too. First, though, I have to check in with Mr. Reed, the gamekeeper. I've been sneaking up when I could, but I *am* nominally employed here."

"Of course." Without a living person to talk to, though, I was less than a shadow. "Only, I wish I knew how to fend off the other spirits. I never know when they'll attack."

"Hmm. Everything I've read says ghosts only come out at night. You're an enigma, really."

"I'm not the only spirit stirring during the day. I hear the voice before sunset sometimes." I tilted my head. "Just the commanding one, though. I wonder what makes us different."

"That's what we're going to find out. I promise."

Fierce determination flashed in his eyes, but I glimpsed fear behind it. He wasn't dead, but something had happened to him too, and not knowing what would be almost as terrifying. I'd been so worried about my own problems, I hadn't given much thought to his.

"Thank you, Mr. Ketley," I said quietly. Selfishness might be another bad habit, but I could change it.

"Don't mention it. I'll meet you back in the library." He gave me a warm grin as he strode away.

I smiled back, and my limbs felt lighter, as though released from invisible shackles. Someone knew I existed and cared what happened to me, an almost-tangible connection binding me more firmly to this world.

Was it possible that being acknowledged made me more real? I supposed not, but as I drifted along, I could imagine that my feet touched the floor and my hands were solid. I haunted the halls, smiling at the unseeing servants and admiring the paintings on the wall. I ended in the kitchen, where Cook stood in whispered conference with George, the butler.

"We cannot tolerate these rumors." George's scowl deepened his droopy wrinkles.

"Don't I know it." Cook banged her spoon against the side of a simmering brass pot. "I've lost two girls already. Say they won't stay in a house what's haunted." She offered the butler a plate of sugary currant scones. "I've heard in the village there was always somethin' irregular about this place. Maybe about Sir Edmund too."

George hesitated, his eyes fixed on the scones still steaming from the oven. He licked his lips and took one. "Just between you and me, Sir Edmund's inheritance was a strange one."

"He's the oldest male relation, isn't he?"

"Only because his father passed away suddenly. Sir Edmund inherited both estates."

"And?" Cook handed him a cup of tea.

George dropped his voice. "The late baronet's solicitor claimed there was supposed to be a will." He took a bite of the scone and sighed contentedly. "It was never found. It might not have changed anything, you understand, but it is—"

"Irregular."

"Just between you and I."

Cook gave a knowing nod and went back to stirring the pot. George sat to enjoy his meal.

Irregular. An understatement when it came to Springett Hall. The voices might be seeking the will. I rubbed the black word on my palm. What had I gotten involved in?

Music floated down the hall, and I hurried to investigate. I peered into the drawing room, where Sir Edmund sat at the piano. If the will named someone else as heir, he was a usurper, and the spirits might be angry over that. Had Sir Edmund and I known each other? Conspired together about his inheritance?

His fingers flew over the keys, pouring torrents of impassioned music through the house. The tide of sound swirled around and tugged me forward until I stood next to the piano, my dress blending into the skirt modestly concealing the instrument's legs. My silent heart ached at the smooth rhythm thrumming from the strings.

Sir Edmund pounded to the end of the song, head hanging, fingers resting on the ivory keys. His back rose and fell in deep breaths.

"That was lovely," I said. "So passionate."

He gave a start and looked up at me. I jumped, and he clutched the edge of the piano.

"Who are you?" he asked.

"You can see me!" Perhaps I was becoming more real. He didn't recognize me, though. Still, he might be willing to help, unless he was hiding something.

"I can see through you," Sir Edmund said, his tone awed. "What are you?"

He could see through me? Philip said I looked solid. I hesitated. Sir Edmund might hate me for haunting his house. Maybe he could even banish me.

"I came to hear your music," I said.

"My music drew you?" His posture relaxed, and a glow lit his wide, blue eyes. "Are you my muse? I think I've felt your presence before."

I cleared my throat. "I was there when you wrote your poem."

"I knew it!" Sir Edmund swiveled on the bench with a manic grin. "I knew some unseen hand was guiding my efforts!" He held out his hands imploringly. "May I ask your name, gentle muse?"

"Lucy, sir," I said, a little guilty for letting him think I was his muse.

"Lucy! You mustn't call me sir. That won't do. Call me Edmund. Surely we'll be great friends. You'll guide me to greatness. Is that why you're here?"

"Perhaps." Lying didn't seem like a wise choice with eternal darkness stalking me. "I awakened when you came to this place. I don't know why I'm here. I think—"

"You *are* here for me! I knew it. My Lucy, my muse! Back to work, back to work!"

I blinked. "But, you see, I—"

"I'm glad to hear you say that, Edmund," John said from the doorway. "I've finally made some sense of the accounts, and there are several tenants you need to meet with."

"Not now, man!" Edmund ran his hands through his blond hair, raking it into a wild mess. "Can't you see that my muse has visited me?"

"Your muse?" John looked around the room. His gaze passed through me.

"Oh, of course you can't see her. She's beautiful—"

I was?

"—and I'm inspired to write. Mundane business can wait. Thank you, my lovely Lucy." He bowed to me and fled the room. I followed for a few steps then clenched my fists.

John stared after him, slowly shaking his head. "Curse it, Edmund. Of all the times to take an odd turn."

He stared down at the ledgers in his hands. Drat. I hadn't meant to distract Edmund from his responsibilities, and after I'd just determined to be less selfish. At least he didn't seem focused enough to orchestrate a dastardly scheme. More likely he was a pawn in whatever game was playing out in Springett Hall.

And he'd seen me! Not everyone could, but it was progress. Certainly when Edmund got past his fit of creativity, I'd be able to talk sensibly to him and enlist his aid. I hurried upstairs, floating on my elation.

"Mr. Ketley!" I called as I raced into the library.

Philip sneezed and looked up from the stack of books he had organized the previous day. "Miss Tregarrick! I've made a good start . . . . What happened? You're almost glowing."

"I overheard the butler talking about a missing will. That might be what we're looking for. And Edmund talked to me! He saw me!"

"Edmund?" Philip frowned. "You mean Sir Edmund?"

"Yes, but he told me to call him Edmund. He said I was beautiful. His muse. He said perhaps I'm here to inspire him."

"Oh, did he?"

"Why are you scowling? Perhaps it's another part of the puzzle. Don't overlook anything, remember?"

Philip rolled his eyes and shoved a book back into the pile. "You think your mission is to inspire that idle, addlepated Edmund Springett?"

I narrowed my eyes. "Show some respect. He's a baronet, after all. And a poet. You should hear him play the piano. It was so passionate."

"He wasn't a baronet a few weeks ago, and I'm sure the addition of a title did wonders for his poetry and musical abilities." Philip leaned back against a chair and folded his arms. "Think what you like about your precious Edmund, but *I'm* not here to inspire him, and I have work to do."

"Why can he see me now, but not before?"

"I don't know. I'm trying to read. You could help."

"I can't turn pages, and this might be important." I stared at the room's reflection in the glass doors of a bookcase, trying to focus on the blank space where I should have been. Why could Philip and

Edmund see me when I couldn't see myself? I passed my fingers over the glass. "What do I look like?"

Philip sighed and set aside his book. "What are you talking about?"

"I don't know what I look like. I can't look in a mirror, and I don't remember. Will you please tell me?"

"Why does it matter?" Philip grumbled.

"Wouldn't it bother you not to know?"

"I suppose." He shrugged. "You have long, dark hair."

I huffed. "I can see that part. What color are my eyes?"

"Brown." Philip picked up another book.

"Just brown?"

"If you want a poem about them, ask Sir Edmund."

"Perhaps I shall."

"They're dirt brown," he said, still focused on his book.

I stepped back and blinked my dirt-colored eyes. "I think you're just being horrid again. The worst part is, I can't even cry when you hurt my feelings."

Philip tilted his head back and exhaled. "They're the color of fresh soil when the gardener first takes his spade to it in the spring. It's dark, and rich, and full of potential—one of the most beautiful colors in the world."

I gaped at him, and he met my stare. He leaned forward, deep blue eyes fixed on mine. Something in my chest trembled at the intensity of his gaze, and I fought the desire to flee. Or to rush into the harbor of his arms. I felt certain I would be safe there, but that certainty filled me with a fear I couldn't understand, and a deep, painful longing.

I shook myself and blinked rapidly. What was I doing? What was I feeling? I hardly knew anything about Philip, and I was *dead*.

He pressed his lips together and turned back to the tome in his lap. "*That* kind of dirt brown."

"Oh." I swallowed.

"The will may be connected to whatever's upsetting the ghosts, but I don't think we can ignore that fact that there was black magic going on here." Philip lowered his voice. "If nothing else, it may be affecting you, or us."

I slid next to him. "I want to help. What if you set the books out with their tables of contents open—the ones that have them, anyway—so I can see if they're worth taking a closer look at?"

Philip glanced at the leaning stack of books. "That's a good idea. It would take forever to actually read every book, and I assume you'd like an answer sometime while I'm still alive to turn the pages." His mischievous grin lit his eyes.

"Hmph," I said. "I suppose."

"Just focus on finding anything about spirits—especially about bringing them back, since that's what we think Sir Jason was trying to do with Lady Henrietta."

He set out several rows of books for me to peruse. I scowled at the tables of contents. One of them caught my attention, and I gasped.

"What is it?" Philip leaned over my shoulder.

"This is Sir Jason's handwriting," I pointed to the scribbles on the edge of the page.

"Yes, I recognize it," he said.

The title of a chapter on binding spells was circled, and in Sir Jason's spidery handwriting were two words: *Philip* and *Lucy.*

Chapter Eight

Philip snatched the book from the table and paced as he flipped through the pages. He stopped, lips curled back, and skimmed the chapter. I slipped behind him and bit my thumbnail to keep silent.

"Blast it!" Philip slammed the book shut.

"What is it?" My hands shook, and I clasped them together.

"Nothing good." His shoulders slumped. "It's not very specific, but it says there are spells that can bind people to a necromancer. Living people, who do so willingly. Maybe he . . . tricked us somehow into being bound to him."

"Tricked us?" I knew what he didn't want to say. We might have done it knowingly. "What would he gain from us?"

Philip eased the book open and perused the pages. "It depends on the spell. He might have been able to draw strength from us."

"Or control us?" I asked quietly.

"Maybe. I'm not sure if it would still work once either of you were dead."

"Sir Jason *is* dead, isn't he?"

"It's hard to imagine Sir Edmund inheriting if he weren't." Philip frowned and turned the book over in his hands. "I've been having nightmares of Sir Jason chasing me in the woods, and I'm sure he means to kill me. I think it has something to do with what happened to my memories."

"Maybe they're just dreams."

He touched the lump on his head. "I don't think so. I'm not sure I'm a good person to be around, Miss Tregarrick. I'm afraid I might hurt someone. I dream other things, so real I almost see them when I'm awake. There's a man beating a woman. I can't see his face clearly, but"—he shut his eyes—"he looks like me."

"You wouldn't do that!"

"Wouldn't I?" Philip dropped into the chair. "I hope not, but I'm not sure, and neither are you. I've seen the nervous way you look at me sometimes."

"I admit it puts me on edge when you're angry," I said softly, "but I don't think you'd hurt anyone. Like with Mr. Parker, the footman."

"What?" Philip asked.

"I was there when you beat him arm wrestling."

"Oh, yes." He rolled his hand into a fist. "When he insulted that maid, I wanted to knock his head against the table."

"Not when he insulted you?"

He shrugged. "I can take care of myself. That poor girl, though . . . I couldn't teach him the kind of lesson I wanted, but at least I put him back in line."

"I have a theory," I said, though a sudden rush of shyness made me bite my lip.

"A theory?" He smiled wryly. "I didn't know you were scientifically inclined."

My cheeks tingled. "I think that our habits are so much a part of us that even when we're dead we don't lose them. Look at my nails."

I held them out and immediately regretted showing off my unfeminine fingers. Well, what did it matter if he thought I had ugly hands?

"What about them?" he asked.

"I bite them. Or I try to, but it doesn't do anything. They look terrible, though. Before I died, I must have chewed them all the time, and now they're stuck like this."

"You remembered that?"

"No, I deduced it."

"Hmm. You are a scientist, then. All right." He held out a wide, strong hand. "I don't think I bite mine."

No, his were clean and carefully pared down to shape. I shook my head. "It's not about your nails. It's about who you are. It's important to you to protect people, help them. You wanted to hit the footman, and no one would have blamed you, but you didn't. That tells us something about you." I curled my fingers in, hiding my nails.

"Do you think I'd stay around you if I thought you meant me harm, especially with all those books about binding spirits?"

He blinked. "I'd never considered that."

"That's my point. You're not in the habit of hurting people."

He nodded thoughtfully then smiled and gestured at the poetry books. "Don't go making me into one of your romantic heroes."

I rolled my eyes. "No danger of that, I assure you." But only because he was so exasperating at times. Otherwise I could easily imagine him riding to the rescue against wicked knights. Or maybe dark magicians.

Philip rubbed his face. "What we really need is to understand Sir Jason better. Maybe we could find his personal papers, see what he really wanted."

"To bring Lady Henrietta back."

"We need to be sure." Philip glanced at the shadows gathering in the corners. "I think we're done for the night, though. It's getting dark, and this doesn't seem like the safest place to be."

I nodded. "We could look for Lady Henrietta, though. She might know what happened."

"You think we can trust her?"

"She doesn't seem to want to harm anyone. Our biggest problem is she can't speak."

Philip shrugged. "I can't even see her, but I'll come along."

I checked to make certain the hallway was clear. We strolled downstairs in awkward silence.

"Lady Henrietta?" I called from time to time, feeling rather silly.

My back sometimes itched with the sense of being watched, and Philip glanced over his shoulder, but Lady Henrietta couldn't or wouldn't appear to us.

Philip cleared his throat. "I missed dinner. Do you mind if we stop in the kitchen? If the other servants are still up, we can find out if anyone besides Sir Edmund sees you now."

"Oh, of course." How had I forgotten so quickly about everyday things like eating?

One of the maids, Miss Matthews, sat at the table, sipping her tea. She smiled, but it was all for Philip; she gave no indication I was there.

"'Ello, Mr. Ketley," she said.

He glanced at me then returned her smile, a picture of mischievous charm. "Good evening, Miss Mathews."

She whisked back a stray hair and smoothed her skirts. "There's a dance in the village tomorrow night."

"Hmm. So I've heard."

"If you're going, I 'ope you dance with me." When she smiled, her eyes twinkled. Blue, not dirt brown.

"If I go, I'll be sure to." He winked, and she giggled as he grabbed a leftover scone and retreated into the hallway.

"You're going to a dance?" I asked.

"I might," he mumbled, not meeting my gaze. "Why shouldn't I?"

Yes, why shouldn't he? He certainly had the right to do as he pleased. "Don't we have work to do?"

"Everyone needs a break sometimes." He walked with his shoulders slouched.

"I suppose," I said. "You can't spend all your time with ghosts, after all."

"No." He sighed. "I suppose I can't."

Shadows shivered away from the gaslights illuminating the halls, but Philip's presence did more than the lights to make me feel safe.

"Are you keeping watch for Lady Henrietta?" he asked. "It's after midnight."

"Of course," I said, though my heart wasn't in it. I was sick of ghosts. No wonder Philip wanted to go dancing. He still had the chance to live. An image bubbled up from my memories of laughing and spinning in a wild dance, strands of my hair whipping loose, and my face flushed with happiness and warmth. None of that for me now, just the oppressive darkness of Springett Hall. I blinked rapidly, not certain how much I wanted to remember after all. It hurt, knowing what I was missing.

Philip poked his head into the drawing room. "Are there any spirits around?" he asked.

"Just me, as far as I can tell," I said.

"Oh. All right, then." He strode across the room and frowned down at the piano.

"Do you think you know how to play?" I asked, hovering behind him.

"It just looks like a mess of black and white to me. What about you?"

My gaze fell to the piano, and its music played in my imagination, floating to the high ceiling, where painted angels gathered to hear it. Mesmerized by the ghostly sound, I let my hands hover over the keys. My fingers stretched for the notes, and memory supplied the tones, so real the vibration rang in my chest. Yes, I knew how to play. Another joy that belonged to the living.

"My fingers remember, but it doesn't matter," I said quietly.

"That must be frustrating." A smile crept over his face. "I'll be your hands for you. Tell me which of these things to press, and I'll play your song."

"They're called keys," I said. "It's not really that easy." Philip's shoulders slumped again. Maybe helping me made him feel less frustrated about his own problems. "You'll have to play quietly," I said, "or you'll have everyone running in to look for ghosts."

With my instruction, he plunked out a simple minuet until it flowed smoothly. It pricked my heart, not being able to do it myself, but Philip learned quickly, and it did cheer me to hear him freeing one of the songs trapped in my head.

"This is more enjoyable than I expected," Philip ran his finger over the tops of the keys. "I wonder why I never learned."

"Most men don't," I said.

"Yet all ladies do."

"Yes, we have to be able to amuse our husbands, show off how ornamental we can be."

"You sound bitter." He turned on the bench to look at me, his eyebrow cocked. I couldn't tell if he was teasing or curious.

"I suppose I am." I pursed my lips. "Of course, I don't remember why. At least I know I had a decent education."

"More than decent. You learned Greek."

I tilted my head. "That feels different. It doesn't come as naturally. The Greek is newer, maybe. I can almost remember studying it. The almost-memories are as frustrating as not being able to play this piano." I pounded my fingers past the smooth keys. "Just out of reach."

Philip nodded. "I know. Sometimes I catch glimpses of things—the past—but when I try to take hold of them, they vanish, like . . . "

"A ghost?" I asked, trying to smile.

Something moved at the corner of my eye. I whirled to find Lady Henrietta staring sadly at the piano.

"Lady Henrietta!"

Philip tensed. She drifted back.

"Please wait." I glanced at the piano. "You used to play too, didn't you?"

She hesitated then floated forward to run her fingers over the silent keys. Philip sat very still, his face pale.

"I miss it too." I chewed my lip. She was as shy as a songbird, and I might only get one chance. "I don't remember much about my life. Do you remember yours?"

She smiled sadly and nodded, her fond gaze traveling the room.

"Do you remember me?" I asked.

Her glance jumped to me then Philip. She made an uncertain, back and forth gesture with her hand.

"Do you know why I was here?"

She flinched and looked away.

"You're frightened of me?"

The clock ticked behind us, marking her long pause. She nodded and slowly pointed to Philip and me. Frightened of us.

"I'm sorry for whatever we might have done," I whispered. "We want to fix it. I think there's something I'm supposed to find. A will, perhaps. Do you know anything about it? "

Her forehead wrinkled. After a pause, she shook her head. Was she lying?

Female voices sounded in the corridor. Lady Henrietta's eyes widened and she raced from the room. Drat! Philip exhaled. The chatting voices grew louder.

"I'm probably not supposed to be in here," Philip whispered and ducked behind a large display of ferns.

Susan strode into the room, blinking like she'd never seen the place before.

"What is it, then?" Nellie asked behind her.

"I don't know." Susan shook her head. "I just 'ad the oddest feeling, like I was forgettin' somethin'. I think I 'ad a dream about it. I'd lost somethin' important and didn't know where to find it. I thought it might be 'ere."

Her gaze brushed over where I stood, with a cold, penetrating look. I shuddered and shrank from her, imagining shadows in her eyes. Was she searching for the will too, or was it a coincidence?

"You and your dreams." Nellie shook her head. "We'd best finish our work. Mornin'll come too soon as it is."

Susan nodded and left, with one glance back. I peered around the room but saw nothing that looked like a will.

Philip stepped out from behind huge, lacy green fronds. "There's a rat back here—a dead one. Let's go somewhere else."

I shivered and followed him out.

"Did you learn anything from Lady Henrietta?" he whispered.

"I don't think she was alive when we were here. She's frightened of us, though, and she might be hiding something. You still can't see her?"

"No, but I could sense her. It made my hair stand on end. It felt . . . wrong. Cold."

My throat tightened. "Is it the same with me?"

"With you?" He looked down. "No, not at all."

"How odd." Were Lady Henrietta and I different types of specters, or did it have something to do with Sir Jason's spell?

The stillness of the house hung over us, slowing our steps, and we glanced over our shoulders as we walked through the entrance hall. The gaslights flickered and dimmed.

"What's that?" Philip asked. "Do you see anyone?"

"No," I whispered, scanning the lofty hall.

Tiny flecks of light darted across the walls. I glanced at the chandelier overhead. Its cut glass prisms trembled, scattering reflected color. Then they darkened as though a cloud had passed over.

"Miss Tregarrick?" Philip asked.

The house groaned, and flakes of plaster drifted from the ceiling like ash. Shadows gathered around the chandelier.

"Move!" I leapt toward Philip, my hands falling through him. He shouted and staggered back. The chandelier crashed around me. Metal grated against tile. The glass prisms exploded, sending broken rainbows flashing across the entrance hall.

Philip retreated into the grand salon, eyes wide. Then his nose flared and he clenched his teeth. The chandelier had landed exactly where he'd been standing. Hissing laughs slithered in the air, and the walls rumbled.

"Are you all right?" Philip asked, his voice hard.

I stood unharmed in the midst of the twisted wreckage. A line of blood welled on Philip's temple where a piece of flying glass had caught him. He could have been crushed.

Shadows darted along the walls of the grand salon toward him.

"Watch—" I froze, choking on the warning.

Come to us, Lucy.

I tried to scream. In the window behind Philip, the tip of the sickle moon cut the edge of the horizon as it sank out of sight. The shadows grew in the deepening gloom.

"Miss Tregarrick? Is it happening again?" Philip followed my gaze out the window. "Look! I wonder—"

Chapter Nine

"Oh!" It wasn't the scream I'd planned, but still a relief after my paralysis, like a deep stretch when waking.

"Miss Tregarrick?" Philip stood before me, a paper-bound book in one hand and a pocket watch in the other.

I sagged in relief. He didn't need me to survive the shadows. He could escape the house if he had to. I was the one who was trapped.

"You're right on time," he said before I could ask what happened the previous night.

"Am I?" I squinted past the rain-curtained window at the cloudy gray sky. "I didn't think I appeared at the same time every day."

"You don't, and I found that strange. Last night, the moon dipped below the horizon just as you disappeared. I thought it might be a coincidence, but I found an almanac." He held out the open book. "You appeared today at the same time the moon rose."

"The moon rises in the morning?"

"Sometimes. The new moon rises with the sun, and it's lost in the daylight. The later the moon rises, the more full it appears."

I leaned over to stare at the chart showing the moon's phases and a series of incomprehensible numbers. "So every day I'll wake up a bit later?"

"Yes. If the pattern holds true, on the night of the full moon you'll wake at sunset and stay all night. Then you'll start to appear after nightfall and vanish in the day. It seems you're out when the moon is, even when we can't see it." He gestured at the rain hammering the window in uneven bursts.

I bit my fingernail. Each night, then, I'd have to spend more time with the darkness and the other ghosts. "Does this mean it's not the shadows taking me away?"

"I'm not sure how it works, but I don't think so. At least not while the moon is up."

I wrinkled my forehead. There was still the voice with its terrible influence over me, but it might not be the same entity as the shadows that attacked us last night. They were waiting for me, trying to drag me into their abyss, but perhaps they couldn't touch me unless I misstepped. "What does this mean? Is it normal for ghosts?"

"No. I've read everything I can find on ghosts. Nothing mentions anything about spirits being affected by the moon, and most are banished by the sun. You're an anomaly, really."

I brushed my hand through the dim light. "It could have something to do with Sir Jason's binding spell."

"Possibly. I haven't found any more about that, but I'll keep looking." He muffled a yawn. Dark circles hung under his eyes, and stubble roughened his jaw.

"Did you sleep at all last night?"

"Maybe a couple of hours." He shrugged.

I gave him a sympathetic look and glanced back at the almanac's depiction of the lunar cycle. "Which one is today?"

He pointed to a waxing sickle moon. I studied the chart, and a shiver rushed down my back.

"Mr. Ketley?" I whispered. "The first day that either of us remember . . ."

"Yes?" He squinted at the almanac.

"It was the day after a new moon. Do you think it's a coincidence?"

He traced his finger over the picture of the darkened moon and sighed. "Given everything else, probably not."

"Could Sir Jason have bound us to the moon?"

He scowled at the almanac. "From what I've read, you have to be able to touch whatever you're bound to. Besides, it's hard to see how tying someone to the moon would benefit Sir Jason."

I fidgeted with a lock of loose hair. The more we learned, the less anything made sense. "What happened after I vanished last night?"

Philip's scruffy jaw tightened. "Everyone was unnerved about the chandelier falling. Mr. Springett said it was just an 'unfortunate incident,' but the other servants aren't laughing about ghosts anymore.

A knife flipped off the table and stabbed one of the footmen in the leg. He almost bled to death. A few people think it was an accident, but most of the ones who were there quit on the spot."

I looked at my translucent hands. "You don't think I'm doing it?" I whispered. "I don't know what happens to me when I'm gone. What if someone else is controlling me, or I turn into some kind of monster?"

"Things get worse when you disappear, but I don't see any reason to suspect you're part of it," he said gently. "It may have to do with the late hour. I don't think the darkness is our ally." He flipped the almanac shut. "My dreams get worse every night. I see Sir Jason chanting, his face distorted by shadows, and a black beast roaming Springett Hall."

"A black beast? Has anyone mentioned seeing something like that?"

"No, but if the other things are real, why not the beast?"

I shivered. "What if it's something else we can't see, like the voice?"

" 'Ello?" Miss Matthews stood in the doorway, a bucket in hand, blinking at Philip.

"Oh, good morning." Philip summoned one of his bright grins. "Can I help you with something?"

"I'm supposed to clean in 'ere." She raised an eyebrow.

"You're probably not supposed to be in these rooms, Mr. Assistant Gamekeeper." I whispered, though the girl gave no sign that I was there.

"Oh!" Philip shifted.

Miss Matthews lowered her voice. "What were you sayin' about a beast?"

"Um, of course. That's why I'm here. In the house. I suppose you're wondering." He glanced around the room and scratched his head. "It's a, uh . . . badger."

"A badger?" She stepped back. "In the 'ouse!"

I laughed. "A badger?"

"A badger," Philip said firmly. "Possibly a badger. It could be something else. Have you seen any animals in the house?"

"I thought it was a rat . . ." Her eyes widened. "It was 'uge, though. It might 'ave been a badger. Are we in danger, then?"

"That's what I'm trying to find out. Just warn everyone to be careful. If you see anything strange, keep away."

"I will!" Miss Matthews hurried off.

"Rats might have been more plausible," I said, laughing again.

Philip rubbed the back of his neck. "Yes, apparently I'm not a very good liar. The gamekeeper said something about a badger this morning, and it was the only beast I could think of."

"At least it will keep people off this floor for a while."

He grimaced. "We have to use the time to search. I think we should focus on finding Sir Jason's papers. I'll check the library for hidden drawers or documents stashed behind the books."

"I'll look in his rooms. Maybe he kept them there."

"What if Sir Edmund sees you?"

I shrugged. "I'll ask him to help."

"Oh, yes, he seems very helpful," Philip mumbled.

"Why do you hate him so much?"

"I don't know." Philip wiped the dust from the clock case with his coat sleeve. "I don't hate him, but what does he spend his time doing?"

"From what I've seen, mostly playing the piano and writing letters and poetry."

"Anything else?"

"No," I snapped, "but contrary to what you seem to think, I don't spend all that much time spying on him, or anyone else."

"How do you think a baronet is supposed to pass the day?"

"Well . . ."

Philip stepped close enough that I should have felt his warmth. "I can tell you what your precious Sir Edmund is *not* doing. He's not paying attention to his tenants, fixing their cottages, solving their disputes. The gamekeeper grumbles all the time about repairs that need to be done around the estate. Sir Jason neglected it, and Sir Edmund can't be bothered to discuss it."

I bit my lip. John had spent all that effort going over the accounts, and Edmund brushed him off. I'd distracted Edmund that time, but he always seemed at least half lost in worlds of his own imagining. Still, wasn't that the cost of creativity, of looking at things beyond the scope of day-to-day life? His poems and music whispered to me of passion, life, and love. I couldn't savor a mouthful of sweet, moist cake or lean into the strength of a warm embrace. The ephemeral things—words, songs, beauty—were all that I had to remind me of joy and hope. I couldn't blame Edmund for his priorities.

"He's new to this," I whispered. "Give him time."

"He probably doesn't have it. Servants are leaving. Sir Edmund's estate is falling apart around him, and he's too busy living like some dissipated romantic to notice."

"Why do you always have to be so hard on everyone! Why can't you just stop and appreciate the beautiful things around you?"

"Why do you have to be such a dreamer? Can't you see that there are things that have to get done?" Philip blinked and stepped back. "Blast it. We've had this argument before."

"What?"

"Can't you see it? Can't you feel it? We've fought like this before. Nearly the same words. They're a habit."

I closed my eyes and focused on the knot of anger in my chest: familiar, almost comfortable. "You're right." I swallowed. "How well *did* we know each other? You don't think we were . . . very close, do you?"

Philip searched my face, his gaze so focused, so intimate as he lingered over my eyes and my mouth that I imagined him leaning down to kiss me. My cheeks tingled in imitation of a blush. I wondered if he could see it, and the prickling intensified.

"I don't think we were what you're implying," he said slowly, his gaze still on my lips. "It seems like it would be hard to forget. Or not remember."

Of course, it had been a silly thought. After all, Philip and I might not have even been friends. "The first time I saw you, I felt irritated," I whispered.

He snorted and rubbed his head. "I'm glad I make such a good first impression."

"No, that's what I'm saying. I don't think it was a first impression. I think I was remembering, like what you said about your feet knowing their way around. You must have found me irritating too, especially with me insulting you."

He folded his arms. "As a matter of fact, I thought you looked charming and wild, like a lost fawn that found its way inside."

"Oh." My cheeks tingled again. Half the time Philip was so cocky it was all I could do to keep from yelling at him and storming out, but then he'd turn around and say something that put Edmund's poems to shame. It was like a spirited country dance: he kept me constantly spinning but never let me fall. I fidgeted with my dark hair, almost the same color as his, and a new thought churned my stomach.

"Could we be related? Brother and sister, possibly?" If we were Sir Jason's illegitimate children, it would explain why we were at Springett Hall.

"No," he said quickly. "I really don't think so. That doesn't feel right."

The tips of his ears turned crimson, and my tight queasiness eased. We probably weren't brother and sister if the idea upset us both so much. We looked at each other, and I squeezed my eyes shut. Did it matter, what we had been in the times we couldn't remember? Of course it did; that was our problem.

Philip grimaced and shook his head. "Let's talk about something else, shall we? We think we lived here with Sir Jason. So, where were our rooms? Our things must be somewhere, right?"

"Our belongings." I blinked. "I hadn't thought of that. You're right, but I've wandered through all the rooms, and I haven't seen any that look abandoned, or familiar."

He sighed. "We need answers. I'll meet you in the library after you check Sir Edmund's rooms."

I nodded and glided down the corridor. The answers had to be here somewhere, though I believed more than ever we wouldn't like what we found.

Chapter Ten

Edmund wasn't in his chambers. Probably off doing baronet-type things, like meeting with his tenants as John suggested. I wished Philip were there so I could gloat.

Since no one was around, I started in the bedroom. The pale light and yellowing wallpaper gave the place a sickly look and dulled the splendors of the garden embroidered on the bed curtains. I brushed my fingers past the neat, tiny stitches of the tree's curling branches, imagining their soft ridges.

Recalling my task, I stuck my head into closets and dressers, looking for secret panels or false bottoms by the light filtering through the cracks, but everything was as it seemed. The bed's wooden canopy would be an ideal place to hide something, but I couldn't float higher any more than I could sink through the floor. Some force—maybe nothing greater than habit—held me near the ground. I drifted out of the bedroom.

The sparse antechamber didn't provide any obvious hiding places. I stepped into the fireplace to search the chimney, and marveled at the low flames crackling and flitting harmlessly around my skirts. The pictures hung too close to the wall to peer through and see if anything hid beneath. I pursed my lips and slipped my shoulder into the wall to peek behind the portrait of Sir Jason and Lady Henrietta. The plaster gave slowly, like thick mud. I recoiled. Why were walls so difficult?

The desk loomed on the edge of the room. I took a deep breath and tiptoed over to examine it. Papers scattered over the wooden surface. A letter in flowing script signed *Faithfully Yours, Miss Elise Ridgewell* lay obscured by scattered fragments of poetry. None of them were about flowers now, just images of night, darkness, and eternity. One caught my eye:

The beast, ghastly death, draws near

Black fur, hot breath scorching my skin
Come to me, dreadful creature
You, who have stolen love from me,
Taken my better part
Rend now my useless heart and blood

I shivered. Could this beast be the one Philip dreamed of? Did Death itself stalk Springett Hall? Miss Ridgewell's letter suggested she was alive, though, so whom did Edmund think death had stolen from him?

"My muse!"

Edmund stood in the doorway, grinning foolishly at me. He bowed deeply, and his eyes darted to the desk. "Have you come to see my latest offerings? I hope they please you?"

"The imagery is . . . striking."

"It comes to me in dreams. Are you the one sending them?"

"What do you dream about?" I asked to avoid his question.

"Strange, wild things like I've never imagined. The moon, but it's huge and painfully bright, some omen of terror. I've considered canceling the ball—"

"The ball?"

"Oh, yes, I had the delightful idea of throwing a ball for my new neighbors on the night of the full moon. That will make safe driving for the guests, but I also love the glory of the moon. Or, I did." A wild look crept into his eyes. "Now it frightens me, and I wonder what mysteries it's holding."

I wondered too, but I just nodded. Lost in his own fantasies and nightmares, Edmund hardly seemed aware of me.

His blue eyes fixed on some distant point. "I dream of love like I never understood before." His gaze found me. "Do you believe love can extend beyond death, Lucy?"

I noticed very distinctly my lack of heartbeat. Was there still some hope that I could find love, that someone would accept me as I was? "Yes, I suppose I do."

"I just have to find the secret to making spirit whole, to making lost love real. Death won't cheat me again!"

Edmund shook his fist at the formless shadows crouching in the corner. Were they just shadows, or was something watching us? I shivered. Perhaps Edmund needed more of the mundane world to touch his thoughts.

"You shouldn't dwell so much on such things. Certainly true love need not fear death. It transcends mortal limits and understanding—"

"No! I must be able to touch, to feel!" He paced, grasping his hair. His harsh tone turned mournful. "You wouldn't understand. You are beyond appetites and passions."

How could I explain how wrong he was? I craved every sensation of life, perhaps more than when I was alive.

His fever-bright eyes searched the room. "I've lost the key, but I'll find it. I will! I must!"

I bit my fingernail. He was searching too. Like me, like Susan. His obsession with souls and death might be more than a poetic notion. Springett Hall's voices and shadows poisoned everyone within its walls.

Edmund stopped abruptly and sank to his desk, snatching fresh paper. His pen scratched madly, splattering heavy droplets of black ink. He twisted his hair into an unkempt tangle, lost in a world beyond my reach.

I stole from the room, and Sir Jason's eyes met mine through the portrait. Cold crept over me for the first time since I awoke: not some imagined chill, but the impossible sensation of actual cold burning my ghostly lungs and cramping my insubstantial fingers. How was this possible? Was I actually feeling, or was Sir Jason reaching from the abyss to torment me?

I fled for the sanctuary of the library, passing John in the hallway. He shook his head and mumbled about badgers. I groaned. The last thing Springett Hall needed was another wild rumor.

Philip had fallen asleep by a stack of books. I knelt to shake him, and my hand passed through his shoulder.

"Now what am I supposed to do? Mr. Ketley?"

He didn't stir. I bent to his ear. "Mr. Ketley, this is no time to rest."

He smiled. "Lucy?" he asked, without opening his eyes.

The gentle way he spoke my name stabbed at me. I wanted to hear it again, but I could never be that dear to him. I blinked my stinging eyes and put my hands on my hips. "What gives you the right to use my Christian name? Wake up, Mr. Ketley!"

He jumped awake, flailing out and knocking over his neat pile of books. "Lu—Miss Tregarrick!" He rubbed his eyes. "Oh, I guess I drifted off, but I was so tired, and there were no dreams. Or at least not unpleasant ones."

Raking back his tousled hair, he gathered the worn leather books, gently closing their faded covers.

"What are those?" I asked.

He sighed. "I'm trying to find out about banishing spirits."

"Oh." I paused. "It wouldn't get rid of all ghosts, would it?"

"I suppose it . . . oh. Of course, we'll look for one that's specific. We don't want to send you away. Um, unless you want to move on."

"No." I shuddered. "I'm not ready. I want to stay."

Philip's expression brightened, and he set the books aside. "There's a chance it wouldn't work on you, anyway. This one"—he tapped the cover of a book—"says that ghosts who are bound to something in this world can't be banished without destroying the thing holding them here. Besides, we know you don't follow the same rules as the other spirits."

If I'd been bound to Sir Jason and he was dead, I might be as vulnerable as the other ghosts. "We'll try it if we have to." I sighed. "Even as a ghost I can't seem to do things right."

"That's not what I meant!"

Philip reached for my hand and, for a moment, I felt warmth on my immaterial skin, seeping through me like water into parched ground. I thought it was just my imagination, but Philip pulled his hand back and stared at it.

"Did you feel that?" he whispered.

"Yes." I cradled my hand, searching for an answer in the tiny creases of my semi-transparent fingers. "What just happened?"

"I have no idea. Hold out your hand."

I did, my palm facing out. Philip held his the same way and slowly brought it to mine. He paused when scarcely more than a hair's breadth separated us then tilted his fingers forward. They passed through mine without a flicker of sensation. We sat like that for a moment before he yanked his hand away.

"I don't understand," I said, my throat thick with unshed tears.

"Neither do I." He scowled at the carpet, his dark eyebrows drawn together. Then he tilted his head. "What's that?"

He picked up a thin brass hairpin and twisted it back and forth, light glinting off its edge. A rushing sensation swooped over me, like I was falling, and images flashed through my mind. I gasped.

"Miss Tregarrick?" Philip asked.

"It's mine," I whispered. "My hairpin. I remember. Sir Jason yanked it out of my hair." I touched the back of my head gingerly, rubbing my long, loose locks. "Then he chased you."

"You're sure?" Philip asked, leaning closer.

"It hurt." The vision whirled again and again across my memory, like a racing carriage wheel. "He grabbed my hair and threw me down. When he raised a hand to strike me, you shouted something, and he gave chase. That's why my hair's loose. It must have been right before I died." I glanced around the library and pointed with a shaking hand. "It was right there." The scene played for me again, and my eyes widened. "When he chased you, you shouted that you had it."

"It?"

"The thing—whatever the voice wants, whatever I failed to protect."

"I don't remember having anything special." He turned out his pockets, revealing a few loose coins, a folding knife, and half of a scone wrapped in a handkerchief. "The knife and the coins are the only things I had when I woke up."

"I'm glad you haven't been carrying the scone around all that time." I wrinkled my nose, and he chuckled. I shook my head. "I don't think it's any of these."

"The voice doesn't know what it's missing. They're good scones." Philip grinned and shoveled the things back into his pocket. He picked up the hairpin and his smile faded. “I’m sorry I didn’t protect you.”

“But you helped me. You drew Sir Jason away. Maybe he did something to you and came back for me.” Despite the terror of the memory, a burden dissolved from my chest. Whatever we’d been, Philip and I weren’t enemies at the end.

“I should have done more. Maybe it wasn’t you who failed. It was me.” His head dropped, and he clutched the hairpin until it pressed a deathly white line into his fingers.

“Mr. Ketley—” What could I say?

“Did you learn anything?” he asked quietly, slipping the hairpin into his pocket. “In Sir Edmund’s chambers?”

I blinked at the abrupt change of topic and shook my head. “Nothing useful. I don’t think Sir Jason kept his papers there. Not anywhere I could see them, at least. I’m concerned for Edmund, though.”

“Why?” Philip frowned.

“He mentioned having nightmares, like you do, and his poems were all about death and a dark beast. We spoke of love lingering beyond death.”

Philip paled. “You did?”

“Yes, he expounded very passionately on the subject. Almost obsessively.”

“That doesn’t seem at all appropriate.” Philip sat back and folded his arms.

“I am his muse.” I smiled sadly. “Are you jealous?”

It was better for both of us if he wasn’t, but I couldn’t help hoping he was, just a little.

“Jealous?” Philip’s head snapped up. “What would I be jealous of? You may be Edmund’s muse, but it’s not like you can be anything else to him. Or to anybody,” he added through clenched teeth.

His statement rocked me back. It was the most horrible thing he’d ever said, because it was true. I could pretend to inspire Edmund and flirt with Philip, but it meant nothing. My existence was a threadbare patchwork of shadows and broken memories; the pains and joys of life had passed beyond my grasp. No one could hold me. No one could love me. I drew in a shuddering breath, and a sob rattled my chest.

Philip jumped to his feet, scattering his books. "Miss Tregarrick. I—I'm sorry. I didn't mean—"

But I fled, racing through the back bookcase into a room I'd never seen before. A skull returned my gaping stare, its hollow eye sockets blacker than the surrounding gloom.

Chapter Eleven

A human skull. Too gruesome to be real, yet there it sat on a desk cluttered with books and papers. A bolt of sunlight from a high, narrow window highlighted geometric symbols scratched into the yellowed bone.

I whimpered. What had become of my body? I'd never given it much thought, but Sir Jason might have used my bones in some foul spell before he died, binding me in this unnatural state. The skull's empty sneer mocked me, and I stumbled back through one of the tall, brass candlesticks stationed around the room.

Something snagged my dress, tugging me off balance. The impossible sensation jolted me out of my shock. My foot rested over a wide silver circle etched around the middle of the room. The hem of my skirt stretched toward an obsidian black altar in the circle's center. I gasped and twisted away, tumbling through the bookcase and past Philip, who pounded on the wall, calling my name.

"Miss Tregarrick! What happened?"

"A skull." I trembled. "It might be mine. Is it mine? That room wanted to keep me—"

Philip held out his hands, and I longed to rush into his arms, to feel warmth and safety. Maybe no one could help me, though. I squeezed my eyes shut, and the skull leered in my imagination.

"You're all right," Philip said softly. "I won't let anyone hurt you. Can you tell me what happened?"

His deep voice calmed my panic.

"There's a room on the other side of the bookcase with a skull on a desk." My voice caught. "Mr. Ketley, what if it's mine?"

He pressed his lips into a thin line. "Did you see a way in?"

"No. I just saw the skull, and a circle on the floor with an altar. The circle tried to capture me. I could feel it. Really feel it. Something's there. It's an evil place. I don't want my skull in there."

"Neither do I," Philip whispered. "We'll find our way in and rescue the skull, whomever it belongs to. I need you to think. Was there a door? The living entered the room, so it must have a way in."

I shook my head. "I'm sorry. I don't know. I didn't see."

Philip nodded and inspected the bookcase, tracing the edges and cracks, pulling on books and tapping the back of the shelves. After a while he shook his head.

"I'm sorry to ask this, Miss Tregarrick, but it may take a very long time to find the door without an idea of where to look. You don't have to set foot on the floor, but if you could poke your head in and see where the entrance might be..."

"You want me to go back?" I felt again like invisible hands tore at me, dragging me into some deep, cold abyss. If Sir Jason had killed me, he might have done it at that black altar. Everything I'd been trying to avoid waited for me in that room. I shook my head, terror clawing at my throat. "I can't. I just can't!"

"Miss Tregarrick, look at me. Please."

My gaze fastened on his. His eyes were deep blue, like the sky on a perfect summer afternoon. I caught a glimpse of my childhood, lying on my back to stare into forever on a cloudless day, and I lost myself in the color.

"I don't want anything to happen to you," Philip said, stepping closer, "but we need the answers in that room. Do you think you could try?"

My image reflected in his eyes, distorted, but still recognizable. I inhaled sharply and leaned in. How could this be? I had no substance, no material form. Of course, to Philip I looked solid. Real. Maybe that mattered more than what the mirror showed. I watched myself nod. "I'll do it."

He smiled. "I knew you could. I'll be right here."

The bookcase gave before me, but the wall pushed back against my hands. I jerked away.

"What is it?" Philip asked. "What's the matter?"

"The wall feels different. Like it's trying to keep me out. It felt like that before, in Edmund's antechamber."

"You can interact with the house? How is that possible?" He reached for my arm, but his fingers passed through. "Do you think passing through the wall can hurt you?"

"I don't know."

He rubbed his face. "I'm not sure what to tell you. We're dealing with more magic we don't understand. If you think it's dangerous, you don't have to go. I'll find another way in."

I clenched my fingernail between my teeth. It could take Philip a long time to find a way, if he found one at all. The room might hold answers, possibly even the key to our salvation. And that skull could be mine. Maybe it gave someone power over me. This might be my chance to free myself from the shadows.

"I'll try again."

"Be careful, Miss Tregarrick."

I nodded and touched the wall again. It resisted, but I pressed through to hover on the edge of the room. A small circle nestled inside the larger one, geometric symbols filling the space between. I pulled my skirts back from the floor, careful not to touch any of the etched designs, and looked around. The walls were solid except for the slit of the single, small window, likewise the floor and ceiling. This couldn't be a room built for ghosts, could it? Perhaps it was a trap! I turned to flee again, and the dark outline of a door caught my eye.

I smiled and plunged back into the library.

"Miss Tregarrick!" Philip grinned in relief.

"It's right here!"

"What?" He raised an eyebrow.

"It's the bookcase. I think the whole thing opens."

"I didn't see any hinges."

"They're on the inside, over there." I pointed to the left.

"Oh, of course!" Philip pushed, but the bookcase didn't give. "There must be a latch." He ran his hands along the sides and stretched to reach the top panel of the highest shelf. "There!"

The bookcase and a narrow section of the wall next to it shifted, and Philip leaned against it. It swung in without even a whisper. I crept behind Philip as he wandered into the room. His movement stirred eddies of dust, a shimmering trail in his wake. He muffled a cough in his sleeve.

"We don't want anyone finding this place," he whispered. He swung the door most of the way shut and reached up to check the latch. "I don't want to get locked in either."

Papers cluttered all three desks and littered the floor, obscuring parts of the circle's silver outline.

"It's a mess. I wonder if it was always like this." Philip stooped to examine the scattered documents.

"Don't touch the circle!" I said.

He nodded and shifted away from it. "This is Sir Jason's handwriting, isn't it?"

"Yes." I shivered at the spidery script.

"We found his papers, then."

We stood side by side, staring at the room. Five tall candlesticks guarded the inner circle, set at even intervals. Lumpy trails of cold, black wax dribbled down their thick brass stems. Darkness emanated from the center of the circle, as if fighting the dim light. Here was the heart of Sir Jason's black magic, the source of the infection oozing through the house, and through us.

I stepped back. I wanted to believe Philip and myself innocent, but as I studied the room, a growing sense of familiarity with the skull, the trappings of magic, and the palpable darkness warned me that the truth was not what I wanted it to be. My instinct was to run, but fleeing the truth wouldn't change it.

I thought of the embroidered bed curtains displaying Eden and the Tree of Knowledge. How had Eve felt with its fruit in her hand? Was it strangely heavy? One taste changed everything, and there was no turning back. It was like stepping across a bridge into a new world. In this room, I might discover things more terrible than I had imagined, but perhaps I could also find the path to redemption and freedom from the shadows.

Philip strode over to stare at the skull. "I really don't think this could be yours. It looks much too old."

I nodded. We drifted apart, each gravitating to one of the other two desks, skirting the silver circle to reach them.

"This one was mine," Philip said from the other side of the room, his voice tight. "It feels . . . comfortable."

"Yes."

I could imagine sitting at the desk and picking up my forgotten tasks. My hands would know what to do, as they had with the piano. Uneven piles of paper sat at odd angles, their flowing writing decorated with loops and curls: the penmanship of someone relaxed and content, if a little bored.

I closed my eyes, wishing I could deny what they told me. "I helped him too, and I did it voluntarily." I'd dabbled in black magic. Necromancy. If I'd hurt anyone, oblivion might be all I deserved. I'd been given this opportunity to mend things, though. I wouldn't waste my chance.

"Yes." Philip strode across the room. "Whatever he was doing, we were in it up to our necks. All right, we're going to find out what happened. Let's start with the papers on the floor. I don't think they fell there by accident."

I stood over his shoulder as he sorted through them, carefully whisking them away from the circle.

"They're dusty." He wrinkled his nose. "They've been like this for a while, maybe since he chased us out of the library."

"Why wouldn't he have come back? Oh, unless he needed whatever we took to finish his work. Or . . ." I shivered. "He might have died the same night I did."

"That's possible," Philip said slowly, "but if it's true, then—" He shuffled the papers and bit his lip.

What had happened to Sir Jason? We hadn't heard any rumors about foul play, but magic might not leave a mark. I could have used a spell against him as easily as Philip. I'd been terrified, and someone was chasing me. I might be a murderess. I squeezed my eyes shut. Not cold-blooded murder, but it would still feel like another stain on my hands.

"What was he writing about?" I squinted at the papers in the dim light. "Different languages, but variations of the same message. Something about drawing near, coming forth."

"Given what we know of Sir Jason, I would guess this is a spell," Philip whispered. "I wonder why he repeated it so many times?"

"Maybe that's how it works—you write it over and over." I skimmed the words. "Or, maybe he was trying to figure it out. He wasn't certain exactly how to do it."

Philip grimaced. "As if playing with magic wasn't bad enough. You think he didn't know what he was doing?"

"Think about all the collections in the library: butterflies, seashells, stones. Sir Jason probably fancied himself a scientist. He was experimenting."

"Yes, but it's one thing to collect rocks and another to toy with summoning the dead." Philip's jaw tightened. "Blast it! We're in the hands of a family of idiots and lunatics."

His comment stung on poor Edmund's behalf, but I couldn't bring myself to disagree. "How did we get ourselves into this? I can't believe I would willingly help a madman summon the dead."

Philip scowled. "Maybe it started as something else and came on slowly, so we just kept wading deeper and deeper until it was too late to back out."

The window dimmed. I shrank from the shadows, but pink and gold streamed in, casting a warm glow over the cold, hard edges of the room.

"Sunset," Philip hissed.

A breeze stirred, whirling the dust into a funnel that glittered in the last light of day. How could something so beautiful exist in a place so foul? I glanced at Philip, hoping to share the moment, but his face was buried in his sleeve.

"Mr. Ketley?"

"It stinks, like sulfur and rotting meat."

A rat dashed out of a dim corner and fled for the library.

The colors faded and the dust turned gray. The twirling breeze centered over the altar. The darkness beat like a pulse, flashing a black so deep it stung my eyes. I couldn't imagine Philip not noticing it, but he scrambled to gather the papers from the floor and Sir Jason's desk.

Dark mist materialized in the silver outline, thickening with each pulse, until the air in the circle roiled with black fog.

"Mr. Ketley!"

He glanced at the circle and swore. "Get out!" Scooping another armful of papers, he fled the room.

The black fog bubbled like a pot coming to a boil.

I hurried after Philip, grasping to pull the bookcase shut behind me. My hands slipped through. I covered my mouth, helpless to do anything against the darkness building within the circle.

Philip tossed his papers on a table and raced for the bookcase.

The hidden door swung shut before he reached it. He stumbled to a stop. The bookcase rattled. Books toppled, thumping to the floor. We slowly backed away together as the wall trembled.

"Can it—*they*—get out?" I asked, my voice shaking.

"I don't know." Philip's breath fogged the air, and his teeth chattered.

The pulse continued, too deep to hear, pounding through me to make my immaterial ears ache. Philip and I clutched our heads.

Disembodied voices glided through the air. If the wall couldn't stop me from passing, it wouldn't hold back this tide of dark, angry energy. The bookcase groaned, and the room shook, rattling the glass cases and leather tomes. Half a dozen more rats appeared from under shelves and behind furniture to scurry for the corridor.

"Run!" Philip shouted.

I followed on his heels, not risking a glance back. At any moment the hungry darkness might burst out to drown everything in an inky black flood. I had felt the strong pull of that circle; if it trapped me, I did not think I could escape, even with the moonset.

We raced past my room to the servants' staircase at the end of the hall. Philip slammed the door shut and leaned against it, panting.

"What did we do?" he asked.

"I think we woke something. We should have left it alone."

"Maybe," he whispered, his voice sharp. "How were we supposed to know? Blast it!" He closed his eyes, the muscles in his neck tight. "There's nothing to do now but press forward."

I shuddered, imagining the swirling dark fog swallowing me. We'd crossed the bridge, and it had crumbled behind us. The only future we could hope for was beyond the blackness we helped create.

Philip stared at me, fear and uncertainty in his eyes. He seemed to need me to agree with him, to tell him going forward was the right thing to do, but I wasn't certain myself. We might only make things worse. It wasn't as if I had much choice, though. He could run away; I couldn't. At least he wouldn't leave me to face the shadows alone.

"Yes," I said. "I think we were already in too deep to escape. We just know it now."

He nodded and set his jaw, though when he met my gaze, I could still see traces of fear in his eyes.

"Shall we go see then?" he asked.

I gave a quick nod, and he opened the door. Gaslights burned bright in the hall, and the shadows slept in their corners. He crept out, with me so close behind I stepped through his heels every time he paused. He scowled at the empty corridor.

"Oy!" he shouted, his voice bouncing off the high ceiling.

"Oy yourself!" called Nellie, tromping up the servants' stairs. "Mr. Ketley? Was that you makin' that racket? What're you doing up 'ere?"

"Uh." He glanced at me, and I shrugged. "Ghost hunting?" he said. "Have you seen anything unusual?"

She laughed. "Just a young man standin' alone in the 'all shouting 'is 'ead off."

"Right," Philip grinned weakly. "You'll tell me if anything else strange happens?"

"Course I will." Nellie rolled her eyes. "Old 'ouses creak and groan sometimes, you know. It's nothin' to get worked up about." She shook her head and returned downstairs.

"Back to the library," Philip whispered.

We paused outside the door.

"I'll check," I said.

"No, let me. Just in case."

He couldn't fight unquiet spirits any better than I could, but it seemed important to him, so I nodded. He swung the door open and peered inside. Motioning for me to follow, he crept forward. Other than the papers scattered over the table and floor, everything looked uncannily normal. I squinted at the shadows by the bookshelves, but they rested in their place.

"Perhaps it—or they—are trapped in the hidden room," I whispered.

"Maybe." Philip picked up the fallen books and gathered Sir Jason's documents. "Let's take these to your room. We need to look through them, and I don't want to stay here."

Back in my room, Philip shut the door and spread out the papers. Some of them fluttered in a draft sweeping the floor.

"It's like a puzzle," Philip said, rubbing his face. "Except we don't know what it's a picture of, and I'm sure some of the pieces are missing."

I grimaced at the jumbled mess. "It's probably a spell, as you said. Maybe more than one."

"So, you're saying we have the pieces of we-don't-know-how-many puzzles here? That's encouraging." He sighed. "Nothing to do but sort them out, I suppose."

He held up the papers one by one, and we began grouping them by topic. Most referred to calling forth and summoning, as we'd expected, but a few rambled on about heart's desires, immortality, and eternity.

I wrinkled my nose. "We can add bad poetry to the list of Sir Jason's sins."

Philip grimaced and started a new stack.

I read over his shoulder as he sorted. The word *limes* caught my attention. "Oh!" My voice cracked.

Philip jumped. "What?"

"It's not English," I whispered, rubbing my palm. My hand looked more opaque now, and the once-faint word stood out in black on my skin. "*Limes*. It's Latin for *boundary*." Memories returned with my understanding. "Not just any boundary: a sacred limit. I was searching through Sir Jason's spells behind his back. I don't recall why, but I came across that word, and it was important, so I wanted to be certain I understood it. I thought it would help us stop him."

"Do you remember how?" Philip leaned forward, his eyes bright.

I pushed against the darkness hazing my memories, but it was like struggling against a stone wall. Were we trying to set a boundary, or break one? I shook my head, and we scanned the paper.

I sat back. "It's instructions for setting a boundary on a spell, but it doesn't say which one. More may come back to me—or to you—as we sort through the rest."

"We'll have to go back for our papers too. When the sun's up," he added quickly.

Distant chimes tolled midnight, giving voice to the silent clock towering above us. The lights dimmed then flared. He froze and stared out at the hall.

"Did you hear that?" he hissed. "It sounded like whispers. The spirits."

I shook my head. We sat in silence, our faces turned to the door, but other than an occasional creak or flicker of the dimmed gaslights, nothing disturbed the night. Slowly we settled back into our work until, in the blackest hours of the night, moonset stole me from Philip's side.

Chapter Twelve

Moments before, I'd been sitting with Philip, reading by lamp-light. Now, daylight streamed into the room, banishing the shadows, and Philip was gone. I blinked, trying to shake the sense that I'd woken from a vivid dream. Or nightmare, as I recalled the hidden chamber in the library. Only the stacks of documents stowed under the sofa proved it was real.

I drifted to the window. The spring gardens stirred under the touch of sunshine and rain, and I longed to wander in them, breathe in the scents of fresh soil and sun-warmed flowers. My hand hovered against the glass.

If I pressed through, I might feel the heat of the sun, or float through the garden on the breeze rising from the woods. At least I'd hear birds calling their mates and see delicate petals unfolding from their winter sleep. Images of shadows and roiling black fog moved across my imagination: oblivion's maw stretching wide to swallow me. I yanked my hand back. It wasn't worth the risk.

Turning my back on the window, I paced again, fidgeting with my hair and trying to discover the cause of my itching restlessness. My gaze fell on the open almanac protruding from beneath the sofa. Where was Philip? He knew what time I'd appear, and this was the first day he hadn't been here when I awakened.

"Mr. Ketley?" I called.

I bit my fingernail. It wasn't as if he had some obligation to greet me every moonrise, but he may have gone back to the hidden room alone. We didn't know what we'd awoken, or if it was any safer during the day. He could be trapped or injured . . . or dead. I paused. Would he be a ghost, then, like me? No, it was a horrible thing to think. Philip still had a chance to live, to be free from whatever curse Sir Jason placed on us. I raced to the library.

John sat at the desk. I rushed by him and through the wall. It gave reluctantly, but was easier to pass through than it had been the previous evening. A spear of light from the window pierced the gloom. A few more papers had drifted across the floor, but otherwise the room looked undisturbed. I backed out, careful to avoid the silver circle.

John puffed rings of smoke as he went through the accounts.

"Put that thing out!" I swatted at his pipe.

His brow wrinkled, and he glanced up before turning back to the ledgers.

I blinked and stepped back.

"Hello?" I said.

John didn't respond. Smoke curled into the air, and I dragged my fingers through it. Some of it caught beneath my palm before circling up through my hand. Amazing! The smoke tickled faintly, like a breeze brushing the fine hairs on my arm. Grinning, I stirred my hand, and the vapors scattered. I waved faster, trying to catch John's attention.

He paused, staring at the odd patterns. I blew the smoke back into his face. He coughed and rubbed his eyes.

"Drafts!" he exclaimed.

"I did it!" I leaned over John's shoulder as he gathered his ledgers. He shivered and stared around the room.

"Did you feel that?" I asked. "Can you see me now? Do you hear me?"

He stormed out, oblivious to my question. I grinned. I was getting stronger. Philip would be proud. He'd laugh when I described John's face.

My smile faded. Where was Philip?

Downstairs, maids gossiped about hauntings in the wee morning hours: a boiling pot exploding in Cook's face, dishes shattering in the cupboards, flames blasting from a fireplace to scorch a maid's dress.

"Did you 'ear about Susan?" Miss Matthews asked her companion in a hushed tone as they scoured plates and cups.

"The one with the dimples?" Her friend leaned closer.

"That's 'er." Miss Matthews set her rag aside. "This morning she said she saw somethin' in the mirror, a ghastly, white face. She fainted dead away, but that 'andsome gamekeeper caught 'er."

"Philip Ketley, you mean?"

"That's 'im." Miss Matthews sighed wistfully.

My shoulders relaxed. At least Philip had been all right this morning. Poor Susan, though. Hadn't she been haunted enough? Maybe Philip was still with her, protecting her. Something twisted in my stomach, an almost-physical blow. I squeezed my eyes shut. It was ridiculous to be jealous. Philip couldn't be mine.

"Mmm." The other maid giggled. "I wish 'e'd catch me."

"'E was supposed to go the Miller's dance, but 'e missed it. Leastwise I didn't see 'im there."

No, he was with me. My triumphant grin quickly faded. What right did I have to keep him from having fun? He wasn't going to spend the rest of his life with a ghost, someone he couldn't touch or grow old with. I didn't want him going odd like poor Edmund. This was why ghosts weren't supposed to linger. I didn't belong to anyone's world anymore.

For now, though, I had to find Philip, make certain he was all right.

Upstairs, Edmund slept at his desk. I stood over his shoulder and glanced at the words peeking from beneath his hand: *eternal love, black-winged dove, endless bliss, deathly kiss*. I tried to smooth the hair back from his pale, haggard face, and he whimpered in his sleep. I left him to his rest and his haunted dreams, my mind still on Philip.

I drifted back up to the floor with my room and the library. The clocks in the house struck noon. My clock's hands forever pointed to twelve. Were they trapped at midnight or noon? Noon was a more reasonable hour for someone to stop the clocks, and a friendlier one.

Philip stood in the library, alone, his back to me. He'd tossed his coat aside, and his cotton shirt stretched across his wide shoulders as he reached for one of the books. I took a guilty moment to study him as he flipped through the tome, his blue eyes serious and his lips curved in a frown. My stomach fluttered. No wonder the maids were giddy over him. It was more than his good looks and easy strength, though. It was the way he didn't give up, he worried about other people, his humor drove away his darker moods.

Had I appreciated those things when I knew him before? Images of Philip's face darted through my mind—instances I couldn't remember, except that he'd been there. I'd watched him, admired him. Perhaps he'd had no interest in me, or something had come between us. My chest tightened with a sense of forgotten loss.

He looked up, and I jumped.

"Did I startle you?" He raised his eyebrows. "I never thought I'd scare a ghost."

"I just wasn't expecting you. I didn't know where you'd gone." I tried not to make it sound like a question. It was none of my business, after all. If he'd been with Susan, maybe I didn't want to know.

"I had to run an errand for the gamekeeper."

"Oh, of course." I smiled. "I scared away John Springett—played with the smoke from his pipe and blew it into his face."

"That's wonderful! I knew you'd get the hang of it." His grin faded. "Sorry I kept you waiting. I'd hoped to get back earlier so we could go back in the room. Not that I'm anxious to face it again, but I think it's the only way."

I nodded, and he set his book aside to swing the bookcase open. We peered in, but nothing stirred at our presence. Philip tiptoed to Sir Jason's desk and frowned at the skull.

"We'll just grab the papers," he said. "I'm sorry about the skull, but I get a dark feeling from it. I don't want to disturb any of Sir Jason's relics until we know what they might do."

"I understand." But I still felt sorry for the skull's owner.

He hurried to his desk, gathering stacks of documents. The silver circles on the floor looked tarnished in the daylight, and I leaned as close as I dared to study them. Could they be a passage to the spirit world? The darkness we'd seen the night before was clearly not the paradise promised in church. I understood oblivion better than I wanted, but now I wished I had more than my imagination to tell me about heaven. I glanced at Philip. At least I had a friend to talk it through with.

"Mr. Ketley?"

"Hmm?"

"What do you think it's like, after a soul passes on?"

He straightened with a frown. "Why?"

"I'm going to have to eventually, aren't I?"

"I suppose. Maybe you don't have to go soon, though. You might be able to stay for . . . a long time." He glanced down at his desk. "I mean, if you wanted to."

"I don't think it's good for people to have a ghost around," I said quietly.

"Some ghosts, but you're not hurting anything. I don't see why you wouldn't be able to stay. It would be nice, and I'd miss you otherwise." He grinned. "Who else would put up with my teasing?"

When he smiled like that, who wouldn't? I swallowed. "You must want someone real to talk to."

"You're real enough." He sighed. "Besides, what am I supposed to say to people? I think my name's Philip Ketley. I don't remember anything past last week, and I may be steeped in black magic. My only prospects are working as an assistant gamekeeper for a half-crazy baronet, and that's if I survive another night of ghost attacks."

"I don't think all that bothers the girls who work in the kitchen," I mumbled.

"Oh?" His boyish grin returned. "Have you been spying again?"

"I'm not doing it on purpose." I picked at my fingernail. "I just miss people. I want to feel connected." I raised an eyebrow. "And they're all saying you're a hero now."

"A hero?"

"Catching swooning maids."

"Ah." Philip shuddered and grabbed another handful of papers. "That wasn't heroic. I came looking for an early breakfast, and some of the maids were talking to me. We heard this horrible laugh, and Sir Jason's face appeared in the mirror. Miss Lamb screamed and passed out. I was so stunned, I just caught her when she fell. If I'd been standing a little to the right, they'd be calling me a lunkhead who drops fainting girls instead of a hero."

"You saw Sir Jason in the mirror? Just in the reflection, not outside of it?"

"Just in the mirror, but if I had any doubts before, I'm sure now that he is among our legion of ghosts."

"Probably the voice—the commanding one," I said. Sir Jason could appear in mirrors, and I still didn't have a reflection, except when Philip looked at me. If I could stay near Philip forever, I would always feel connected to this world, but that wouldn't be good for either of us.

"You never answered my question," I said quietly. "What do you think heaven's like?"

"Hmm." He leaned on the desk. "I'm too practical for these kinds of questions. I can only imagine it's similar to here—whatever good or bad we make of this life just goes on with us. Though I suppose it wouldn't be heaven if it didn't offer a measure of justice that's missing from this world."

My gaze found my desk, where I'd written about black magic, possibly helped compose spells. "I think I'd rather have mercy than justice. Do you believe in second chances?"

"I guess I do." He waved the papers. "I think I have to." He pulled out his desk drawers to peer behind them. His eyes narrowed. "What's that?"

I hovered closer and tried to see. He reached deep inside the desk and carefully pulled out a long, folded piece of paper.

"Could it have fallen there on accident?" I asked.

"I don't see how. It looks like I hid it."

Philip set the other documents aside to smooth it out. The color drained from his face as he read it.

"What is it?" I asked.

"It's Sir Jason's will," he said so quietly I had to lean in to hear. "He named me as his baseborn son and sole heir."

Chapter Thirteen

I covered my gasp.

"Blast it! I don't believe it." Philip crumpled the will and tossed it into the corner.

I didn't want to either, but it explained how he knew the estate so well and why he was working with Sir Jason. There was no resemblance between the two of them, but that didn't necessarily mean anything. Of course, if Philip was the sole heir, it still didn't tell us anything about me. He rubbed his face, his expression full of anger and self-reproach.

"You can't help where you came from," I said softly.

"Maybe not, but I feel unclean just thinking of it." He wiped his hands on his coat. "Why did I hide the will in here?"

"Would you have wanted to inherit?"

"Be the heir of all this?" He gestured to the circles, the candlesticks, the skull. "No, probably not. If this is my legacy, all the more reason to put it behind me." He glared at the crumpled paper. "Do you still think that's what we were keeping from Sir Jason?"

I studied my memory of Sir Jason attacking me in the library. "I don't know. If you hid it, he would have wanted it back, but it doesn't seem like enough to explain his actions, or why he still cares about it."

"It doesn't feel right to me either. We're missing something."

He snatched it up and smoothed it back out, adding it to his armful of documents. We hurried them to my room.

He shut the door and scowled at it. "This won't do much against spirits, I suppose."

"Aren't there ways to keep ghosts out?"

"I don't want to keep you away." He flashed a warm grin, and my cheeks tingled. His smile faded, and he sighed. "I read that salt works, but when I went to the kitchen to, uh, borrow, a handful . . . it burned me."

"What?"

He shifted the books and held out his hand. Dozens of tiny red welts marked his palm. "It hurt me to touch it. I suppose I've eaten some and it didn't bother me, but carrying a handful of it was too much."

I reached out, wishing I could soothe away his blisters and the worry in his eyes. "You're not a ghost," I whispered. "Why would it affect you?"

"I don't know. Maybe it's not ghosts it keeps away, but darkness." Bitterness seeped into his words. "I'm stained with a fair serving of that, aren't I?" He turned away.

I whisked in front of him. "You're trying to fix things. You're not a bad person."

"Maybe it's the magic the salt works on, then." He shrugged and met my eyes, and his expression softened. "Regardless, the only way I see to keep anyone safe is to unravel Sir Jason's spells and send the other spirits away."

Philip laid out the documents in my curly handwriting for me, keeping those covered with his own neat letters for himself. At least I could read: a strange way to interact with the world without touching it. The connection was so intimate and real, it was easy to forget it was all mind and spirit. Until it came time to turn the page. I missed the smell of paper and ink more than I longed for sunshine or food as I watched Philip thoughtlessly flip past page after page.

"These all go in the stack about summoning," I said sometime after the clocks struck midnight. The lamp flickered in the draft. Dark gathered on the edges of the light, eerily silent after so many haunted nights. It would almost be less frightening if the doors would creak or the lights flicker a few times. I kept looking over my shoulder, expecting to see spectral eyes in the shadows.

"All right, just a moment." Philip set his papers down and stretched. I yawned in sympathy, my mind numbed by the flood of words that hovered in my vision when I closed my eyes.

"Anything helpful?" he asked.

"I wrote about dissecting human corpses for spell components.

Do you want to know the three magical uses for a dead man's hand?"

Philip grimaced. "It's amazing how much I don't."

"I only hope I was copying it and not writing from personal experience."

"I know." He stacked the papers, tapping them into a neat pile. "I've been reading about forecasting the future using the livers of various animals." He shuddered and pulled out the next set of documents. "If you want a change of pace, I have some of Sir Jason's poetry, or whatever this is."

I skimmed the page.

Eternity set by bounds, yet eternity is boundless. Can one bind the unbindable? Can one tie soul and heart to one plane? They stretch over many planes. How many can we touch at once? If we touch just one at a time, can we be held to it? Can a soul die? Can a body be made immortal?

"He's rambling. He was a madman."

Philip snorted. "I think we can agree on that, but we have to try to make some sense of it."

"This sounds more like philosophy or theology than magic." I trailed my fingers through the papers. "I almost feel sorry for him. He must have gone mad when Lady Henrietta died. Edmund and John said it changed him."

Philip leaned back against the sofa. "You've seen her clearly, but never any of the other ghosts. I wonder if she isn't a normal spirit either. Maybe he found a way to call her soul back, but she got stuck somehow. After all, he may not have known what he was doing."

A lump knotted in my stomach. "What if I was an experiment?"

"You think . . ." Philip's dark brows drew low. "You think he murdered you to see if he could keep your spirit here or call you back?"

"Maybe. He might have come back for me after he chased you out of the library."

"I'll kill him." Philip jumped to his feet.

"He's already dead, remember?"

"I—" He bared his teeth. "I don't care. I'll banish him to Hell where he belongs. I've seen enough of these spells. I could do it, make him suffer."

"No, Mr. Ketley!" I scrambled up. "You're talking about black magic. That's not the way to fix our mistakes, or his."

"He shouldn't have touched you! Someone needs to make him pay." He slammed his fist against the wall, denting the wood panel. I shrank back.

He stared at his knuckles and sank onto the sofa. "What's wrong with me? I'm afraid I am the man in my dreams, always shouting and hitting." He rubbed his eyes then looked up at me, his face creased by fear and pain. "I'm sorry. I think I need to get some sleep. I'm not feeling entirely myself."

"Of course." My shoulders relaxed. "I wasn't thinking of how late it must be for you."

"It's more than that. I dream of lashing out with magic. It's so real, I can feel the power flowing through my hands. It might be memories. I wake up with this hate and anger trying to claw its way free, like they're living things inside me." He dropped his head into his hands. "I'm afraid of what I might do."

"You don't want to hurt people," I said softly. "You can keep your temper in check."

"I hope you're right, Miss Tregarrick, but it'll be easier to do if I have some rest. Do you want to keep working?"

The stacks of documents surrounded us, piled up like an accounting of all our forgotten sins. My stomach sank. I wanted to throw them out the window, take Philip's hand, and run somewhere far from this world of ghosts and magic. "I'd rather take a break," I managed to say.

He stashed the papers under the sofa and bid me goodnight. The room felt empty without him. I drifted into the hall. The lights flickered, and I flinched from the shadows. The other ghosts stayed quiet, but I was alone now. No wonder Lady Henrietta was skittish.

Light glowed from Edmund's antechamber, promising refuge. I don't know if I hoped to find him awake or asleep, but he wasn't there. I frowned. Where would he be in the middle of the night? It wasn't my business, but it seemed unhealthy to be wandering so late. I glided to his desk and stared at the flowing handwriting. More poems.

I bind myself to you, and you to me
To wake as one or sleep eternally.

I rolled my eyes. He was getting worse. Another scrap read:

Cursed. Dark beast prowling.
Ripping, tearing, shredding my heart.
Clawing its way free.

It sounded like Philip's nightmares, almost the same words he'd used. Were Edmund and Philip dreaming the same things? I needed to see more. Narrowing my eyes, I slid my hand over the papers. My fingertips tingled, but the poems didn't move. Philip and Edmund's well-being might depend on what was written here, and perhaps my own salvation as well. The top paper shivered when I huffed. I wet my lips and funneled air at the page. It fluttered aside.

I'd done it again! If only Philip could see! I noticed what was written on the page, and my smile faded.

Where does the soul dwell?
What plane does it touch?

Cold clutched my chest. The words were too much like Sir Jason's.

"Midnight muse!"

I whirled. Edmund staggered in from the hall, rubbing his eyes.

"I've had the oddest dream. When I woke up, I was in the library. I felt like I'd lost something, and I might find it there."

"Lost something? In the library?"

"Yes." He yawned and ambled to the desk, squinting at the papers. "My! What imagery! Did I write these?"

"You don't remember?"

"I think I'm doing things in my sleep. It's astounding. I'm so inspired, the poems won't let me rest, even when I'm so tired I beg for slumber."

I shook my head. "That isn't right, Edmund. You need sleep. Will you lie down now?"

"Yes, if you command it, darling Lucy. I need to see to my plans for the ball, but that will wait for morning."

He stumbled into his bedroom and collapsed, fully dressed, through the bed curtains. I shook my head. He sounded a little more rational than usual, but all this talk of doing things in his sleep . . . and these horrible poems in Sir Jason's words.

My chest tightened. If Sir Jason was the voice commanding me, he might also be speaking to Philip and Edmund as they slept, possibly guiding or controlling them. I'd assumed Edmund could see me because he was a romantic, looking beyond the everyday, but it might be because Sir Jason was influencing him. Perhaps it was all tied together: his reaching for grander visions made him more susceptible to dark influences as well as noble ones.

What of Philip? He'd seen me first, and he dreamed of using magic. Sir Jason might be manipulating him to perform some spell, finish whatever dark work he'd left undone. What would that do to Philip? I couldn't let him sleep if it allowed Sir Jason inside his mind.

I didn't know where to find Philip, though. I flew out of the room and down the halls toward the kitchens. As I hoped, a scullery maid slept on a pallet in front of the stove, warmed by its banked fire.

"Where do the men sleep?" I asked.

She didn't stir. This would be a problem. A rat scuttled past us in the dark, and the maid shifted. I leaned down by her ear.

"Where can I find Philip Ketley?"

Her eyelids fluttered.

"Philip Ketley. Where can I find him?" I pleaded. "Where does he sleep?"

She groaned and rolled over. At least in her sleep she could hear me. I'd never considered trying to talk to people this way before, but if it was easier for me, it must be for Sir Jason and the other ghosts as well.

"Where's Philip Ketley?" I shouted.

"Outside, with the stablehands," she muttered. "Go back to sleep."

Outside. I wanted to think him safe, not being in the house, but he had nightmares even out there, dreams of working spells.

The back door was locked for the night, but that didn't affect me. Sir Jason's spells might, though. He could have bound me to the house. What would happen to me if I stepped outside? I could be gliding into oblivion's grasp. But what might happen to Philip if I didn't? I wouldn't leave him in danger.

I pushed my hand past the solid oak then drew it back in. It looked normal, at least for me. Whispers rolled around the kitchen, and the hanging pots jangled against the wall.

Stop.

The voice. Was there a chance it was trying to help, to warn me? My movements slowed as I struggled against its control. No, a friendly spirit wouldn't coerce me to its will. Sir Jason wanted to stop me, which had to mean I was doing the right thing.

I inhaled and threw myself against the door. It pushed back against me, but I twisted through, the chains of Sir Jason's command slipping from my mind. The glimmering nighttime world opened before me, black and silver in the moonlight. I stretched my arms wide and marveled.

The quarter moon sat heavy on the western horizon. In just a few minutes it would vanish, and so would I. If I disappeared outside, would I be gone forever? I spun back to the door and paused, thinking of Philip. I had a few minutes; it would have to be enough.

I ran past the kitchen garden, searching for the stablehand's quarters. A light glowed from the stable loft. Not pleasant accommodations, but it made sense. I raced through the stable door. The horses jolted awake, neighing and rearing. I shrank from their rolling eyes and pounding hooves.

Shouts sounded from above.

"What's all this, then? 'Orse thieves?"

"It'd better be a good fight if they're dragging us out at night."

The other voices laughed, and a cavalcade of young men holding lanterns and pitchforks trotted down the stairs. Philip trailed behind them. He saw me, and his eyes widened. I rushed outside as the stablehands began their search of the stalls. Philip slipped after me into the dark night. The frantic horses quieted behind us.

"Miss Tregarrick!" Philip whispered. "What are you doing here? I didn't think you could come outside!"

"I had to warn you not to sleep!"

"Not to sleep?"

"Yes. He's in your dreams. I saw—"

Oblivion seized me, whisking away my warning.

Chapter Fourteen

Prickles crawled over my skin as I flowed back together, like pins and needles on my limbs. I gasped at the new sensation and stared at my translucent hands.

I'd survived my excursion outside, at least. Philip slept on the sofa in front of me. His brow furrowed, and my chest tightened. Sir Jason might be harassing him even while the sun shone.

"Mr. Ketley!" My hands scrambled helplessly at his shoulder. "Please, don't sleep!"

He jerked awake with a gasp, lashing out. His angry glare softened when it fell on me. "Miss Tregarrick?"

"I think he's in your dreams! Edmund had all these awful poems—"

"Wait, wait." He rubbed his eyes. "I'm a little groggy, so you'll have to slow down. I tried to stay awake like you said." He looked at me, curiosity and a warmth I didn't understand in his expression. "You came outside to find me. When did you stop being afraid to leave the house?"

My cheeks tingled. "You were in danger. I had to warn you. You shouldn't have let yourself fall asleep."

"I'm alive," he said softly. "I have to sleep sometime. In here, though, I didn't have any nightmares. I don't know if it's the daylight, or if you were guarding my rest."

I almost scolded him for teasing, but he wasn't laughing. I bit my lip. I wanted to believe I could protect him somehow, but I wouldn't gamble his safety on a romantic notion. "I don't know. It may be safer to sleep during the day, when the other ghosts aren't around."

He nodded and leaned forward. "So, what happened to upset you?"

"I went to check on Edmund last night—"

"Oh?" Philip scowled and raked back his hair.

"He wasn't around, but I looked at some of his writings. They sounded like Sir Jason's notes and your dreams, about the plane where souls dwell, being bound together, and black beasts. Then Edmund came in, and he said he was doing things in his sleep: writing poems, searching for something. I thought, what if Sir Jason is manipulating him in his sleep, and you as well?"

"That makes sense. My dreams frighten me." Philip shuddered, and he dropped his voice. "The man I see beating the woman? I think he's my father."

I blinked. "But Sir Jason's will—"

Philip shook his head. "The man looks so much like me, and I remember bits and pieces of it. He'd come home drunk and lay into whomever was close with his fists or whatever else was at hand."

"Oh, Mr. Ketley." I sank by his side, my eyes stinging.

"I stood up to him sometimes. He gave me this crooked nose and a handful of scars as reminders that I was never strong enough." Philip's eyes blazed dark with raw pain and anger.

"You tried," I whispered.

"It was never enough, though. I just wanted to be stronger. Strong enough to stop him. Strong enough to hurt him." He swallowed, his eyes fixed on a distant point. "I think that's how Sir Jason lured me here. Sometimes I hear his voice telling me he can make me strong enough."

I could hardly blame him for his choice. I stood beside him and stared at the same distant point, just beyond the reach of memory.

Finally Philip cleared his throat. "I just don't understand why Sir Jason would lie and make me his heir, unless he wanted to keep the estate from Sir Edmund for some reason. If only we knew what Sir Jason did to us, what power he might have over us . . ." He grimaced and rummaged under the sofa, pulling out the stacks of papers. "Let's go through the rest of them."

I read over his shoulder, helping him sort the documents. Disappointment settled around me as I stared at the results of our work. Somehow, I'd expected to find something momentous, like a journal detailing every jot of Sir Jason's monstrous plan.

"It's a mess," Philip said. "I didn't see any notes about black beasts or the moon, but there are definitely enough about binding spells."

He spread that stack out, and we both scanned them.

"These talk about setting boundaries." I pointed to several notes. "It sounds like by putting limits on the range of your spells—your power—you can concentrate its strength. I wonder if those were the boundaries I was looking for."

"That makes sense, like directing light through a magnifying glass. It would make it stronger, but if you broke the glass, the light would dissipate." He flipped through the documents. "This is similar. It says you can pour your power into one object to give it focus."

He shuffled through more of the papers on binding spells, and we scanned them.

"These don't tell us anything new." Philip tossed them back in the stack and pulled out several more documents.

One of Sir Jason's spidery notes caught my attention, sending a chill pouring over me. "Mr. Ketley?"

"What is it?" He leaned closer, and I wished I could feel his warmth.

"This spell. I remember speaking these words." I could still taste them on my lips, gritty and bitter. *I bind myself to Jason Springett, strength given to strength, will to will* . . . I looked away. How could I have been so foolish?

Philip snatched up the paper and scanned it, his face turning pale as he read. "I remember it too. I hated the words. They were like thick sludge going down my throat."

We both stared at the paper, rereading the terrible promise that had given away our futures.

"Sir Jason said we had to bind ourselves if we wanted to share in his power and knowledge," I whispered.

Philip's gaze turned distant. "There was something else, too, wasn't there? Something we had to touch to complete the spell?"

"I . . ." My hand tingled. "Yes, something cool and smooth." I curled my fingers over the memory. "It fit in the palm of my hand."

"So we were bound to an object. Both of us. One that tied us to his magic." Philip tapped his chin.

"That could be what we took from him. Would he need it back?"

"Yes, especially if he was using it to channel his power." Philip pulled out the page describing how to use an object as a focus for power. We read it more carefully, and he nodded. "If this is correct, he would need it to complete whatever spell he was trying to create."

"No wonder it's so important. Could all of this just be meant to bring back Lady Henrietta?" It was a darkly poetic notion, but it went beyond the limits of my romantic tastes.

"Maybe. It doesn't sound like it's that difficult to summon a spirit, but maybe something about the circumstances made it more challenging." He sighed. "We should see what's in those poems Sir Edmund is writing, find out if there's any clues to Sir Jason's intentions. What would be a good time to sneak into Sir Edmund's chambers?"

"I don't know. He doesn't seem to keep regular hours."

Philip looked away. "You know him well enough to guess, I'm sure. You went to his chambers last night."

"Mr. Ketley! What are you implying? Be reasonable. I was frightened, and I'm concerned for him. I think he's wrapped up in all this, and I don't think we can just ignore the danger to him. We are living in his house, after all. Well, I'm *dwelling* in it, and you're sleeping in the stables, but still . . ."

"Yes, I see your point." Philip paced. "If I'm caught in his rooms during the day, I can say I'm looking for him, but if I go snooping around at night, it'll look much more suspicious. We may as well go now." He gestured with a half smile. "Lead on, my lady."

His lady? The words fluttered in my chest, but I forced them to be still. He'd said it himself: I couldn't be anything to anyone now. At least, not what I'd like to be.

Edmund's antechamber was empty. I motioned Philip inside. He tiptoed over to the desk and sifted through the dozens of papers in a jumbled heap on the desk.

"Blast! He writes too much poetry!" He lifted one from the mess. "Oh, here's one about you."

"About me?" I hurried over. "Really?"

"Midnight muse? Lovely Lucy? Yes, I'm sure." He set the paper aside, face down, and wrinkled his nose. "It doesn't do you justice."

My fingers slid uselessly past the paper. "You're just being cruel. Wouldn't you want to know what someone said about you?" I folded my arms. "I hear the maids talking about you."

"Oh?" He didn't look up from the poem he was scanning. I frowned. I couldn't win if he didn't react. Before I could think of another jab, he straightened. "Here's more of what you were talking about. *Black beast rending. Darkness rising. Bind me to this mortal plane. Prison of flesh, prison of stone.* It goes on. It doesn't even seem like poetry, just raving."

"Yes, I do think Edmund is unstable. At least he finally moved that picture." I pointed to the bare spot in the antechamber where the portrait of Sir Jason and Lady Henrietta once hung. My gaze traveled through the open door to the bedchamber, and my throat tightened. "That doesn't seem right."

"What?"

"He hung it in there. Why would he want a picture of his uncle in his bedchamber?"

Philip studied the picture. "Maybe it's not the uncle he's interested in."

"What do you mean?"

"Lady Henrietta. Edmund might by fascinated with her now too."

"His aunt?" I wrinkled my nose and slipped past him to stare at her portrait.

Philip came up next to me. "His aunt by marriage." He cleared his throat. "She looks familiar, maybe from my dreams. If Sir Jason is influencing his nephew's mind, Sir Edmund might've picked up his uncle's obsession. Miss Tregarrick, this could make him dangerous."

"You don't think he'd hurt someone?"

"Under Sir Jason's influence? Possibly." Philip squinted at the embroidered bed curtains and traced the stitched outline of one of the tree branches. "This is beautiful." His frown twisted up. "What do you think, knowledge or life?"

"What?"

He motioned to the embroidered panel. "Is it the Tree of Knowledge or the Tree of Life? Both were in the garden, but there's only one tree in the picture, and someone spent an incredible amount of time on it. It may have meant something to Sir Jason."

"Oh, I never thought of that." I stared at the beautiful tree with its tempting fruit. Knowledge or life? What was Jason more obsessed with? "Which would you choose?"

"Me?" Philip asked. "Given how much I hate not remembering, I can understand why Eve chose knowledge. What about you? You have a different perspective on it."

If I could have my life back, but no memory, would I take it? What about remembering everything, but staying as I was? Why couldn't it be possible to have both? "I don't know."

"Hello?" Edmund called from the antechamber. "Is someone here?"

Philip grimaced and backed behind the curtained bed.

"What are you doing?" I whispered. "I thought you were going to pretend you needed to talk to him."

"In his bedchamber?" Philip hissed. "That would look a bit odd, don't you think? Get him out of here!"

I stepped back so I could see the antechamber while watching Philip's hiding place and called, "Edmund, it is I."

He smiled broadly and flung his arms out as he stepped into the bedroom. "Midnight muse! Moonlight maiden! I bathe in your inspiration, I drift in the dreams you send me as if I slept in your arms."

Philip's eyes narrowed. I focused on Edmund, whose gaze darted restlessly around the room.

"But Edmund, dark forces invade your dreams. You must beware of those who would use you for their own purposes."

"You're an angel, darling Lucy, always looking out for me. Perhaps you're right. I would sleep more peacefully if you could stay with me. Will you visit me tonight?"

Philip twisted the edge of the bed curtain in his fist.

"I may not be able to, Edmund," I said quickly.

"Of course, darling Lucy. You're sent to me by the gods, by the moon herself. Thank you for your warning."

"You might do best to sleep only during the day."

His bloodshot eyes turned distant. "It's by looking deep into the darkness that we find the truth. If I keep searching, it will become clearer."

"Look in the light, Edmund. Darkness only confuses, gets us lost."

Philip made a shooing gesture.

"Will you show me what you've written?" I asked.

Edmund shook off his vacant expression. "Yes, of course." He wandered to the desk, gesturing at the sloping, haphazard stack of poems.

"You've been busy." I scanned the papers. "It's very vivid. Can you tell me about it?"

Philip peered out of the bedroom.

"It comes to me in visions," Edmund whispered. He plucked at the collar of his shirt and stared into the shadowy corner with wide eyes. "The dark animal chases me. The walls close in. She's forever eluding me."

Philip tiptoed for the door.

"She?" I asked.

"The lost soul. I have to find her, bring her back, make her immortal."

"Is there not immortality in words? in memory?" I asked as Philip reached the hallway.

"It's not enough!" Edmund shouted. "It fades, it dies. All things are forgotten. All things die and pass beyond our grip." He paced, tearing at his hair. "If I were only stronger, I would keep her here forever."

He collapsed at his desk, sobbing like a child. Scattered poems drifted to the floor.

I couldn't comfort him, so I whispered in his ear, "Rest, Edmund, while the light protects your dreams."

He closed his eyes and turned his face from me. I slipped out.

Philip walked next to me in silence. Finally, he said, "I see why you worry for him, but I don't like the way he talked to you."

"Oh?" I smiled sadly. "Some of it was rather sweet."

"You like hearing all that nonsense about being his muse?"

I winced and looked away. "Everyone likes to know they inspire someone. We want to know our life matters." My voice dropped. "Or mattered."

Philip's boots beat a heavy tread over the carpet in the long gallery. "Sometimes we might not be able to tell people they inspire us. We can't all be poets, after all, and it's frightening to think of pouring one's heart out, especially if the other person would think us a fool."

He scowled at the floor, and I bit my lip. I longed to be the one who inspired him, but I wasn't truly a muse.

"Miss Tregarrick?" he asked.

"Yes?"

"I probably ought to go back outside, since I'm supposed to be, uh, watching for poachers or something."

"You don't know what an assistant gamekeeper actually does, do you?" I smiled.

"Not as such." He flashed his boyish grin. "I don't want to be dismissed, though, especially not now. I was thinking, since you've ventured outside the walls of the house now, that you could come with me. Maybe a change of scene will give us some fresh ideas."

"I suppose it might."

We went down the back staircase and through the servant's area of the house. A maid passed us and smiled at Philip, but he didn't notice.

"Oh, dear," I said once the girl was out of sight.

Philip's head snapped up. "What?"

"You must be worried about something. You missed flirting with that poor maid completely."

"Blast. Did I?" He looked over his shoulder.

"Now she'll spend the day wondering what she did to earn your displeasure."

"I wouldn't want that." His teasing smile glinted in his blue eyes. "I promise to flirt extra next time I see her."

I laughed. "You know you're wicked, don't you?"

"I just like to hear you laugh." He grabbed his bowler from the hat rack and swung the back door open for me.

"You don't have to do that."

"I'm being polite. I'm not going to stand by and let you float through the door." He smiled and waved me through with a bow.

"People will think you're insane." I paused at the threshold.

His smile faded, and he sighed. "They may be right. Are you ready?"

"Yes."

I stepped into the sunshine.

Chapter Fifteen

The light shone through me without casting a shadow. I stumbled to a stop.

"Are you all right?" Philip hurried to my side.

"The sunlight..."

"Does it hurt?" He turned to shelter me in his shadow.

"No, but it doesn't warm me either. I'd hoped to feel something from it, I suppose."

"Would you like to go back in?"

The house loomed behind me, its battlements cold and gray against the bright afternoon sky. "Not yet. What did you want to show me?"

"Everything, I guess."

We stood on the south side of the house, facing the kitchen gardens and stables. Beyond them were orchards, pastures, and woodlands.

"There are formal gardens behind the house," Philip said, "and a hedge maze on the north side, though I suppose you might cheat and just glide right through."

"Perhaps." I grinned.

He chuckled. "Then you could help me find the way out. Do you want to see the lake too?"

I nodded, and we walked around the front of the house. The lake glittered in the sunlight as we strolled past. A pair of rowboats sat beached on the shore, oars poking over their sides invitingly, but I wasn't sure what would happen if I tried to sit in a boat or go over the water. On the far side of the house, we found the entrance to the maze. Its dense, green walls cast deep shadows.

"Would you like to race?" he asked.

"I might cheat, remember?"

"Not if you swear not to. I know your word is good."

"I suppose I have to be honest after that." I wrinkled my nose. "I promise. Have you found your way through before?"

"Maybe." He winked. "We'll see who can reach the center first. Ready?"

I tossed back my loose hair and nodded.

"Go!"

We started in different directions, but I wheeled to follow him. His boots pounded over the gravel, and he didn't look back. I pushed myself to glide just behind as he darted down the shady, twisting paths. Philip didn't hesitate as he raced through numerous turns.

The center of the maze opened before us, marked by a white globe on a pedestal. Philip laughed and slowed his pace, reaching for the stone. I sprinted ahead, dashing through him to reach the pedestal first.

He shouted and stumbled to a stop. I smiled, and he chuckled and wiped his forehead.

"Were you behind me the whole time?" he asked.

I nodded, and we laughed together. Our merriment faded, and we stood grinning at each other. The maze seemed bright and warm despite the deep shade. Philip reached to flick back a stray lock falling over my shoulder. He stopped himself and took off his hat to rake his fingers through his hair. I bit my lip and looked away.

Philip cleared his throat and leaned against the pedestal. "That was a good trick." He smiled, but it didn't reach his eyes. "It wasn't cheating, either, I suppose. You're not even out of breath, are you?"

"Of course not, but it was almost . . . tiring. How strange." I tilted my head, trying to analyze the change, but the feeling was gone. The light shifting over the stone drew my gaze. "That's beautiful."

"Hmm? Oh, it is, isn't it?" He tapped its iridescent surface.

"It almost looks like trapped sunshine," I said. "I wonder what it is."

"I have no idea. Shall we find our way out?"

I nodded, and we strolled together out of the maze's high walls. As we left the tall hedges, I noticed a vague heaviness pulling me back, an echo of what I'd felt passing through the walls of the house.

"Do you feel anything odd?" I asked.

Philip tilted his head. "No. Why?"

"I don't know. It was difficult to move for a moment. Let's keep walking. I want to get out of the shadows."

He gave me a concerned glance and guided me to the gardens stretching behind the house. The sense of something tugging at me faded. Low boxwood hedges divided the back of the estate into a patchwork of open spaces, like outdoor rooms carpeted with turf and furnished with walkways, arbors, stone benches, and flowers. Daffodils created drifts of yellow and white in front of us. Between them, green tulip blades pierced the soil, breaking free from their winter tomb, and fragile vines bursting with colorful flowers climbed for the sun.

"Oh! Sweetpeas." Memories flashed across my mind of burying my face in a bouquet of their flowers and tracing the delicate, curving petals. "They're blooming so early."

"The gardeners said they were overrunning the greenhouse, so they brought them out."

"I think they're my favorite." Maybe I'd been the one growing them. It was encouraging to think I might have done something in my time at the estate that had pleasant results.

Philip plucked one of the flowers and twirled the stem between his fingers. "You seem more like the type to like roses."

"The type?"

"You know, young, pretty, romantic."

"You think I'm pretty?" I raised my eyebrows.

He snapped his mouth shut and shrugged. "Pretty enough. This way. Don't dawdle!"

I drifted behind him, grinning foolishly. He led me back to the south side of the house. In the orchard, blooming trees dripped pink petals that fluttered through me. Horses grazed in the nearby pasture, their foals racing on long, knobby legs. Two of them ran up to the fence, but they reared and shied away.

I backed up. "I'm sorry. I think they're frightened of me."

Philip reached through the fence, and they snorted and ran from him. “Of me too. The horses panic every time I walk in the stables.”

“I wonder why?”

“Maybe they sense that I’m tainted too.”

“Is that what we are? Tainted?”

“I don’t know.” He looked toward the woods, his eyes troubled. Then his expression brightened. “There’s a place you’ll like. Come with me.”

He hurried for the trees. Tangled branches choked the path, but I didn’t need to worry about tearing my dress or even stumbling, so I glided after him into the shade. Philip looked back from time to time to motion me on, his face lit by a smile. Finally he stopped.

“Can you see with your eyes closed?”

“No.”

“Good. Close them and keep walking. Don’t look until I say.”

“Walk with my eyes closed? What if I run into something?”

He raised an eyebrow. I glanced at the mossy ground visible through my bustled skirts and looked up sheepishly. “Oh, of course.”

He grinned. “See, nothing to be concerned about. Just head toward the stream.”

“There’s a stream?”

“Can’t you hear it?”

“No.” I cocked my head. “That’s strange. Your ears must be very keen.”

“I suppose.” He shrugged. “If you can’t hear the stream, just go straight ahead; you’re facing the right direction.”

I shut my eyes and pressed forward. Somehow, I kept my sense of the ground’s gentle ups and downs. “Am I going the right way?”

“Yes, just a bit farther.” He paused as I glided forward. “There, you can open them.”

A carpet of flowers spread around me like a low purple cloud. Bees hummed among the nodding blossoms, and orange and white butterflies flitted across patches of sunshine.

“Oh, Mr. Ketley! It’s so beautiful my heart might break.”

“Is that a good thing?” His deep voice sounded close to my ear.

“Yes.”

"Then I'm glad." I heard the smile in his voice.

"I wish I could stay here forever."

"Who says you have to haunt the house? You could be a spirit of the woods. The flowers won't last forever, but they'll come back every year."

"I think I'd get lonely."

Philip rubbed his jaw. "I'll build a little cottage out here, and you can haunt that. Maybe over there by the stream."

I didn't want to admit how much I liked the idea of just Philip and me cozy together in this beautiful place.

"Shall we go look?" he asked.

I nodded, and he forged a path around the flowers, careful not to tread on them and spoil the effect. He gestured for me to join him on a large, flat rock. On one side, the cloud of purple blossoms spread away from us, and on the other a little stream gurgled over the rocks. A silvery fish flashed under the water, and tiny, long-legged insects darted over the surface.

Philip sprawled out on his stomach to gaze down at the stream. I settled next to him. We stayed in our comfortable silence as the sun moved across the sky and shadows shifted in the woods.

He stretched and smiled at me. "I think this must be what heaven is like."

"Quite nearly." I sighed and touched the rock where the sun's heat should have soaked into my fingers.

His gaze focused on me, turning serious. "Yes, quite nearly." He reached for my hand, and I inhaled slowly, praying to once again feel a hint of his warmth. His fingers slid through. I stared at him, while he stared at his hand, clearly visible through mine. The sadness on his face echoed the misery tightening my throat.

Knowledge or life? It wasn't a difficult decision.

"You can't feel that, can you?" Philip asked quietly.

"No." My voice caught.

"How can you be so close, yet so far out of reach?" His gaze found mine, and he searched my face. "Thought and feeling without any substance. Maybe those are the things that matter most."

"Yes," I whispered, "but I miss the rest of it."

He pulled his hand from mine. "So do I."

My chest ached as if my silent heart were twisting. Philip hopped off the rock and held out his hand for me then curled it into a fist. I jumped down, smoothing my skirts. We walked a meandering course through the woods as the sun dropped low in the sky, igniting the clouds with pink and orange. Birds darted and trilled overhead, and a breeze whispered through the shimmering green of new leaves.

"Thank you for showing me," I said, forcing cheer into my voice. "You were right. It's good to have a change of scene." After all, how many more beautiful moments might I enjoy before I passed out of this world? If Philip was right, and we made our heaven in this life, I hoped this afternoon could be a part of mine. "Mr. Ketley?"

"Yes?"

"Would you . . ." I shook my head. "Nevermind."

"Oh, no." He stopped and folded his arms. "I know that trick. You want something, and you're not going to tell me, so I have to guess, and if I get it wrong I'll never hear the end of it. Come on, out with it."

I looked back into the woods. "I don't have the right to ask."

"Who says what rights you have? Tell me, how can I be of service?"

"Don't show anyone else," I said in a rush. "I don't want to share . . . that place."

He watched me solemnly, his gaze almost tender. "I promise. It's yours." His expression lightened. "Besides, who would I show?"

"Oh, I hear the rumors."

"Rumors?"

I looked away, regretting my loose tongue.

Philip's brow drew together. "What rumors, Miss Tregarrick?"

"It doesn't matter," I whispered, hurrying forward.

"It matters to me." Philip ran ahead and stepped into my path.

I could have passed through, but I stopped with a sigh. "The girls are all infatuated with you, and they say you're a bit of a rake . . ."

"A rake!" His face fell. "You don't really think that of me, do you?"

"That's just what they say. It's not my business." The tingling on my face was so intense, it must have colored me bright red.

"Maybe not, but it's mine. I don't want you thinking I'm some sort of scoundrel. Whatever I may have done in the past, I'm not the type to . . ." He pressed his lips together and stared at the ground. "At least, I hope that's not what I was," he said more quietly. "I think less of all those maids flirting with me, if that's their opinion. I'll make amends by being perfectly solemn and not flirting back."

"Don't make promises you can't keep." I whispered, shying from his dark gaze.

"I would never," he said, his expression so earnest I couldn't help believing him. He squinted into the evening gloom. "Blast, you've distracted me," he said, though his cheerfulness sounded forced. "Where are we?"

We'd wandered out a different way than we came in, and the trees grew thick around us.

"The house is that way." I pointed to the battlements peeking through the treetops, glad for the change of subject.

Philip blazed a trail through the thick undergrowth, stopping short when the ground dipped down. A small, narrow building made of gray stones huddled in the dense trees in front of us. It had no windows or doors that I could see, and a low roof. It couldn't have held more than one room.

"What's that?" I asked.

"I've never seen it before, but I'm not surprised since it's tucked in this little corner of the woods. Maybe it's one of those false ruins the gentry build to remind us how cultured they are."

"They're called follies," I said, "and I think they're romantic."

He laughed. "I'd be disappointed if you didn't. Do you want to explore it?"

"It's getting dark."

"All the more reason to avoid the house. Besides, wouldn't ruins be more romantic at night?"

I cocked an eyebrow. "I think you might have a poetic soul after all."

Philip winked. His teasing grin warmed me when his touch—even the sun's rays—could not. I tried to wrap the feeling inside me and store it with the other memories of the day.

He pushed his way around the side of the stone building: a gray block lost in a tangle of clawing branches. His coat was snagged and dirty by the time we found the front. He straightened his hat and stared up, his face going pale.

"Miss Tregarrick, stay back."

Greek columns guarded the gray façade, with the name *Springett* engraved across the top in thick, heavy letters. Deep shadows hung under the portico, almost hiding the rusted iron door in the dark recess. Philip dropped back next to me.

"It's a mausoleum," I said.

Chapter Sixteen

"Maybe we should walk away, pretend we didn't see it," Philip whispered, shuffling back from the gray tomb.

"What's wrong?" I'd never seen Philip squeamish.

"I didn't want you to have to think about it." He rubbed the back of his neck and looked away. "Try not to be angry with me, but I've been searching for your grave, and Sir Jason's too. I thought we might learn something."

"Oh. I appreciate your consideration, but you needn't shelter me from those sorts of things." I glanced at the mausoleum. Clambering, dried vines, not yet touched by spring, crossed the stones like withered veins. "You haven't found anything before this?"

"I'm not even sure how Sir Jason died. The servants said a local woman hired to do the laundry found his body in the upstairs corridor. Apparently there were no signs of foul play, but when I tried to ask the villagers about it, they looked at me as if . . . as if I might have been responsible."

"You weren't," I said firmly. "They found him near my room, then?"

"That's what they say. It's one of the reasons the servants avoid the third floor if they can. They say it's the most haunted part of the house."

"I suppose maybe it is. Have you learned anything about what happened to me?"

"Nothing, thankfully. I don't like thinking of you that way." He blushed. "I mean..."

"Mr. Ketley, I'm dead," I said quietly. "I think it's important for both of us to remember that."

Philip scuffed a furrow into the ground with his boot. "Of course, I haven't forgotten." His expression still bore traces of guilt mixed with his sadness. He cleared his throat. "Shall we go inside?"

I nodded. Work would be a good distraction from the regret wrenching my chest.

Philip pulled open the heavy iron door, and its rusty hinges squealed. Two stone caskets sat side by side in the dim light of dusk. The foot of one was engraved *Henrietta, Beloved Wife*. The other read, *Jason Springett, Baronet.* A pedestal stood at their head with a white globe resting on it. It reminded me of the one in the maze, but the gloom dulled its polished surface.

"So, I suppose . . ." I gestured at the coffins.

Philip groaned. "We probably should make sure. Stay here. I'll do it."

I hovered outside as he crept in. He pushed aside the lid of Lady Henrietta's tomb, the strain flushing his face red. He glanced in and gagged violently into his sleeve. With a grimace, he shoved the lid back in place then walked slowly to Sir Jason's tomb. I bit my fingernail. Could Sir Jason, whose presence haunted us waking and sleeping, really lie moldering here in his grave?

Philip inched the lid to the side. Covering his nose, he peeked in, his face pale. Then he pushed the lid back; the scrape of stone echoed in the dim vault.

The iron door shuddered. A chill swept past as it swung through me and clanged shut. Philip shouted from inside the crypt. I bolted through the door into solid blackness.

"Mr. Ketley?" My voice bounced off the stone walls.

"Blast it. I can hardly see. Is that you by the door—the silvery shape?"

"I suppose. That's where I came in." I lifted my hands, but my eyes might as well have been shut. I certainly didn't see anything silver. The darkness had a grasping, cloying feel, like it would wrap around and suffocate me if I stayed too long.

"Thank you, Miss Tregarrick. I think I've found the handle." Philip's voice was close to my ear, and I caught a blur of movement against the dark.

The door rattled but didn't open, and Philip swore under his breath. He rammed his shoulder against it, and it swung out with a groan. Philip hurried into the still evening air, making his way toward the house. I rushed to keep up.

"What happened?" I asked.

"The door might have been an accident. I should have braced it open, but . . ." Philip hunched his shoulders and walked faster. "I heard whispers in the dark."

I shuddered and wrapped my arms around myself. "Aren't the ghosts trapped in the house?"

"You can leave, can't you? We don't know what rules they follow."

"Or if they have to follow any rules at all." I suspected most of my own limitations came from habit and fear. What if they'd moved beyond those things? If Sir Jason reached into the minds of people as they slept, how far might his influence extend? "What about the coffins?" I asked quietly. "Were they . . ." I hesitated, not certain which answer would upset me more.

"Sir Jason and Lady Henrietta are both there. They're . . . definitely dead. It doesn't make sense, really. If Sir Jason was planning on bringing Henrietta back like we suspect . . ." He stopped at the edge of the lawn and closed his eyes. His voice dropped to a horrified whisper. "Please, no."

A chill trickled down my back. "What are you thinking?"

"We've been assuming Sir Jason was trying to bring Henrietta back, but what does that mean?"

"He summoned her spirit, or at least I imagine that's why she's trapped here." I thought over his ramblings, or Sir Edmund's, about making spirit whole and immortal love. "He was trying to raise the dead, wasn't he?"

Philip shook his head. "Miss Tregarrick, they were terribly decayed, especially her. Nothing I've read suggests black magic can restore rotted flesh, but it can allow a spirit to possess a living body, especially one already tainted." Philip paced. "Did he just happen to choose us as his assistants? Male and female, young, healthy, and bound to him. He lied to make me his heir." He drew a long breath. "Maybe he and Lady Henrietta planned to move into our bodies, start over. When they grew old, they'd do it again. It would be a dreadful sort of immortality."

I recoiled. "You can't really think they'd do that! Even Sir Jason couldn't be that much of a monster."

"It feels true," Philip whispered.

He was right. Something inside me recognized the truth. It explained our presence here, the binding spells, the will. My stomach twisted and I covered my face, wishing I could throw up. Anything to empty myself of the terrible thought of Sir Jason possessing Philip and summoning his wife to possess me. "We couldn't have known from the start."

"No, not that part, anyway." Philip clenched his jaw.

The last of the sun's rays slipped away. I looked up at the house, blazing with gaslight, and caught a glimpse of a familiar, sharp face in an upstairs window. My instincts screamed at me to flee, but I stood petrified, unable even to look away.

"Sir Jason!" Philip stepped forward.

The image slipped to the side and vanished.

"It was just a trick of the light," I said, my hands shaking.

"No, it wasn't." Philip kicked a tuft of grass. "He's watching us. He knows what we're doing, and he's getting stronger, while we're no closer to banishing him. Blast it! There may even be a way for him to finish the spell, take over my body and find a new one for Henrietta." He shuddered. "We have to stop him."

"Are you certain it's safe to go back inside?" I asked, but Philip marched to the house.

I shivered and raced after him, but my gaze was on the windows. Sir Jason appeared in glass and mirrors, but none of the other ghosts did. I couldn't fathom how he accomplished that trick. And I never saw him in the corridors like Lady Henrietta or the shadows. He seemed to have all the advantages, but there had to be something we could use against him.

Philip held the door for me before stepping in, and a passing parlor maid gave him a strange look. He scowled at her, and she hurried off. Apparently, he was serious about not flirting anymore. I moved at a half-run to stay with him as he strode up the stairs.

The lights in the hallway flickered and dimmed. Sharp-edged shadows darted along the walls. I huddled close to Philip. He stared down the corridor, his face pale and lips curled back in a snarl.

"Can you see that?" I whispered, pointing at the shadows.

He nodded, eyes narrow. "It's not going to work, Sir Jason!"

The portraits trembled as dark shapes swam around them, and the one of Lady Henrietta crashed to the floor. The frame shattered, ripping the canvas. The floor rumbled and a roar echoed down the corridor.

A rat fled past us, and the shadows mobbed it. The creature shrieked and writhed, slamming itself into the wall several times before falling still. My stomach turned, and I looked away. The hissing shadows slithered back up the walls.

"What's happening?" I asked, my voice trembling.

Philip reached for my hand, letting his long fingers rest over my insubstantial ones. His warmth crept into my skin, as it had in the library, and I gasped. He looked at our overlapping hands, eyes wide. Then, the feeling vanished. I whimpered and leaned closer, aching for the lost comfort of his touch.

The lights flared up, and Philip shielded his eyes. After blinking a few times, he crouched in front of the ruined picture, smoothing the pieces together. The jagged tear severed Lady Henrietta's face.

"I don't understand," Philip said. "Why would he do this?"

I hovered behind him. "Perhaps he didn't mean to. Or it was the other spirits. We don't know that they're working together."

Philip let the torn canvas fall and rubbed his face. "We need answers. Come on."

I followed him down the hall to my room. Philip sat in front of the sofa and studied the stacks of papers. He picked one and spread the pages across the rug.

"These are all the pieces of the summoning spell," he said. "Maybe there's something here to help us reverse his magic."

I chewed my lip and studied the notes. A drawing in my script showed one circle nestled inside another, like those in the hidden room, but on the paper a pentagram covered the center. It gave me a sick, unclean feeling, as if I needed to wash my hands. The text beneath was underlined: *Circles of unbroken silver.*

I traced my finger over a line of text in Sir Jason's handwriting. "Oh, dear."

Philip glanced between my face and the paper. "What?"

"He wrote *revenīte.*"

"That's Latin for *return.*"

"Yes, but it's a command to more than one person. He wasn't just calling back Lady Henrietta. He could have summoned any number of spirits."

Our papers spilling past the edge of the rug reminded me of the mess in the hidden room. I glanced again at the line *Circles of unbroken silver.* "I think the spell room *is* a spirit trap. He could have held them in the silver circles. Then the papers spilled and covered the lines."

Philip's eyes widened. "We cleaned them up, so the circle is whole again."

"Yes, but how many spirits might have escaped while the circle was broken? I'm not even certain the gateway is closed. There's a dreadful darkness lurking there." I rubbed my palm. "Maybe that was the boundary I was worried about."

"There's also the other boundary Sir Jason mentioned—the boundary of his powers. I suppose it could have been either of them. I don't understand why he would want to summon so many spirits. Unless . . ." Philip looked ill as he set the papers aside. "The spell he used to bind us let him draw strength from us, right? So, what if he was doing the same with the ghosts?"

There was so much darkness in that circle. I shivered. "It would make him very strong."

Philip drummed his fingers on the floor. "Yes, but if we banished the other spirits, it would weaken him. We can't let the ghosts loose, anyway. Imagine a plague of angry spirits roving the countryside."

I groaned. It seemed much too large a problem to solve, and it just kept expanding, like a stain on a linen napkin soaking up spilled wine.

Elsewhere in the house, the clocks tolled midnight. The gaslights in the corridor flickered out. Our paraffin lamp sputtered and shrank, as if darkness sucked away the flame. Philip swore and turned up the wick. Shivering light danced against the walls, and shadows swayed in the corners.

A shape moved in the doorway, and I screamed. Lady Henrietta hovered in the corridor.

"What is it?" Philip jumped to his feet.

"Lady Henrietta's here. She startled me."

Shadows crept along the floor behind her. She backed into the room. The dark shapes rolled into a pool of inky blackness. Grotesque shapes rose from the dark puddle into angular, vaguely human forms. The muttering shadows lurched closer.

"Mr. Ketley?" I darted to his side.

"I see them. Stay in the light."

He lifted the lamp. The black shapes swarmed for Lady Henrietta. She rushed to join us behind the shield of the light, and the shadows recoiled.

"They're after Lady Henrietta," I whispered, my eyes fixed on the shadows testing the limits of the brightness.

"They escaped Sir Jason's trap. Maybe they're looking for revenge."

"Do you think he would help us?" I asked, glancing around for some sign that Sir Jason might offer assistance against the darkness inching nearer.

Lady Henrietta shook her head.

"We can't trust Sir Jason? What about the other ghosts?"

A frantic headshake.

"Are you talking to Lady Henrietta?" Philip whispered, tightening his grip on the lamp.

"She says not to trust any of them."

"Can we trust her?" he mumbled. "She might want Sir Jason to bring her back."

She clasped her hands and shook her head again.

The darkness pressed through the doorway. Philip lunged forward, wielding the light. The shadows wavered, but one slithered into the room. The roiling black mass mimicked human shape, head and limbs bubbling up and melting back into formless darkness.

A clawed hand reached for Philip. He swung the lamp. The shadow shrank back with a hiss. Another black form slunk behind Philip.

"Watch out, Mr. Ketley!"

He wielded the lamp right and left, but more of the dark things drew near. The lamp sputtered down to a scant flicker. Lady Henrietta screamed soundlessly, and the walls rumbled.

There had to be something I could do. The spells! If only I knew a spell for banishing spirits. It was just words. Maybe I didn't need a body for that, but the only ones I remembered were for summoning, and I didn't even know if they worked.

Black shapes massed together, rising like a dark wave over Philip.

"No!" I flung myself through him, bracing myself between him and the ghosts.

"Miss Tregarrick!" His hand scrambled for my arm; he passed the dying light through my body.

The shadows roared.

"Leave us alone." I held out my trembling hands and steeled myself, too frightened to move. The black wave might drag me into the abyss and drown me in eternal night, but that was likely my destination anyway. I might buy Philip time. Time to escape, to defeat Sir Jason, to live.

The cresting black wave shuddered and rolled back. I blinked and stared at my hands. This time I could see their faint glow against the darkness. I stepped toward the shadows. They scattered apart, scuttling like giant spiders. I walked forward, herding the hissing, roiling mass to the door.

They bolted down the hall. The walls trembled, and a crack opened, tearing the wallpaper. A fading wail echoed down the corridor then everything grew still.

"Impossible," I whispered.

"You did it!" Philip grinned widely.

"What did I do? I don't understand."

"At this point, I'm not going to question it," Philip said. "We knew you were different. You have some power over them."

"I don't want to be some kind of . . . monster among monsters."

"It's fascinating—"

"Fascinating!" I turned on him. "How does that help us? Is this just some curious adventure to you?" Philip recoiled, anger and hurt mingled in his eyes. My shoulders sagged. "Let's find a way to end this. We need to put the ghosts to rest. All of us."

Lady Henrietta nodded. Philip looked away, his expression tight. I wanted to reach out, tell him I was sorry, but what would it matter? If we were successful, my mission would be fulfilled, and I would cross into the abyss, hoping that I had righted enough of my wrongs to find peace in the next world. He would move on with his life, and some day this whole incident would just be a strange nightmare to him—and me along with it.

We settled down to the documents in stiff silence. When I froze at moonset, I waited for oblivion, for once welcoming its numb forgetfulness, until I remembered the beautiful afternoon in the clearing. I longed to be welcomed by carpets of purple flowers instead of blackness, but my dreams of light and warmth vanished with the moon.

Chapter Seventeen

The bright glow of the afternoon sun as I rematerialized didn't burn away the terror of the shadows' attack or the taint of black magic binding me to my cursed existence. My heart sat heavy in my chest. On top of everything else, I'd driven away my only friend. Philip was nowhere to be seen.

A flash of color on the sofa caught my eye, and I crept over. A bouquet of sweetpea flowers rested there like a kaleidoscope of butterflies in white, pink, purple, and blue. Beneath them was a note in Philip's neat handwriting.

I hope you're feeling better. Meet me in the library when you're ready.

The kind words pierced my insubstantial chest. I sank and tried to stroke the porcelain-fine petals, remembering Philip's bright smile when he showed me the garden. Why did he have to treat me like a living, breathing person? Everything would be easier if we just fixed our mistakes and moved on. But then I would never see Philip again. Tearless sobs shook my body as I huddled by the sofa.

Finally, my crying slowed. I felt hollow and drained as I turned my back on the flowers I could never touch or smell. Maybe Philip had found an answer to end this misery. I drifted down to the library.

Philip lounged in a chair by the bookshelves, his face half-turned from the door. His brow furrowed as he skimmed a book. I paused to memorize the strong line of his jaw, the waves of his dark hair. If I could take the images with me—the memories of his eyes, his smile, his warmth—there would be a glimmer of light even in the darkest abyss. With a silent sigh, I glided to his side.

"Miss Tregarrick?" he asked without looking up.

I blinked. "How did you know I was here?"

"Can't you sometimes sense when someone's standing behind you?" He closed the book and gave me a wary glance.

"I suppose." I shrugged. "Real people, anyway."

"You're real enough to me." He stood, and I resisted the urge to back away. "I'm not here to have a lark hunting ghosts in an old house. The shadows last night would have been enough to chase me away if that were the only thing keeping me around. I want to fix my mistakes and make sure both of us are free from Sir Jason."

"I know. I'm sorry," I whispered. "I was frightened, but I shouldn't have taken it out on you. You're my friend, and I wish . . ." I swallowed. What *did* I wish? Too many things.

Philip's gaze softened. He slowly lifted his fingers to my cheek. I closed my eyes, praying I would feel even a memory of his warmth. Enough to pretend, for a moment, he could touch me.

The door banged open. We jumped.

John walked in, focused on the ledgers in his hands. Philip lowered his hand and straightened to attention. John stopped short, nearly dropping his book. Then his eyes narrowed.

"What are you doing in here?" he asked.

I didn't dare look at Philip, but I prayed he would think of something better than badgers.

"Pardon me, Mr. Springett," Philip said. "Mr. Reed, the gamekeeper, asked me to find a map of the estate."

John's scowl relaxed. "Oh, you're the gamekeeper's boy, are you?"

Philip's expression tightened. I scowled at John's dismissive tone and strolled to his side to peer at the account book open in his hand. Nothing helpful there.

"I work for Mr. Reed, sir," Philip said.

"Then I have a few concerns to raise with you. You've been negligent in your duties."

This was too much. John seemed to be doing his best to hold the estate together in difficult circumstances, but I wasn't going to listen to him lecture Philip about responsibility. Wrinkling my brow in concentration, I slid my palm over the open ledger. The pages flipped. John jumped and dropped the book.

"Drafty in here," Philip said mildly.

John snatched the book from the floor, looking around. "Yes, too drafty to work. Take whatever maps you need to Mr. Reed, then do something about the rats. They're everywhere!"

"Yes, sir," Philip smiled at John's retreating back. Then he laughed. "Nicely done. You'll make a believer of him yet."

My smile faded. "Would that do any good? Most of the servants believe, and they're still in danger."

"You're right." Philip rubbed his face. "We should encourage everyone to leave. It's only going to get more dangerous."

"Oh!" I stepped back. "And Edmund's planning a ball the night of the full moon! There will be crowds of people!"

"Maybe you can get him to cancel."

"I'll try, but the more time passes, the less he listens to me."

"Then you should talk to him right away. I'll start piecing together a banishing spell from what I can find in Sir Jason's books."

"Resorting to magic, then? Isn't there a way to win that doesn't leave us more tainted?"

"Maybe we'll find something," Philip said, though he didn't sound hopeful. "But we can't rule out the only weapon we have. I'll meet you back in your room."

I hurried to Edmund's chambers. He paced the floor, his hair hanging over his face, his steps dragging, his eyes veiled by his long lashes. I wasn't certain if he was awake or walking in his sleep.

"All is lost! All is lost!" he muttered.

"Edmund?" I asked.

His head snapped up and he blinked rapidly. His vacant expression warmed into a smile. "My muse! Darling Lucy! You've saved me from a dreadful dream." He clutched his chest, dragging wrinkles across his white nightshirt. "I don't remember the details, but there was so much despair."

"I came to talk to you about the ball."

"Of course!" His expression brightened again. "I should have thought to ask you for guidance! It's such a momentous step."

"It is?" I scrambled to hold on as the reins of the conversation slipped from my grasp.

"Yes, but you can tell me. . . . Will Miss Ridgewell say yes?"

"Yes?" I asked then groaned as the pieces fell into place. He was proposing to Miss Ridgewell at the ball. This would make things more difficult.

"She will? Oh thank you!"

"Er . . ." She probably *would* say yes, so I wouldn't look like a liar. "The ball could be dangerous, though. The dark forces in this house might not be happy to have a new mistress. You should cancel, or hold it in the village instead."

"Nonsense! This is my house now, and I'll hold the ball here. Miss Ridgewell's going to say yes. Nothing can go wrong!" He grinned and paced with renewed fervor.

His words gave me a chill. "But, Edmund—"

"I know. I should be writing. The poems in my head are shouting."

He sank to his desk. Apparently, I was dismissed.

As I turned to leave, a flash in the looking glass caught my eye. I shifted to see better, and it moved in perfect harmony with me. I gasped. It wasn't my reflection, exactly, but something of me showed in the mirror—a faint bauble of light. Was this another sign I was getting stronger?

For now it did me little good. Edmund wasn't listening to me. His imagination twisted everything to fit his whims. After all his sweet speeches, I was a little surprised by my lack of jealousy at his announcement, but I was never a real person to him, just an extension of his fancies. I drifted slowly down the corridor. A rat squeezed out from under a door and scuttled along the hallway beside me.

"Get away!" I walked faster, turning down the long gallery toward the back staircase that would take me to my room. Another rat joined the first one, and then another. They glanced at me from time to time, their sharp eyes tracking me, but showed no intention of doing anything.

Susan opened the door to the back staircase, balancing a tray of tea, probably summoned by John or Edmund. They must have lost quite a few servants if a housemaid—even one with charming dimples—was waiting on the master of the house or his brother.

The rats surged forward. She screamed and let the tray clatter to the floor. She backed into the staircase, kicking at the teeth and claws closing in on her. I leapt into their midst, but unlike the shadows, the rats were fearless.

"Philip! Edmund!" I shouted as Susan cried for help. They probably couldn't hear us from so far away.

A whisper slid around us, rising from the hissing of the rats.

Find it. Finish it.

"I won't help you, Sir Jason! You can't control me!"

The rats darted forward, climbing Susan's apron. She twisted, nearly tumbling down the steep stairs. The rats clambered higher, their claws shredding her dress. I swatted uselessly at them.

Finish.

I covered my mouth. He was holding them hostage. The whole house. He could manipulate them, fill their sleep with nightmares, send rats to attack. If I agreed to help him, I might save Susan and the others from his wrath, but I would be allowing him to finish his spell, condemning Philip or Edmund to be his new vessel.

A rat tore the cap from Susan's head. I swung helplessly at the creature. Susan cried and screamed as the next one clawed her shoulder. Another tangled in her hair, drawing blood from her scalp. She shrieked.

"Stop!" I shouted. "I'll do it! Leave them in peace, and I'll bring you the object!"

The rats streamed away like a filthy tide. A few of them staggered to the ground, twitching several times before lying still. I covered my face and heaved. Susan sank to the ground, crying hysterically.

"I'm sorry. I'm so sorry," I stood between her and the rat corpses. "Sir Jason won't hurt you anymore."

But I'd doomed myself. Worse, I'd doomed Philip or Edmund.

Susan's gasping sobs slowed. I knelt next to her. I might not be able to redeem myself, but perhaps I could help the others, counter Sir Jason's influence. He didn't care about them as long as he had access to his magic again. Susan seemed especially susceptible to the whispers of spirits, maybe even when she was awake. I leaned closer.

"You need to leave. It's not safe here. You can find something better than this."

I'd encourage Edmund to give her—all the servants—good references, despite quitting without notice. Maybe he'd actually listen.

Susan dabbed her eyes with her sleeve and touched her bleeding scalp. "I can't do this. I'm leavin'!" She stared up at the high ceiling. "Do you 'ear me? I quit!"

She raced down the stairs. A bittersweet lump lodged in my chest. I felt like I was losing a friend, though she didn't know I existed and wouldn't want me around if she did. I wasn't certain what I'd done was wise, either. How was I different from Sir Jason, manipulating people like this? I might have to help him, but I didn't have to be like him.

Finish it.

Sir Jason's presence felt close enough to touch, but each time I turned, I saw only the shadowed walls.

"I still don't know what I'm looking for," I shouted at the dim stairwell.

A tug jerked me back. I shuddered.

"Isn't there another way?"

The pressure in my head built until I felt like I would fly apart if I didn't obey. It was worse than ever, possibly because I'd already given in to him once. I was losing pieces of myself already. I took a reluctant step in the direction of the command, like a fish on a taut line. The tension pulled me back up the main stairs and into the library, depositing me in front of the glass cases. The hold on me dissipated.

"Well?" I asked.

Silence.

I sighed and studied the case. It was Sir Jason's collection of crystals and semi-precious gems, ranging from pebbles the size of my fingernail to glittering specimens as large as my head. I cupped my hand. A stone would fit what we remembered of the object Sir Jason bound us to. I squinted and searched the case until I saw a label sitting by an empty spot almost hidden by its neighbors. Moonstone.

I stepped back. That must be it. I knew what we were looking for! It might even explain the moon's hold over me. I turned to the books. Philip would know which ones to search. He could help me make sense of it.

But I didn't want to involve him with Sir Jason.

I drifted slowly back to my room. Philip smiled when he saw me, and a bittersweet ache spread through my whole body, the pain nearly crumpling me. How much could I tell him? He wasn't likely to leave, even in the face of being eaten by rats or possessed by Sir Jason. There was even a chance he'd let his temper rule and turn to magic to fight back. Somehow, I had to get him and Edmund away from Sir Jason.

"I take it you didn't have much luck with Sir Edmund?" He set aside his book.

"No. And the rats we've been seeing? I think Sir Jason's controlling them. They attacked Susan. Miss Lamb, I mean."

His expression darkened. "Is she hurt?"

"Not badly. I . . . chased them away."

"Well done," he said, though his voice sounded weary. "We have to stop him before he gets stronger."

I bit my lip. "Do you think it would be wrong if I talked to people in their sleep? Told them to leave? I want to help them, but I don't want to be like Sir Jason."

Philip sat back with a thoughtful frown. "It's a clever idea, but I'm a little uncomfortable with the idea that someone's whispering in my ear while I'm unconscious. Of course, if it were you, I might feel differently about it." He winked, and my throat tightened. "I suppose it wouldn't hurt if you played the muse for more people while they're awake."

A rat stopped in the corridor, just out of sight of Philip. It sat up to watch me with its sharp, black eyes.

Philip shut his book. "The light of the full moon might weaken the ghosts. That would be the perfect time to perform a banishing spell on Sir Jason and the other spirits."

The rat's whiskers twitched rapidly. Sir Jason would kill Philip before letting him do the banishing spell. I had to distract Philip. I had to lie. He might hate me when he found out, but hopefully he would be safe.

"I . . . remembered something," I said. "The object Sir Jason bound us to? I think it's a moonstone."

"Moonstone?" Philip jumped up and paced. "Yes, that feels right, and it might explain your unusual situation."

"I think we should focus on finding it."

"Hmm. Maybe. We don't want Sir Jason to get it, but I need to finish this spell."

The rat stepped closer. I shifted between Philip and Sir Jason's creature.

"If he's so interested in the moonstone, we need to make that our priority," I said. "I need your help finding it." Sir Jason had to know that Philip wasn't an immediate threat, and that I was trying to cooperate. I lowered my voice. "If he finds it first, he might be able to finish the spell."

Philip glanced at his half-written spell. "I suppose you're right. I'll have time to finish this later." He smiled at me. "I'm glad one of us is keeping a clear head."

I bit my tongue, wishing I could feel the pain. Cold. Silence. Darkness. They all might be better than I deserved.

Chapter Eighteen

The next day, Philip and I started our search for the missing stone in the library.

"I read about moonstones this morning," Philip whispered as he peered behind the velvet curtains. "They have their own magic. Some people think they're made of moonlight trapped in solid form."

"I suppose that explains how Sir Jason linked me to the moon." I sighed and poked my head through a locked desk to squint at the dim interior.

"I wonder why it doesn't seem to affect me." Philip's voice sounded muffled through the wood.

"Probably because you still have a body." I straightened. "It is a bit of an advantage."

He gave me an odd look, half curious and half sad. "Sometimes." He pulled up the cushion on a chair. "Moonstone is also supposed to bring good luck and love."

"Perhaps that's why Sir Jason used it," I said.

"Maybe. I wonder, though, if the moonstone's magic might have interfered with Sir Jason's, twisted his spells in ways he didn't intend."

We spent several fruitless hours combing through every item in Sir Jason's collections then moved on to the vacant rooms along the corridor, ending with my chamber. As the household settled down for the night, we snuck down to the guest bedrooms and the long gallery, searching each vase, sculpture, and lacquered side table for familiar-looking stones.

Philip rubbed his face and frowned at a painting of a half-man, half-beast stalking a sleeping woman. "We're assuming I lied when I told Sir Jason I had it. What if I really did?"

"You could have hidden it outside, or he might have taken it from you." I mulled over my fragmented memories. "It's possible that he had it when he returned for me, and I'm fairly certain he did come back and corner me in my room. The fear and the feeling of defeat were so strong, even worse than when he threw me down in the library; it seems like that must have been the end."

Philip gave me look full of sorrow. "Maybe we should check your chamber again. The stone might be smaller than we're expecting."

In my chamber, he knelt to examine every crevice in the wood-paneled walls. I searched as well, but my mind wandered. Obviously, Sir Jason didn't know what had happened to the stone or he would just tell us. Was he watching, even now? I looked over my shoulder for rats.

Philip's paraffin lamp flickered, and we both froze. No whispers or shadows approached.

"Odd," Philip said. "The draft seems to be coming from this wall, not the window." He took the glass hood off the lamp and moved the light around, studying the flame's twisting dance. Finally, he straightened. "I have an idea."

"What's that?"

He grinned. "It's when a thought pops into your head unexpectedly."

I rolled my eyes. "What's your idea?"

"This is the same spot I walked up to before, as if I remembered it. We didn't think there was anything here, but I can feel air moving past."

"You think there might be another secret door?"

"It makes sense, doesn't it?"

"It does!" I hurried to the wall. "I'll check."

I stepped through, but the wall pushed back against me. I struggled through onto a landing with steep, narrow stairs leading up. Moonlight filtered through a tiny window at the top. "Oh!"

"Are you all right?" Philip's voice came faintly.

"Yes! You were right! I just didn't know what to expect." I studied the wood-paneled wall. "There's a handle on the left. Your right, I mean."

After a few moments, the door clicked and swung open. Philip stood at the threshold, lamp in hand, and stared at the staircase.

"Do you remember it?" I asked.

"Not exactly, but it's familiar." He closed his eyes and dashed up the stairs two at a time. I raced after him. He paused at the top, his lamp throwing dancing light against the plain wooden doors on either side of the landing. Philip swiveled to the left and put his hand on the brass knob.

"This is my room! I'm sure. It feels right."

I looked to the other side. "Then that one was probably mine. This is very strange, though. Why would we have rooms up here?"

"They might have been servants' quarters once. Maybe Sir Jason converted them for our use." His eyes shone. "We may be able to piece together our lives by exploring our rooms. Who goes first, you or I?"

"You," I said quickly.

"What are you afraid of?" He stepped away from his door, a smile quirking his lips.

"I don't know." I glanced at the door. "The truth."

He cocked an eyebrow. "Maybe not a bad thing to be scared of. Best to face your fears, though. You go first."

I tried to push him back, but he stepped through me and swung open the door to my old room.

It stretched back across the top of the house, long and narrow. Once it might have housed several servants, but now there was a single bed draped with gauzy white curtains. The ceiling sloped down to a small attic window on the far side. I glided to it, my taut nerves relaxing at the sight of the moonlight illuminating the white flowers in the garden. I turned back to the disorganized room: clothes tossed on chairs, books open on the floor, flowery doodles on the wobbly desk pushed against one wall. A comfortable mess. Home.

"Oh, yes, this is my room."

"Were you leaving in a hurry, do you suppose?" Philip asked, lingering in the doorway. His gaze flicked over the mess.

"I think this is how it always was." My cheeks tingled. "It feels right this way."

"I thought you liked to be organized."

I shrugged. "Maybe I needed a place to relax."

"It's a wonder you were able to get anything done. Half your clothes aren't even put away." Philip grinned and set down the lantern to pick up an airy, pale pink dress draped on a chair by the door. "Look at all the bows and lace. I don't know how women can stand it."

He held the gown in front of himself and twisted back and forth to swish the skirt. I laughed and put my hands on my hips. "They're beautiful. And delicate. Put it down before you damage it." I drifted over and stared at the dress, remembering the soft, light touch of the fabric against my skin. "I wish I could wear one of them again, maybe for the ball."

"You're going to the ball?" He carefully set the dress aside.

"I imagine not, but it would be lovely to go dancing one more time."

"With Sir Edmund, I suppose?"

"No." It was Philip's strong arms I longed to feel around me, spinning me through the room. "I'd just like to dance again."

"Hmm." He shifted through the books stacked on the chair. "All this poetry. We know you're a romantic. *In Memoriam*?" He flipped through the pages. "Blast! Is this entire poem about somebody dying?"

I snatched at the book, but it eluded me. "It's soul-stirring. Not that you'd understand. It's about carrying on after death, and the many faces of love."

"You have an unhealthy fascination with death." Philip studied the books, his tone light.

"You mean I had."

"Oh." He met my eyes, then glanced away. "I guess so. I'm sorry. Does any of this help you remember?"

I pivoted, drinking it all in. "Not exactly. I feel comfortable, but sad. Safe. I remember loving the books. The dresses, too, but I don't think I got to wear them very often. Not the fancy ones, anyway."

"I wonder why you had them, then?"

Memories trickled back: running my fingers over folded silks and moirés in a bouquet of fresh colors, selecting the ones I liked, giving orders to a dressmaker as I handed over my coins. "They were part of a dream," I said softly. "A daydream, I mean. I think Sir Jason gave me money to buy what I liked: fancy dresses I wanted to wear someday, books I hoped to read. I suppose it was silly, given how things turned out."

"It's not silly to dream."

"I wish I could read the poems again, at least."

"I'll read them to you," he said softly.

"Really? You'd do that?" Happiness mingled with the grief aching in my chest.

He chuckled. "Not that monstrous *In Memoriam*, but some of these others look more palatable." He waved a copy of Shakespeare's sonnets. "After my room, though."

The other room was so neat and orderly it hardly looked like anyone lived there. Philip walked to the little closet, digging past a few sets of clothes and a heavy-looking bag that clinked with coins. Of course he'd been more practical with his earnings. He shrugged and shut the door. Two books sat on the dresser: one a copy of Shakespeare's sonnets identical to mine and the other a leather-bound notebook.

"Is that a journal?" I asked.

He grabbed it and frowned. "No, a sketchbook." As he flipped through the pages, I caught glimpses of animals, flowers, and a girl with dark hair that might have been me. He glanced at me and closed it quickly, blushing faintly. "Nothing that helps us now."

"Those looked lovely. Doesn't that interest you? You can draw."

"What good does it do us?"

The dull despair in his voice startled me and brought flashes of memories, like fanning through the sketchbook: images of his face smiling, frowning in concentration, sometimes angry.

"I'm sorry." He rubbed his face. "I was just hoping for something more."

He tossed the sketchbook aside and picked up the sonnets, shaking his head as he skipped through the pages. "I think you must have been a bad influence on me before, but I did promise I'd read to you." He straightened and smiled faintly. "Here's something from Shakespeare: 'Let me not to the marriage of true minds admit impediments. Love is not love which alters when it alteration finds, or bends with the remover to remove . . .' "

Philip's deep, rich voice soothed my worries away like a warm bath. I closed my eyes as he went on. " 'O no! It is an ever-fixèd mark that looks on tempests and is never shaken; it is the star to every wandering bark, whose worth's unknown, although his height be taken.' "

He paused, and I glanced at him. His gaze drifted from the page, but he kept speaking. " 'Love's not Time's fool, though rosy lips and cheeks within his bending sickle's compass come: love alters not with his brief hours and weeks, but bears it out even to the edge of doom.' " His eyes met mine, and he finished, " 'If this be error and upon me proved, I never writ, nor no man ever loved.' "

We stared at each other. I trembled under his searching gaze, his eyes full of raw longing. Could he see as much in mine?

"I remember something else," he whispered and strode across the room.

My knees locked as he brought his hands to my face. His fingers gently brushed my cheek, warm and real. Tingles raced over my skin. I inhaled but didn't look away, afraid to break the spell. He leaned close, but when his lips reached mine, the sensations of his touch vanished.

Chapter Nineteen

Philip jerked back with a cry. "Did you do that on purpose?"

"What? No!" I lowered my voice. "I don't think so."

He ran his hands through his hair. "You were always running away. I could never get close to you."

"What do you remember?" I whispered.

"Just bits and pieces, but I loved you."

My eyes burned, and I shut them against the pain.

He took a deep breath. "Being near you made the slavery to Sir Jason bearable. You were smart and funny and beautiful. You were always drawing back, though, sometimes friendly, sometimes coy, never quite close. I tried to talk to you about how I felt, but you said you were afraid. You never said of what. You don't remember?"

"I don't," I breathed out in a tight whisper. "I'm sorry."

"You can't tell me, then, if you ever loved me too?" The hope flickering in his eyes dulled. "No, you said I irritated you. I suppose that's not the response of love."

He turned away, his hurt and frustration so close and hot that I was afraid they might burn me. More images emerged from the murky haze in my mind. I'd seen him like this before.

"I remember too," I said.

He jerked around. "What?"

"I was afraid of you," I whispered.

"Y-you were?" He stepped back, eyes wide.

"Not in the way you might think." I squeezed my eyes shut, trying to capture the fragmented memories. "You were so serious. So . . . intense." The feelings welled up as I spoke, and my hands trembled. "I knew if you got to know me, you couldn't really love me like you thought you did. I cared for you. I couldn't bear for you to find out what I really was."

Philip's brow furrowed. "What you really were?"

"A failure. A joke." I wrapped my arms around myself, echoes of mocking voices stirring in the depths of my mind. "I ran away to work for Sir Jason because he tricked me into thinking I might be able to do something for once, but everyone was right."

"Everyone?" Philip's face darkened. "What were they right about?"

"I'm silly. Absentminded. My parents, my brothers and sisters, my teachers and tutors, they all told me so."

Once I started, the rest of my confession slipped easily from my tongue, the jagged pieces of memory flowing together as I spoke. "I wanted to learn Latin and Greek like my favorite poets and travel the world—Rome, Greece, maybe China and India—actually see all the things I've only read about or looked at under glass in science exhibitions. Everyone laughed. Girls don't do those things." I lowered my voice and looked away. "Whenever I told young men about my dreams, they couldn't get away from me fast enough. My brothers moaned and complained that they'd be caring for me when I was an old maid, locked in my room with my books and maps of the Grand Tour. I wanted to prove that I could do things, that I wasn't just a flighty daydreamer. Even working for Sir Jason . . ." I shrugged, keeping my gaze down. "My Greek wasn't good enough. I wasn't good enough. He constantly reminded me. I tried, but it turned out I was a failure after all."

My words hovered in the room. I was too ashamed to look at Philip, too frightened to see his reaction.

"You were good enough for me," he said softly.

I flinched. It just made my loss that much more bitter. "You never knew me. I never let you."

"You think I couldn't see what you really were? I got frustrated with you for daydreaming sometimes when there were things to be done, but I knew you were smart. When you focused on something, you were so systematic about it. Besides, how many people learn Greek at all? You tried, which is more than the rest of them can say. You were better at Latin than I was."

"I was?"

"I didn't let on, but you picked it up faster. I liked that. You challenged me to be better. As much as Sir Jason goaded and belittled us, he wouldn't have kept either of us around if we weren't good at what we were doing. You inspired me. I just needed you to hold still long enough that I could tell you."

I sank to the ground. Had I been so busy running away that I'd missed seeing what was right in front of me, including my chance at happiness with Philip? If I didn't even know myself, it would have been easy for people like Sir Jason to turn me into their puppet. Now I'd put myself in Sir Jason's hands again. I was making the same mistakes, probably headed toward the same failure and the same all-consuming darkness.

Philip knelt by my side. Heat stung my face. I touched my cheeks, and my fingers came away sticky with tears. "This isn't possible," I whispered.

"You really can't believe that someone could love you?"

"No. Perhaps." It hurt too much to consider. "I mean the tears. I couldn't cry before. Why can I now?"

"Maybe because you're not running away any more," he said quietly.

"Aren't I? I'm still scared."

"Even so, you're here, trying to figure it out. You're being very clever about it, too. You just had to forget what everyone else said and then you could be yourself."

Myself? I still wasn't entirely certain who that was. I wanted Philip to be right, though, wanted to believe he saw me more clearly than I did. "Now that I remember, it feels so true." I wiped more tears from my cheeks.

"Do you trust me, Miss Tregarrick?"

I looked into his blue eyes and saw my reflection there. "I think so."

He shook his head. "You need to give me a real answer. Do you trust me?"

I sniffed. "Yes."

"Good. I don't know why people would say such things to you—

how they could miss seeing who you really are—but I can see you, and you're not a failure. You learn quickly, you don't give up, and you're brave enough to stand up to Sir Jason and try to protect people from him even after you've lost nearly everything." He paused. "Also, I like the way you hum."

"Hum?"

"Yes, when you're concentrating on something, you hum. Mozart, especially. Sometimes Beethoven."

"That doesn't seem like something one is good at," I said, though a flicker of a smile forced its way through my tears. I'd made some terrible, foolish mistakes, but I hadn't been entirely wicked. Maybe it wasn't too late to take the good parts of who I'd been and leave the rest behind, if I could get free from Sir Jason.

"Your humming is splendid," Philip said. "It made me smile, even when it broke my concentration."

"You smile all the time."

He sat back and picked at the edges of the worn gray rug. "Only when you're around. I was angry. At the whole world. At my father. There was no one to help us: my mother and my siblings. Nobody cared what happened to the brats of a poor factory worker, and even if they'd listened, we might have ended up in the workhouses."

I reached a hand through his.

He sighed. "Then Sir Jason came, promising he could make me stronger. I wanted to believe him."

"Like I did, when he told me I had potential. He said I could do anything, escape into my dreams or chase them across in the world."

Philip nodded. "He knew how to manipulate us. He wasn't lying, either, just not telling the whole truth. Once I realized what I'd gotten into, I hated him just as fiercely as my father and everyone who turned a blind eye to his actions. I think you were the only reason I didn't do something rash."

"I'm sorry I didn't let you closer when we had the chance." Fresh tears rolled down my cheeks.

"When we had the chance?" He looked at me, puzzled.

"Certainly you don't still love me now?"

He leaned closer, and a smile curved his lips. "Weren't you listening? 'Love is not love which alters when it alteration finds. It is an ever-fixed mark, even to the edge of doom'. I fell in love with you all over again this week. I thought I was insane, developing feelings for a ghost, but now it makes sensee." He cleared his throat. "Especially if, possibly, you've come to love me too?"

"I do," I whispered. "I think I loved you before. I was just too afraid. I didn't trust. But I do now. Please forgive me for taking away our chance at happiness."

He grinned. "Who says our chance is past?"

"I'm dead, Mr. Ketley. You can't spend your life with me, can't even touch me." I looked away, blushing. "Shouldn't you be with someone real?"

"You *are* real. Besides, Jason bound both of us. As much as I hate that, I like to think it also means we're tied together. Wherever you are, I'll be there too. Someday I'll be dead. It's the one thing we can count on." He smiled broadly, and I rolled my eyes, laughing and crying at the same time. He went on more seriously, "Then I think I should be able to hold you. In the meantime, I won't pretend I don't long to touch you, but we can still be together, at least while the moon is up."

He reached for my face. A tear slid off my chin and flashed when it hit the ground.

"What was that?" Philip asked.

Another tear splashed on the floor, disappearing in a burst of light. Ferocious roaring shook the walls and rattled the doors. We ducked, covering our ears. A scream froze on my lips, and everything snapped out of focus.

Chapter Twenty

Back in the room, with sunlight pouring around me, I screamed, but Philip was waiting for me.

"Lucy! Lucy, it's all right. I'm here. We're together."

I blinked and inhaled deeply, trying to convince myself I was safe. Then Philip's words sank in. "Lucy?" I asked.

"Oh, well . . ." Philip grinned shyly. I raised an eyebrow. When was he ever shy? "I suppose I never asked you formally, but I thought agreeing to spend the rest of eternity together was rather like a proposal, and you seemed to accept. I hope I don't presume too much?" A smile gleamed in his eyes.

I shook my head at the sweet, preposterous idea. "Who on earth would perform the marriage? Don't I have to be alive for that? Wouldn't the priest need to see me?"

"Maybe we can find one of those non-conformist preachers crazy or romantic enough to see ghosts." He cleared his throat. "What I'm hoping to accomplish is getting you to call me Philip."

A smile crept over my face. "Philip." His name tasted sweet. "Of course." We grinned at each other, and more than ever I longed to rush into his arms. Or just feel his warmth again, even for a moment. My grin faded. "What happened last night? What was that noise?"

"Sir Jason, I think. He seems to get more active just as you disappear. I believe he's stronger when there's no light from the sun or moon. Another reason to perform the banishing spell in a couple of nights, when the moon's full."

I glanced around, searching for rats. Did Sir Jason have other ways of watching us? I couldn't let him think we were distracted from finding the stone. "All those people will be here for the ball. What if the spell endangers them?" A house full of victims if we made Sir Jason angry.

Philip's lips twisted into a frown. "Blast it. The ball's a bad idea."

"Yes." I sighed. "I still wish I could go."

"I wish I could take you. I'd love to see you in one of those gowns."

"I thought you said they were silly."

He grinned. "They are, but I like to see you happy."

A blush tingled over my cheeks. Keeping the truth from Philip hurt worse than ever now. As soon as I could get him out of the house, I had to tell him everything and trust he'd be reasonable. We could solve this together. It was probably the only way we would solve it.

"About the stone," I whispered.

"Yes, I've been thinking about that. How do we know it ever made it out of the spell room?"

"We . . ." I'd held the stone at some point, but I didn't remember where. Was it in my hand when Sir Jason knocked me to the floor and chased Philip? When he returned to find me kneeling by the sofa? "Maybe it didn't."

"I think that's where it would have been when everything started. Sir Jason assumed one of us took it, but what if we tricked him, and it never left the room?"

"It'll be dark soon, but we'll have to check." We needed to protect the stone, but if Sir Jason knew we had it, he'd force me to turn it over or use it. Unless Philip took it and ran.

We crept over to the library, and Philip opened the bookcase. I paused on the threshold. Even in the safety of the evening light, darkness radiated from the circle, alert and hungry. Philip pushed the door shut and strode to his desk, yanking out drawers and knocking on the sides for secret compartments.

I snuck up behind him and whispered, "If you find it, don't show any reaction. Just slip it in your pocket." His brow furrowed, and I said, "Trust me. I'll explain."

Concern flickered across his expression, but he nodded once and went back to searching. I paced the room, pretending to look, but mostly scanning the corners for rats and watching the light slowly fade in the window.

The darkness over the altar billowed like a black sheet in the wind.

"Philip!" I hissed. "Get out!"

"What is it?"

"It's almost sunset. The shadows are stirring."

Philip squinted at the black haze and nodded. "The circle should hold them, but better not to take chances."

He fumbled for the latch on the door. Whispers hissed around us. I backed against the wall. It gave slowly, like pressing into taffy. I pulled away, but my hand held fast.

"Philip!"

He swung the door open. "What's wrong?"

"My hand's stuck. The wall won't let go."

A moan echoed in the room. The darkness in the circle broke into separate forms wavering like black flames in the dusk. The shapes pressed against the outline of the circle. Featureless human faces formed from the roiling dark. Outside the circle, muttering shadows hovered in the corners.

Philip grabbed for my free arm. His warmth flashed over my skin along with the pressure of his firm grip, but then his hand slipped through. "I don't understand. If the wall can hold you, *I* should be able to."

"It's pulling me in." My voice shook. I sank further. Did Sir Jason somehow know I planned to betray him, or had the spirits found a new way to attack?

Philip pounded on the wall. The house groaned, and the pressure tightened on my arm. Slivers of pain jabbed my skin, and I gasped.

"Stop! It's crushing me!"

He recoiled. I leaned away from the wall. It sucked at me like quicksand. I whimpered as more of my arm disappeared.

"No!" Philip put his face by mine. "Lucy, look at me."

Trembling, I tore my gaze from the wall to find his eyes.

"Lucy," he said softly. "Focus on me. On my voice. Don't think about anything else. Can you do that?"

"Yes."

"Good. Take a deep breath."

"I can't. I don't—"

"You do, at least when you speak. I've seen you. Focus. Try."

Remembering what it felt like to draw breath, I forced my lungs to expand. Air crept down my throat and filled my chest. I could feel the dry tickle of it, but my excitement vanished under the pulses of pain shooting up my arm.

"Good," Philip said. "Close your eyes. Focus on each breath."

I did. My lungs tingled, and the air scratched my nose and throat. Pain throbbed through the bones in my hand, all the worse because I had felt nothing for so long. Heat flowed through my free arm, down my side to my waist, but I kept my eyes shut, and the pain in my pinned hand eased.

"Lucy?"

I opened my eyes. Philip grinned at me. His arm was around my waist. My jaw dropped. He was touching me, his warmth spreading over me like the dawn.

"How—?" My voice choked. It was too miraculous to be true. Had I found a way to dream?

"Shh. Don't think."

He swung me out of the room and slammed the bookcase behind us. I cradled my throbbing arm. The pain was real. Unbelievably, terribly, delightfully real! More than just hints of warm or cold, or ghostly chills and tingles, true sensations raced over my skin.

Philip took my hand gently in his, checking for injuries. He ran his fingers over my wrist, and I winced. The contrast between the ache in my arm and the caress of Philip's gentle touch made me shiver.

His eyes widened, and he looked at my face. His fingers, suddenly cold, brushed my throat.

I inhaled sharply. "What are you doing?"

A grin spread across his face, and his eyes shone with wonder. "Lucy, you're not dead."

Chapter Twenty-One

"What?" I couldn't have heard correctly.

He laughed. "You have a pulse. I wasn't sure, in your wrist, but feel your throat. Your heart is beating!"

I laid my fingers next to his on my neck and found the steady rhythm. The throb of my returning heartbeat ached as it pounded through my arteries. I leaned against Philip, and he caught me in a fierce embrace.

"How is this possible?" I breathed into his chest. I could smell him: pine and licorice and something musky.

"Maybe some things we shouldn't question," he whispered, his breath stirring my hair.

"No. I think we need to know. People don't just stop being dead." I pulled back to look myself over. "I'm still a little hazy—not quite solid."

"Maybe we broke Sir Jason's spell. Or, because you didn't want to disappear anymore—"

"You think I wanted to be dead? Invisible?"

"Not exactly." He rubbed the back of his neck. "You do have morbid tastes, though, and you wanted to escape."

My face burned. "Not like that! How can you even say that?"

"Wait, Lucy! It was just an idea. I'm sorry."

I sighed, and my racing pulse slowed. How did I ever take my heartbeat for granted? "I was always hiding, running away. But I never wanted to disappear completely. I just wanted to find a place where things could be better, where I felt like I mattered."

"Of course, I know." He shifted from foot to foot. "You're happy about this, right? You know, I won't hold you to what you said about us, if it was just a romantic fancy."

I stared at him. "A romantic fancy? What do you think of me, honestly? Are you trying to insult me?"

"No." He held up his hands. "I just don't want you to regret anything."

"Do you regret it?" I asked, holding my breath. My dizzy, confused happiness hovered, ready to crash into despair.

"Not at all." He looked down. "I just don't want my heart broken again."

My heart—my living, beating heart—skipped at his forlorn expression. I stepped up and ran my fingers over his warm, stubbly face, blushing at my boldness. Hadn't he said we were engaged, though? "You need to shave."

"I will, twice a day if you'd like," he said solemnly.

I pulled his face close to mine. His fingers trembled slightly as he traced my jaw. Then he kissed me softly, like he was afraid I would break. Or vanish. I drew him closer. He wrapped his arms around me and lifted me off the ground, my skirts rustling as he spun me about and kissed me again. Finally, after all this time, I was truly floating.

My legs nearly buckled as he lowered me to the floor. I still didn't feel solid against the ground. "Oh!" I grinned foolishly.

Philip laughed. "I take it you still want to marry me?"

I gave him a look of mock horror. "You think I would have kissed you otherwise?"

He laughed and took my hand, lacing his fingers with mine. "We could leave, you know. Start over somewhere else, away from this cursed place. We'll have each other, and Jason Springett can't hurt us anymore."

I leaned against his chest, listening to his strong heartbeat as his warmth seeped through me. Safety and home were right there in his arms. Now we could escape, be together, leave all of this behind.

But the room behind us was filled with dark magic we'd helped create. Ghosts roamed the house, getting more powerful each day. Sir Jason was willing to kill to get what he wanted. No one else had any idea what to do about it. I couldn't be content in a new life knowing what we'd done and what we'd run away from.

"We can't," I whispered. "We have to finish what we started."

His chest rose with a sigh. "I know. I was just dreaming."

I drew back. "There's more. The romantic in me might like to believe it was our love that brought me back—"

"Wasn't it?" Philip grinned. "In fairy tales, love usually breaks the spell."

"It feels like it should." I blushed again, pleasantly distracted by the memory of our kiss. "I think I need to understand what happened to me—to us—before we can move on. We don't know what kind of spells are still affecting us."

"You're right, of course." Philip kissed my hand and released me. "Back to work. No peace for the wicked."

"Philip! That's not funny."

"It is a little." He winked.

I rolled my eyes and caught his outstretched hand, never wanting to let go. A rat huddled under the sofa, as still as a statue. My stomach twisted. Had Sir Jason been watching our private moment? Did my being alive change anything?

"Wait!" I pulled Philip to a stop. "I was hoping we could go outside."

Philip raised an eyebrow.

I stood on tiptoe to whisper in his ear. "We need to talk away from the ghosts."

His smile hardened into forced cheerfulness. "In that case, I know just the place," he said, his voice a little too loud. Pulling me to his side, he guided me down the servant's staircase.

At the back door, a snarling hiss tore through the hallway.

Stop.

I tried to step forward, but my boots dragged back over the thick carpets, tugging me from Philip's embrace.

"Lucy?" He reached for me.

"I can't. Sir Jason . . ." I swallowed.

"You left before, and now you're whole again. He can't control you."

He took my hand and pulled me toward the door. I felt like I was walking through walls, pushing myself against Sir Jason's command.

We reached the threshold and I jerked to a stop as if a chain circled my waist. Philip's hand slipped from mine.

"No!" He took my wrist. "You're stronger than him, Lucy."

I struggled, but my muscles tightened and my head throbbed. I shook my head. I'd let Sir Jason in, and now I couldn't break his hold. "Help!"

Philip wrapped his arms around me and spun me out of the house. I gasped as the pressure knocked the air from my lungs. Then I was breathing again, the coils of Sir Jason's power slipping away. Philip set me down. I staggered and caught myself on his arm.

"Run!" Philip squeezed my hand, and we raced into the dark.

As we reached the woods, another tug yanked me to a stop. I tightened my grip on Philip and plunged forward, and the final cord of Sir Jason's control snapped. Twigs snagged at my dress and hair, but we didn't slow until we reached the clearing. Philip led me to the flat rock. I marveled at the rough, cool texture of the stone and the breeze caressing my skin.

Philip sat beside me. "I always feel safe out here. What did you want to tell me?"

He needed to know about Sir Jason's threat against everyone in the house, but he might be furious that I'd kept it from him. Could I make up an excuse for not telling him earlier? I bit my lip. I didn't want him angry with me, but I didn't think happiness could be built on a lie.

I took a deep breath and met his eyes. "When Sir Jason attacked Miss Lamb, he ordered me to bring him the moonstone. His rats would have killed her if I didn't agree. I told him I would." I wet my lips. "I didn't tell you because I was afraid of how you'd react."

He studied my face in silence then looked away. I clasped my hands and held my breath.

"I think you did the right thing helping Miss Lamb." He stared across the moonlit clearing. "You really didn't think you could tell me?"

I exhaled and grabbed his hand. "I'm sorry. I wanted to, but I didn't know if it was safe."

"Safe for me?"

I nodded. He sighed and pulled me against his shoulder. My racing heart slowed. He wasn't happy, but we weren't about to have a big argument either.

"I'm grateful, I suppose, that you were willing to take on that burden alone, but you know you don't have to do that now."

"I know." I wrapped my arm around him, rejoicing in his warmth. "So, what do we do? I've bought us a little peace, but in the long run things will be worse."

"We're going to fight Sir Jason. Trick him. He'll probably guess you've told me, but we'll play along. We need to find the stone anyway, but when we do, I'll try to be ready with whatever we need to destroy it and unravel his magic."

"He'll be watching."

"Yes, so we'll have to be fast and clever. I'll need to do more reading, though." He leaned his head against mine, and I closed my eyes. "I'd love to stay like this forever, but there'll be time for that when we're done. The banishing spell is even more important now."

I nodded reluctantly and let him lead me back into the house. We returned to my chamber—actually, the antechamber to our rooms, I realized—and he scooped up our stacks of documents. I grabbed a stray paper and grinned as it crinkled in my fingers.

"Where are we taking them?" I asked.

"Somewhere we won't worry about being disturbed, either your room or mine."

I hesitated, my face warming. How strange it felt, after being numb for so long. "Our bedrooms? That's not proper . . . I mean, now that I'm alive."

"Oh." Philip's forehead wrinkled. "I suppose that could be a concern." He smiled. "We'll meet in the middle. We'll store the papers in my room, where they're less likely to get lost"—he winked—"and sit together on the landing if we need to read them."

"I'm being silly, aren't I?" I asked. "I mean, we're alone together anyway."

"No, it's probably good for us to have some space that's our own. I think we can trust ourselves, but it's wise to have boundaries.

Speaking of which"—he hefted the stack in his arms—"let's get these somewhere safe so we can search for the moonstone."

He stashed the papers in his room and looked around with a frown. "Our rooms would have been a good place to hide the stone. I doubt Sir Jason ever came here."

"I don't know if we would have had time to hide it up here, but I suppose it's worth looking. I'll start in my room."

"Yes, he'd never find it in there." Philip gave me a wicked grin.

I smirked and sashayed across the landing as his laughter faded behind me. I paused at the threshold, glad to be alone for a moment. Though I felt my heart beating, I still suffered an odd sense that I was visiting my own grave as I surveyed the last vestiges of the life I was trying to leave behind.

I gathered books, put dresses in the closet, and picked up discarded bonnets and ribbons, taking the time to caress each one, searching for memories hidden in the abandoned treasures. Occasionally I discovered a flicker: staying up too late reading a thrilling novel, modeling a new bonnet, or mending a tear in a dress. Little hints of the life I could never reclaim, and perhaps didn't even want to.

Finally, I'd put the room in order, but without any sign of the stone.

I turned my back on the room and nearly tripped over Philip in the landing. Of course, searching his room wouldn't have taken long. He'd fallen asleep with his head against the wall and papers scattered around him. I gently collected the documents and a few books, frowning at the titles about banishing spirits. One of the notes was a letter in Sir Jason's handwriting, more faded and yellow than the others.

Dearest Henrietta,

I began preparations to leave as soon as I received word that you were ill. I will be on my way home to you at first light. How I long to be at your side, instead of wandering far off in the strange, cold world, away from the warmth of your smiles. With any luck, I will reach you before this missive, but still I send my love along with it. I promise we will be together again soon. Please get well. You know I cannot go on without you.

Eternally yours,

Jason

Tears blurred my vision, and I set the letter aside, feeling wrong for having read such private emotions. Was this the illness that claimed Lady Henrietta's life? Had Sir Jason made it back in time to say goodbye?

I glanced at Philip, longing to trace the strong line of his jaw, sink into the comfort of his embrace. Now that I had him, I never wanted to let go. Sir Jason was twisted, but I could sympathize with his pain. And what about poor Lady Henrietta? She must have loved Sir Jason. Perhaps she still did, even while she feared what he had become.

Moonset tugged at me.

"Philip!"

I grabbed his hand to haul him back from his rest, lest sleeping after moonset put him in danger. He opened his eyes, and my hand froze in his. No! I wanted to scream, to beg the moon to let me stay. The voices in the abyss cackled and howled.

Philip jerked up to stare at me. "Lucy? Oh, the moon's setting. But I thought—"

Chapter Twenty-Two

The antechamber solidified around me. Tingling pain shot through my limbs. Blood pounded in my ears. The warmth of the sun streamed over my skin. I drew a deep breath and sighed.

"Yes," Philip said from the sofa. "Maybe we ought to find a way to actually break the curse."

He sauntered over and presented me with a bouquet of sweet-peas, their white petals veined in scarlet.

"They're beautiful!" The soft blossoms tickled my nose, and the spicy-sweet scent wrapped around me. "Thank you." I touched his smooth cheek, and a thrill shot from my fingertips to my heart.

"I'm happy to try love's kiss again," he said with a grin.

I blushed. But we were engaged—how strange that still sounded!—so it wasn't improper, and with the curse hanging over us, I wanted to savor every moment with Philip. I closed my eyes and leaned into his kiss, running my fingers up into his hair to keep him close.

He rested his forehead on mine and smiled. "If this *is* the result of insanity, I wish I'd caught it sooner."

I laughed, but my grin faded as I toyed with his dark hair. "Have I only been gone one day?"

"Of course. You've never missed a moonrise. Why?"

"Your hair is longer."

"So I need a haircut too?" He raised an eyebrow. "Are you always going to be this hard to please?"

"No." I smiled a little. "Well, perhaps. Your hair does seem longer, though."

He shrugged. "Maybe you just never noticed it."

"I suppose." I hadn't been able to touch it before, but it looked wilder.

"As pleasant as this is," Philip said, his arms warm around my waist, "I have something else for you."

"Oh?"

He reached beside the sofa and, with a flourish, presented me a basket of food: cucumber sandwiches, sliced meat, cheese, and strawberries. "I brought a picnic. I think we need to search outside for the stone, but this way we don't miss dinner. We don't know how long it's been since you last ate."

I hesitated. "I should be hungry, shouldn't I?" I had watched with envy as Philip nibbled on scones or bread and cheese while we worked, and I longed to enjoy food again, but I didn't feel hungry or thirsty.

"You've gotten used to not eating, but your appetite will come back."

I took his arm, feeling the hard muscles through his coat. When we reached the corridor, distant voices floated along the ceiling. We froze, searching for shadows, but the sounds were warm and merry.

I eased my grip on Philip and laughed. "That'll be guests arriving for the ball!"

"The ball? I thought it wasn't for two more days. It's not the full moon yet."

"Yes, but guests who have far to travel will come early and stay at Springett Hall. That's probably Miss Ridgewell's party."

He frowned. "That's not good news. We don't want more people here."

"I know, but I'd hoped to sneak a look at Miss Ridgewell. I think she'll be the next lady of the house soon."

"Jealous?" Philip asked, his voice a bit tight.

I squeezed his arm. "Not even a little."

"Very well." He cocked an eyebrow. "Remember, though, people can probably see you now."

"Oh, of course. At least with all the guests around, we won't have to make up an explanation for why I'm here." My stomach fluttered. If the servants got to know me, I might make friends with them. I was sorry that Susan was gone, though it was a selfish impulse. "My hair!" I brushed back my loose locks. "What will they think? I look . . . improper, wild."

"You can fix it if you're concerned about making a good impression." Philip smiled and pulled my hairpins from his pocket.

"You've been carrying those around?" I asked, plucking one from his palm. It was warm from his hand.

"Yes," he said, and his shy smile turned teasing. "You should be grateful. I've saved your reputation."

I smirked and slipped the pins into my hair then took a moment to smooth out my dress. Despite all my adventures, it was still clean. "I shan't look disreputable now. Those other girls will wonder how an assistant gamekeeper managed to capture the fancy of such a proper young lady."

"I was very lucky."

I blushed, and Philip offered me his arm again to lead me down the back stairs.

We weren't the only ones curious about the guests. Some of the servants lurked on the edges of the entrance hall to catch glimpses of the gentlemen and ladies with their top hats and silk gowns. Philip and I watched from the doorway of the drawing room. A few of the maids spotted us and shot me dark glances. I sighed. However much I might know them, I was still an interloper, unlikely to ever be accepted.

"Sir Edmund's here," Philip whispered, "and that'll probably be his lady."

I peeked around the doorframe to the heart of the bustling activity. I'd imagined the future lady of Springett Hall as a tall, fair, imperious woman, as fashionable as Edmund. Instead, she was short, plump, and pretty with dark hair and a simple gray traveling dress. She looked like the type who'd mothered dolls and pets as a child, more suited as the wife of a farmer than a baronet. She made such an odd contrast standing next to Edmund that I stared.

Miss Ridgewell turned her smile on Edmund, and adoration lit her eyes. He grinned and stood close to her, bending to whisper, his expression calmer and happier than I'd ever seen it. She straightened his cravat, and he laughed and snuck a kiss on her hand. I smiled. They might not be a matched pair outwardly, but their hearts fit. She could be like the string to his kite, keeping him aloft but not letting him drift too far.

"Well?" Philip asked.

"I like her! If we can get rid of the ghosts, I think Springett Hall will be in good hands."

I turned to find Lady Henrietta hovering behind us, watching Edmund and Miss Ridgewell with a frown. She had been mistress of this house once, beloved by its master, and now she had to watch someone else take her place. Jealousy might make her dangerous. I stepped closer and recognized her expression. She wasn't angry, or even sad. She was afraid.

"Lady Henrietta?" I said softly.

She blinked at looked at me. If she could tell I was solid now, she gave no indication.

"What's wrong?"

She stared after Edmund and Miss Ridgewell as he escorted his guests upstairs to their rooms. Longing filled her eyes then she shuddered and turned away.

"We can make them safe if we find the moonstone," I whispered. "Do you know where it is?"

She fled past me.

"Well?" Philip whispered.

"I'm not certain. She either can't answer or won't. We should probably go search for the stone."

I hesitated and glanced over my shoulder at the piano.

"What?" he asked.

"Do you think . . . ?" My fingers ached to touch the instrument's smooth ivory keys.

"Oh, of course. We'll just be quiet." He grinned and led me to the bench with a bow. The edge bit into my legs as I adjusted my dress. I glanced at myself in the huge mirror. I looked pale, but otherwise as I'd seen my reflection in Philip's eyes. Choosing a quiet song, I poured my happiness and fears into the keys, closing my eyes as the notes spilled into the air. When I reached the end, I sat for a moment, listening to the sounds fade in the enormous room.

"Beautiful," Philip said. "I guess you were humoring me when you said I played well."

I spun to smile up at him. "No, you did well for your first try. It just felt so good to play again." I glanced at my fingers. I had thought them ugly when I first awakened, but they were beautiful to me now.

"I'm glad to know my future wife is so capable of—how did you put it?—amusing her husband." He winked.

His wife. I was going to be his wife. I thought my heart might flutter from my chest. I couldn't even find a reply to his teasing. Still, that life was only a dream until we'd stopped Sir Jason.

Philip leaned on the piano. "Do you want to play again?"

"I missed it more than I realized, but we do need to search the estate tonight."

I stood, and several of the keys fell on their own, clanking out a discordant racket.

"What—" Philip's brow furrowed.

"It's not me." I stumbled back from the bench.

The piano continued playing a mournful string of minor chords.

"Do you hear that?" Philip asked. "The voices . . . they're whispering something about the beast."

I shook my head. I couldn't see or hear any shadows, but goose bumps stippled my arms. Human voices sounded down the hall.

"I don't want to be questioned," Philip whispered.

I nodded, and we fled, our fingers laced together. The piano stopped. Philip pulled me around a corner as footsteps headed to the drawing room. I squeezed his hand, waiting for the sounds of screams, but heard only the confused babble of women's voices. Whatever game the ghosts were playing, they weren't attacking anyone at the moment.

"Outside," Philip said.

We slipped into the dusk. A light wind ruffled the lawn, reflecting the fading daylight in shimmering waves. Beyond it, the lake glittered black and gold.

"Why do you think you hear the voices sometimes and I don't?" I asked.

"I don't know. Maybe they're trying to tell me something. I've never heard Sir Jason; he seems to only speak to you."

"Perhaps, but I don't like not knowing. What if they're trying to influence you?"

"To do what? They can't control me. I feel like I'm getting stronger all the time. My senses are sharper, too, like I'm waking up a little more each day. I'm able to hear noises the other servants can't. It's possible the voices are just too quiet for you to hear."

I nodded, though I was uneasy thinking of the magic affecting Philip. He offered me his arm, and I took it, savoring the warm pressure of his touch. The breeze sighed by, and I shivered.

"You're cold?" he asked, shucking off his coat to wrap it around my shoulders.

The smell of pine and licorice—his smell—wrapped around me, and I snuggled into the coat.

He gestured at the shore. "Do you want to have our picnic by the lake?"

The deep, cold darkness of the water reminded me of oblivion. "Why don't we find somewhere warmer?"

I led him down the lane. As we passed the lake, I felt the whisper of a pull toward the house, but I pressed on, and it dissolved.

"Where are we going?" Philip asked with a smile, the basket of food swinging from his arm.

"I suppose the village is out of the question?"

"It might lead to an awkward situation if everyone expects you to be dead," he said quietly.

"Oh. You're right, of course."

He squeezed my hand. "There's a knoll over here, though, where we can see the village. It'll make a nice spot to eat."

We rambled up the little rise by the road. The grass rustled softly around us, stirring up a warm, earthy scent, and the lights from the village twinkled below like a reflection of the darkening sky. Philip beckoned me to sit by him and presented the basket.

"Don't eat a lot to start with, but you need to try something."

I nodded and bit into a strawberry. The crisp, sweet-tart flavor rolled over my tongue and the tiny seeds tickled my mouth. It tasted of spring, flooding me with memories: gathering berries with my sisters, eating the strawberries with cake or fresh sweet cream for my birthday. When I tried to swallow, though, I choked and coughed it into my napkin.

"Lucy! Are you all right?"

"I don't think I *can* eat." I gave him an apologetic look. "It feels . . . wrong. I think, whatever's happening to me, I'm still not quite as alive as I should be."

"Are you sure?" He scrambled through the basket. "Maybe you should try some bread?"

"No, I really don't think so. My appetite might come back later." I doubted it, though. All the minor, day-to-day sensations I associated with being alive—thirst, hunger, fatigue—were only noticeable by their absence. My heart pounded in a body that remembered what it was to live, but might never return to normal. I couldn't guess what I'd become or what it meant for my future.

Philip set the basket aside, his expression concerned, but I caught his arm. "You should eat. I'll feel badly if you starve yourself on my account."

"I suppose." He picked up a sandwich and took a bite.

A bark echoed over the lane. We tensed as a farmer with a lantern trudged along after his bounding dog.

"Ho there, Brutus," the farmer called. "Who's there?"

Philip stood and stepped forward. The dog gave a yelp and darted behind its master's legs.

"What's the matter with you?" the farmer asked the trembling creature. He turned his gaze back on us. "Who's up there?"

Philip cleared his throat. "It's Philip Ketley, sir, from Springett Hall."

"Oh, aye." The farmer's voice was wary. "And Miss Tregarrick, too, is it? Haven't seen you around lately. Thought you'd left Springett Hall like everyone else."

"No, sir." I stood, glancing at Philip with an eyebrow raised.

"It's a bit late for young folk to be wandering about." The farmer swung his lantern at us, almost as if he expected us to cringe or flee like shadows. Maybe the villagers understood more about Sir Jason—and us—than we suspected. "The beast may be wandering these hills still."

"The beast?" Philip asked.

"You must've heard o' the beast. It appeared the night Sir Jason died."

"What did it do?" Philip gripped my hand.

"It wandered the lonely spots o' the village and howled like the keening o' a banshee, enough to set women and children to crying and grown men scurrying for cover. In the morning, we found upwards o' a dozen cattle with their throats torn out." He pointed his walking stick at us. "You'd best get inside before it gets any later, and stay away from the woods."

He whistled for his cowering dog and hurried on down the lane.

"The beast is real, then," Philip whispered. "Suppose it's another thing Sir Jason summoned, and we let it escape? It may just be a matter of time before it kills someone."

"Can we banish a monster?"

He rubbed his chin. "I don't know."

"The villagers don't think I'm dead."

"No." He brushed his hand over my sleeve. "Maybe because there was no body to find. You weren't killed, just made immaterial."

"Possibly. I'm not really alive anymore, though. At best, I'm something in between."

"You're alive, Lucy," he said firmly, as if trying to convince himself. "We're going to undo whatever curse Sir Jason's magic laid on us."

I glanced at my hand, slightly luminous in the moonlight. Would a banishing spell send me away too? Despite the steady pulse of my heart, I no longer belonged to this world.

Philip picked up the basket and we strolled back toward the estate. I checked over my shoulder occasionally, wondering where the beast was now and if it obeyed Sir Jason as the rats did.

"Do you think you had time to hide the stone?" I asked.

"I think Sir Jason was close on my heels. It was probably him who gave me that lump on the head. The first place I remember after I woke up was our clearing, so that might be where I was heading."

"Are you certain he found you? You might have evaded him."

Philip's arm tightened against mine. "No matter how important the stone was, I never would have let him go back after you."

No, Philip would have protected me. I couldn't help smiling. "Maybe you hid it before he reached you."

"The woods are an awfully big place to search."

"Don't sound so hopeless." I nudged him with my elbow. "We'll retrace the most likely paths."

But he was right; there were countless little nooks in trees and under rocks. If Philip had simply tossed it aside, we might never find it. So much the better, though, if that meant Jason never did either. We'd find a way to banish him and break the curse before he realized the search was futile. We reached the clearing. Hundreds of small, smooth stones lined the stream bed.

"It could take a lifetime to sift through those." Philip scooped a handful and plopped them back into the water. "I'm not doing that in the dark."

He pulled me close, and we strolled a circuit around the front of the estate, past the hidden mausoleum, the lake, and the maze on the far side of the house. Springett Hall's battlements looked like a neat row of gravestones in the moonlight. I squinted at the windows, trying to guess which room was mine.

I tilted my head. "What if I had the stone and threw it out the window before Sir Jason could reach me?"

Philip grinned. "That's a brilliant idea. We'll look."

We crept across the lawn, walking a drunken line and stopping occasionally to examine something on the ground. In the garden, some of the sweetpea flowers had already wilted, as if winter had returned to claim them. I sadly caressed their limp, faded petals, and they clung to my fingers.

"Moonstone!" Philip said.

"What?"

He pointed. On the far edge of the garden, a stone like the one in the maze stood on a pedestal, gleaming in the darkness. "Those garden ornaments are made of moonstone!"

My heart skipped. "They're too big to be the one we're looking for."

"True." He pulled me forward. "Sir Jason must've been obsessed with moonstone, though."

Faint bands of color formed a muted rainbow just beneath the stone's cool surface. I ran my fingers over the nearly imperceptible ridges. "It's beautiful."

"I suppose it appeals to your romantic nature." I heard the teasing smile in Philip's voice.

I blinked and forced myself to look away from the colors shifting deep inside the white globe. "It's not just the stone. It's . . . being alive. Being able to feel and touch and interact with the world." I turned back to him and traced his jaw. "You need to shave again."

He laughed and took my hand, running my palm over his cheek. I giggled at the tickle and looked around to make sure we were alone, but of course no one was around in the middle of the night. Philip kissed my palm and drew me into an embrace. Goose bumps raced over my skin.

"The moon's setting. Kiss me good night?" He looked at me with undisguised sorrow and longing. My heart twisted.

"Of course." And I did, clutching his waistcoat as I froze, wishing, if I held on tightly enough, I'd never be torn from him again. There was no chance of that, though, unless we broke the curse. I vanished with the warmth of his lips lingering on mine.

Chapter Twenty-Three

The next evening, I again found myself staring at the eternally silent grandfather clock. Philip's coat was gone from my shoulders. My hair hung loose around me. I'd returned to the exact place where I began every day.

"Philip?" I asked.

"Lucy?" he called from the secret staircase behind me. I smashed into the closed door and stumbled back, rubbing my forehead. Now, I couldn't get used to being solid.

I managed the hidden latch and opened the door to find Philip reaching for the handle on the other side.

"Sorry, I lost track of time." He kissed my cheek and whispered, "I've been working on the banishing spell. Are you all right?"

"Yes." I blushed. "I ran into the door."

"You tried to run through it?" He flashed his boyish grin.

I nodded and fought my own smile. He held out his hand, offering my hairpins.

"You found them!"

"I saw them fall when you vanished." His shoulders slouched. "I guess I'll just hold onto them while you're gone."

I twisted my hair back, my heart heavy. Philip started up the staircase.

My legs ached, climbing the steep stairs, and I had to pause for breath at the top before I asked, "Do you think we'll get tired of this?"

Philip glanced around and dropped his voice. "Once we undo the curse, we won't spend all our time piecing together spells and searching dusty corners for moonstones."

"I meant all these problems we have."

"Oh. It will be frustrating at times, I'm sure, but I think all couples face that. Our problems are so dramatic they might keep things interesting. Remember Shakespeare? 'Love alters not with time's brief hours and weeks?' Though, I think he was wrong about that."

"You do?" My heart sank further.

"Yes, I think love changes. Everything does. If we keep working through the problems, though, it can get deeper, richer, over time. Like a garden. The more work you put into it, the more beautiful it becomes."

I grinned foolishly, my heaviness melting away in the warmth of his hope. "Careful. That was almost poetic."

He grimaced. "Back to work, then."

We sat with our knees touching, and even that simple contact filled me with courage. Philip pieced together the banishing spell from hints in the books and papers, hiding his actions from Sir Jason with mundane conversation. I scoured every source for a solution that didn't involve magic. The sun sank as we read, and Philip shifted and fidgeted.

"What's wrong?" I whispered, searching for the watching eyes of Sir Jason's rats.

Philip leaned closer. His voice was little more than a warm sigh against my ear. "I just can't make sense of this. It almost sounds like Sir Edmund's poetry. Sir Jason's rambling on about heart's desires."

"We know he raves at times," I whispered.

"He keeps repeating it, in different languages, with slight variations: heart desire, soul hunger, life yearning. And this idea of eternity and permanency."

I took the paper. "So, it's a spell." My forehead wrinkled. "But why? It seems like the other spells would give him what he wanted: he and Lady Henrietta together forever." I bit my lip. But Philip had just said that love changed. Everything changed. I kept my voice to a low murmur. "What if he wanted to create an anchor of some sort?"

"Blast it!" Philip's grip tightened, crinkling the papers in his hands, and he tossed them aside. "Let's get back to searching outside. There's plenty of ground we haven't covered."

He gave me a significant look, and I nodded. He'd found something. We laced our fingers together and hurried down the servant's staircase to the back door.

"What is it?" I asked when we reached the edge of the woods.

"We really do need to find the stone. We can't banish a ghost tied to something in this world unless we first destroy the thing it's bound to, remember?"

"Oh, drat." I shuddered. "But *we're* bound to Sir Jason."

"Through the stone, so I think we're safe if we can destroy it. If he'd bound us to himself directly, we'd have a whole different set of problems. The good news is I've pieced together the banishing spell. We can use it tomorrow at the full moon to send away the other spirits and weaken Sir Jason. After the guests have left the ball if you prefer."

I rubbed my arms. "I still don't like using magic again. Isn't there another way?"

"Not that I've found. It's my idea, so I'll do the spell."

My stomach turned. "Philip, if anything happened to you, I don't think I could bear it."

He sighed and pulled me close. I relaxed into his arms, listening to the rhythm of his heart. "I'm doing this for us, Lucy."

I smiled, until I remembered why Sir Jason had cursed us all in the first place. "I'm not certain that having a good reason for something makes it right."

He pulled away, his eyebrows drawn together. "You mean like promising to help our enemy complete his spell and then lying about it?"

"I was keeping you—everyone—safe!"

"You didn't trust me to fight my own battles. How long would you have hid it from me if you'd stayed immaterial?"

"Are you going to hold all my mistakes against me?"

The moonlit stillness hung between us for several heartbeats.

"I'm sorry, Lucy," Philip whispered hoarsely. "You did what you had to. That's what I'm trying to do."

I nodded and slipped back into his embrace. He stroked my hair, soothing the ache of our disagreement.

"The stone's probably inside," he said. "We haven't had a chance to search the ground floor thoroughly. Maybe while you're gone tomorrow I'll start sorting the ones in the stream bed."

I didn't envy him that task. We snuck back inside. The house was in an uproar preparing for the ball. The guests' valets and lady's maids mingled with the few servants remaining from Edmund's staff. With so many strangers, no one paid us much attention as we wandered through the downstairs rooms looking for moonstone, but I worried for all the extra people. The spirits were quiet, possibly because of the waxing moon, but the stillness in the corners had a tense, watchful feeling.

"I guess you won't be able to perform tonight with everyone around," Philip said as we passed the drawing room where a pair of valets played cards by the piano. Philip caught my hand and pulled me close, spinning me through a few waltzing steps across the entrance hall. "Do you want to sneak down to the ball tomorrow?"

I laughed and led the way into the old library. Refreshment tables had been set up in preparation for the ball, and maids busied themselves rolling up faded carpets and dusting the stale room. It would be lovely on the night of the ball, full of men in black suits and women in pastel dresses. "I'd love to go," I whispered, "but what if Edmund recognizes me?"

Philip's face darkened. "Don't let *him* ruin anything." A grin twisted his lips. "You can wear a mask and one of your fancy dresses. Then, when the moon sets, you'll disappear and leave the mask and dress behind."

I chuckled, imagining everyone's shocked expressions. "You said the full moon doesn't set until the sun comes up. I think even the most devoted dancers would be gone by then." I paused. "Do you really think we could?"

He opened his mouth to reply, but something on the ground caught his attention, and he knelt to examine it.

"What is it?" I asked.

He scratched at a faint white mark on the floorboards and rubbed the substance between his fingers. "I think it's chalk. Look. It makes a circle. You can see it now that they've moved the rugs."

I squinted, and the circle came into focus. It was scuffed and almost faded away, but traces of it remained. Philip crawled a short distance along its circumference, ignoring the confused stares of the maids coming and going. He paused again, staring at a spot on the floor. "Blast."

This time I saw it too: remnants of black wax ground into the wood. I walked the circle and found five such spots evenly spaced around it. Philip stood and stared at the ceiling.

"What's above us?" he whispered.

"I would guess Edmund's chambers, and on the next floor"—I lowered my voice further—"the spell room. We're directly beneath it. I thought he just moved his library to expand it, or maybe so no one found his spell books and the secret room—"

"He could have put the spell room somewhere else, though, like in the attic where he hid our rooms," Philip said. "It seems there's something special about this location."

A flash of movement jerked our attention to the wall. It rippled beneath the blue and white wallpaper. Lightning-shaped cracks tore through paper and plaster. A massive bookcase, so tall it nearly reached the ceiling and almost as wide, swayed over a maid who straightened its ornamental plates and curios. Teacups tumbled out like the first rocks announcing an avalanche, shattering on the floor. The maid screamed, and Philip jumped forward.

"No!" I yelled.

Philip leaned into the tilting shelf. It groaned. Books and knickknacks crashed around him. His muscles strained beneath his coat, and he grimaced, but the shelf creaked and stopped. Other maids and footmen came running, pausing to stare in astonishment. A few of the men jumped forward to help, but Philip shoved the huge case back against the wall.

The maids gasped and cried out, flocking around Philip. His eyes met mine, and I shook my head in wonder. He shot me a smug smile. Once he extricated himself from the grateful girls, he took my arm and walked on with a nod to the crowd of servants.

"That was impossible!" I said when we'd climbed the stairs and left everyone behind.

"Obviously not." He raised an eyebrow. "You don't think I'm strong?"

"Of course you are, but that thing was enormous. It could have killed you."

"I wasn't going to stand by and watch some poor girl get crushed. It didn't feel all that heavy, really."

I shook my head in disbelief.

"Look!" He grinned manically and swung me up into his arms. "You weigh nothing. Maybe you're a ghost after all."

I laughed. "I know you're strong. You don't have to impress me."

He lowered my feet to the floor and leaned close, something fierce and wild in his gaze as he searched my face. "I want to impress you. I want you to know I'll always protect you."

He pulled me into a crushing embrace and kissed me, a growl rumbling in his throat. His fingers dug into my back through my corset as he kissed me again, deeply, like he would drink me in. I leaned in, wanting to lose myself forever in his long, hungry kisses.

The lights flickered, and hissing laughter emanated from the shadows.

"Wait!" I pulled back, flushing in embarrassment. "What are you doing?"

He recoiled, his eyes wide. "I'm sorry. I'm not thinking. I don't know what's wrong with me." He rubbed his face. "There *is* something wrong, though, isn't there?"

"You don't seem quite yourself," I said slowly.

"That case should have crushed us, but it didn't even feel heavy."

"I saw you straining to hold it." I touched his forehead. "See, you're sweating too."

"I don't feel well." He leaned on me. "Don't leave me tonight. I promise to behave."

"I know you will. I'll stay with you as long as I can."

We reached the stairs to our rooms. Philip pushed against the wall, dragging his feet up each step. By the time he reached the top, he was pale and shivering, though sweat beaded on his face.

"Am I dying?" he asked.

"No." I said firmly, trying to convince myself. It *had* to be true; I couldn't lose him now. Still, my voice shook. "You're staying here with me. You're just unwell."

"I'm cursed too." He leaned against the wall. "I knew I must be. What did it feel like, to be immaterial?"

"Nothing. That was the problem." I tightened my grip on his arm. "But that's not going to happen to you."

He stumbled into his room and curled up on his bed, his teeth chattering. "Then what's going on?"

"I don't know," I whispered, "but we'll figure it out."

I sat next to him and stroked his hair. He shut his eyes, and his breathing grew steady. Even in sleep, though, he twitched and mumbled, his brow drawn.

A rat peeked its head through the doorway. I gritted my teeth. Couldn't Sir Jason give us a moment's peace?

"Philip's sick! Unless you're going to help, you may as well leave us alone tonight." I threw *A Treasury of Necromancy* at the rat, and it skittered aside.

The rat paced the threshold, its movements growing slower as the night wore on, until finally it collapsed, its legs twitching. I covered my mouth and turned away. When I looked back, the rat had stilled. Gagging, I used the necromancy book to scoop it out of the little window on the landing, but I couldn't help feeling pity for the creature. It wasn't the first one I'd seen die under Sir Jason's control, and I doubted it wanted to be his pawn.

The documents still sat in the hall, so I brought them to Philip's bedside. There had to be an answer somewhere. I wasn't going to lose everything just as I learned the value of what I had. I'd do anything . . . My hands paused. Would I? I'd already risked my soul to protect Susan and everyone else in the house. What was I willing to do for love? How much would I give for Philip? He wouldn't want me to be foolish, but love wasn't rational.

As moonset approached, my despair deepened. Tears slid off my face, flashing away when they hit the documents without smudging the ink or staining the paper. Another symptom of my oddity. Even if I did remember everything I'd been, I wasn't certain I'd understand what I'd become. I wiped a tear and studied it on my finger, but it glistened as any tear would. It dropped to the floor, where it shimmered and vanished. The house rumbled.

I threw the notes aside and shouted at the walls, "Leave us alone!"

Chapter Twenty-Four

Philip. My gaze found him the next evening as soon as I had awareness. He was curled up on the sofa, clutching his head, his teeth bared in a snarl.

"Philip!" I called.

His hand lashed out. "Stay back!"

"You're still unwell. Why are you out of bed?"

"I felt better in the morning. Now . . . I can feel the moonlight. It's so bright it burns. My mind is on fire."

I stepped closer, but he shrank away.

"No," he whispered. "I don't want to hurt you."

I pressed my lips together and dashed to pull the draperies over the moonlit window. "You wouldn't, Philip. I know you. I trust you."

"Do you? Every bit of me? Don't we all have something dark inside of us? Sir Jason knew that. He fed on it, manipulated it. What if he gave it life? The dark beast—"

"You're *not* the dark beast!"

"Aren't I?" he snapped. "He made your weakness weaker, what if he made my strength stronger?"

I shrank back. His hair was longer, the stubble on his face now a thick beard. His teeth glinted sharply in the dim light.

"Get out, Lucy. Lock me in. Don't let me hurt anyone. Please. Do whatever you have to."

"Philip—"

"Go!" he roared.

I fled into the hallway and slammed the door. Philip screamed and growled behind the door, and I sat against it, tears stinging my eyes. A side table decorated the hallway. I hauled it over in front of the door. The edge bit into my fingers, and I gritted my teeth, glorying that I could feel the pain. It meant I could protect Philip.

Music and happy voices sounded from below. My heart froze.

The ball! A nightmare now, not a fairy tale, with all those people. I sank in front of the table blocking the door and bit my fingernail.

A bang rattled the door, breaking the rhythm of the distant waltz.

"Philip?" My voice shook.

A deep growl rumbled from the antechamber.

"Philip?" I had little hope of an answer.

The door shook. Another boom, and the heavy wood cracked. He'd lifted that enormous bookcase into place yesterday. He was beyond human strength.

A bang splintered the wood and knocked the table from its place. I shoved it back and sat on it. He'd lifted me like I was nothing, though. I scooted to the edge and braced my feet against the floor. The next crash jarred my teeth. My boots slipped on the deep carpet. Raspy animal growls escaped from beneath the door. Something scratched at the splintered wood.

Another bang. The crack in the door widened. Thick, dark fur flashed through the broken wood. The next crash sent me tumbling from the table. It didn't matter how solid or real I was; I couldn't stop him.

The bits of spells I'd picked up ran through my mind. I could try one of them, but they were all dark magic. I didn't want to taint myself further, and I wouldn't harm Philip. He'd said to do whatever it took, though.

Music drifted upstairs. Another waltz. I had to warn everyone to leave. Edmund would probably listen. I ran down the hall, stumbling to a stop at the top of the stairs.

They wouldn't just leave. They'd hunt Philip, try to kill him. Of course, that was what he meant when he said 'anything,' but I couldn't let them do it. Not when there was a chance Philip would return to himself, just as I had.

Maybe I could convince everyone to leave for another reason. I could start a fire. Yes, that would chase everyone out and leave Philip's condition a secret.

The door burst apart. A huge animal sprang into the hall, part lion and part wolf. The thick mane covering its massive shoulders was the same deep, almost-black as Philip's hair. I was too late.

It stalked toward me, head low, lips peeled back. The beast had come from Philip, possessed him, but there was no trace of his intelligence in its expression.

I stumbled away, and its snarl rumbled against my pounding heart. The edges of my vision narrowed so all I could see was the beast prowling closer. Instinct screamed for me to run, but the monster would give chase, catch me. Would I wake up again with moonrise tomorrow? Even if I did, what of Philip? He would never forgive himself for hurting me, not to mention everyone down below, even if it was the beast controlling him.

The creature was so close I could see its eyes. Deep blue, like a perfect summer afternoon. Philip didn't want to hurt anyone. Maybe he was still in there.

"Philip?" My voice cracked.

The monster's ears twitched.

"Philip." I forced my voice calm. "I know you can hear me."

The beast stepped forward, muscles tense beneath its dark fur. Shadows gathered against the walls, edges sharp as blades. Their whispers filled the hallway, not the single voice of Sir Jason, but an ocean of angry words. The monster's ears flicked to catch them.

Black beast. Right hand of death. Do our work.

The creature roared and stepped forward, tail lashing like a whip. I held out my hands.

"You're strong, Philip. Stronger than the beast. You don't want to hurt anyone. Not really."

Blood. Death. Revenge.

It growled. The hair along its back rose.

"I trust you. You wouldn't hurt me. I won't let you hurt anyone else."

Drink your fill. Eat their flesh. Make them pay.

The beast lunged past me. I dove for its neck and hung on. It snarled and thrashed around, hot breath on my sleeve. I wrapped my fingers in its thick fur. Sharp teeth stopped short of my arm, but the beast dragged me down the hallway as if it didn't notice my weight.

The shadows laughed.

"Stop, Philip! Please!"

A growl thrummed under my fingers. We reached the stairs. Below, I could hear the strains of the violins and the indistinct chatter of the crowds enjoying the dance. The creature dragged me down the first flight of stairs, and I thudded along, the steps jabbing into my side.

"I love you, Philip," I whispered into the monster's pricked ear. The words—the feeling behind them—were the only things I had strong enough to stand against the beast, to save Philip. "Don't let Sir Jason win!"

It snarled. No, best not to mention Sir Jason.

"Stay with me, Philip. You promised."

The beast hesitated, and I caught a glimpse of something intelligent in its eye. Philip was still there. Then the glimmer was gone.

I looked up. Lady Henrietta stood before us in the hallway, eyes wide. Below, I glimpsed servants and guests in their finery. Any moment, someone would see the beast. They would scream, and the night would end in blood.

The monster growled, the sound resonating in my chest. Lady Henrietta stepped back.

"It's Philip," I said. "He's cursed. Just like me. Like you. Can you help him? Help everyone down there?"

She stretched out a trembling hand. The beast snarled again, but shrank from her touch.

"He can see you!" I said. "Push him back more. Please!"

She nodded and slowly walked forward. The beast backed away from the grand staircase, its throat rumbling. I readjusted my grip, the fur sticking to my sweating palms, but I didn't let go. The beast lowered his head. Lady Henrietta tried to shoo it back, but it circled around, dragging me over the carpet. Its eyes flicked from the people below to the ghost floating in front of the stairs.

"Philip," I whispered in its ear. "You don't want to go down there. Please stay. I need your help. I want you to protect me."

The beast froze. Its body trembled. Philip was fighting it! Tears of relief blurred my vision as I locked my fingers into the thick ruff around its neck and pulled. Its muscles remained tense under my hand, but it let me half-drag it back up the stairs and down the corridor to the splintered door. Its nails clicked on the wooden floor where the worn rug didn't cover.

"Upstairs, Philip. To your room. We'll be safe there."

The beast hesitated, but I pushed and it loped up. I shut the secret door behind us and followed. It waited at the top, head low and eyes reflecting the dim light.

"Good boy," I said.

It snarled, and my heart jumped.

I swallowed. "I'm sorry. I didn't mean to patronize you. Will you please go into your room?"

The creature just stared at me. How much did it understand? At least Philip was keeping the monster in check. I walked in, and it trailed behind, sniffing along the floor and growling to itself. I shut the door and the growl deepened. The beast paced to the door and roared.

"Philip, please, come away."

I searched for anything that might call him back to me. My gaze found the book of sonnets. They'd helped him remember that he loved me once before. I grabbed the book, and it fell open to the same poem.

"'Let me not to the marriage of true minds admit impediments.'"

The beast turned to me, lips curled up to bare sharp, white teeth.

My hand trembled, but I kept my voice even. "'Love is not love which alters when it alteration finds, or bends with the remover to remove.'"

It cocked its head and slowly stepped forward. I drew a long breath.

"'O no! It is an ever-fixèd mark that looks on tempests and is never shaken.'"

The beast sat at my feet, watching with intense blue eyes.

"'It is the star to every wandering bark, whose worth's unknown, although his height be taken.'"

With a yawn, the beast curled up beside me and rested its head on its paws. I laced my fingers through its thick fur to hold it there and read until it fell asleep. I didn't dare move for fear the spell would break and it would bolt off. The two doors between the beast and the rest of the house wouldn't hold if it charged them.

So I sat all night, with the beast possessing the man I loved sleeping by my side. The same worry played through my thoughts repeatedly as the moon made its slow journey across the stars: what would happen when it set at dawn, and I was no longer there?

Chapter Twenty-Five

The hollow darkness of night greeted my reappearance. Someone had removed the broken hallway door from its hinges and picked up the splintered wood, but Philip's usual place on the sofa was empty. My heart seized. Anything could have happened in the hours since the curse whisked me away. It wouldn't be fair to lose Philip after finding him again, but black magic knew no sympathy, no mercy, no love.

I raced upstairs and flung open Philip's door. Clothes and papers lay spilled across the floor. Had the beast done this, or had someone found our secret rooms? I flung the clothes aside, searching for hints about what had happened. The little bag of money tumbled to the floor with a muted jingle. A burglar wouldn't leave it behind, and neither would Philip if he'd planned on going somewhere.

His sketchbook sat on the rumpled bed with a fresh vine of sweetpea flowers as a bookmark. I let the pages fall open and ran my fingers over a drawing of a bird so real it could have flown from the paper. I flipped to the spot marked by the flowers, blank except for a line in Philip's neat writing:

I love you. I'm sorry.

My fingers froze over the words. Sorry for what? Becoming the beast? I flipped through the pages, but there was nothing else. A sense of foreboding washed over me. The words sounded too much like a farewell.

I dropped the book and dashed through the halls. Philip preferred being outside. I ran to the stable, where lights burned in the windows, and banged on the door. A couple of the stableboys pulled it open, clutching their pitchforks as they peered into the darkness.

"Please," I panted. "Have you seen Mr. Ketley today?"

"No." One of the young men leered. "I thought 'e found somewhere warmer to sleep."

I blushed, remembering my disheveled hair. Who cares what they thought? I fled from their chortles. Where would Philip go?

Of course, I knew the answer. I plunged through the brush along the stream, brambles tearing at my dress. It would probably restore itself at moonrise. If not, I didn't care. I'd spend all of eternity in a torn dress if I could find Philip safe.

Our clearing opened before me. Philip sat on the flat rock with his back to me, his head resting in his hands. Tears of relief brimmed in my eyes, and I tiptoed forward.

"Lucy," he said without turning. "Stay there."

"How did you—?"

"I can smell you. You smell like lilacs, and you're frightened."

"Of course I am! I woke up, and you were gone. What are you doing?"

"I thought the moon would bring out the beast again, and I know a farmer who's fast with his gun. When I didn't change, I wasn't sure what to do."

"Philip!" I gathered my skirts and tromped over to him. "Listen to what you're saying! How dare you talk like that?"

He kept his face from me. "What do you expect me to do? I'm dangerous, Lucy. I can't let myself hurt someone."

"Philip—"

"There was nothing but the smell of blood for me last night. I wanted to taste it. I would have gone for Sir Edmund first."

"But you didn't!"

"Aren't you listening?" He whirled on me, his eyes wild beneath his shaggy hair, and his face covered in thick stubble. "I'm a monster! I got what I wanted. We both did. That's the hinge of Sir Jason's spell, of the curse: to get what we wanted."

"What?" I stepped back.

"You wanted to escape from everything, and you did. I wanted to be strong. Strong enough to hurt everyone I hated. Now I am."

"Maybe," I whispered. "We both wanted something else, though, didn't we?"

"What?"

"Each other. And we got a second chance."

"What kind of second chance is this?" he snarled. "We still can't be together. It just makes the curse that much more potent."

He stood and turned away from me. I reached for him but drew my hand back. What if he was right? Maybe second chances were just another of my daydreams, and it was time to run again.

I glanced at Philip, whose shoulders hunched in fear or pain. Philip, whom I finally had the chance to love. I'd seen last night that I couldn't run anymore. Fear only gave power to the shadows. It was another habit I had to break.

"Why can't we be together, Philip Ketley?" I folded my arms.

He barked out a laugh. "Because I nearly tore out your throat last night." He turned and rested his fingers over my pulse, and I resisted the impulse to swallow. "I could hear your blood pounding . . ."

I grabbed his hand. "Stop being so dramatic. That was the beast, and you were stronger. You won."

"It could happen again," he said quietly. His eyes pleaded for reassurance.

"Every time you defeat it, you'll be that much stronger. If it makes you feel better, we'll build a cage for when you feel like you're changing again, until you know how to control it."

He shook his head, and his teeth flashed in a grimace. "I could do that, but I can't have you around."

His words knocked my breath away. "Y-you don't want me anymore?"

"Oh, I want you." The longing in his gaze warmed my cheeks. "I want to stay with you always, but I also want to protect you, even from myself."

"I thought you meant it when you said 'Love is not love which alters when it alteration finds.' Just because the alteration is in you, does that mean your love stops?"

He cringed. "I still love you." The words softened the edges of the pain and fear digging into my chest. "That's why I'm trying to keep you safe."

"I appreciate that." I stepped closer. "If I thought the danger was real, I would agree that I might have to love you from a distance. But you *didn't* hurt me. As for leaving me alone . . . what happens if I go invisible again? Wandering around with no one to talk to? Maybe forever? Don't I get a say in all this?"

"I—" He stopped, hope as faint as starlight softening his expression. "I don't think you're being rational."

"Of course I'm not. As for rational: do you really want to let Sir Jason win? If you give up and walk away—or worse, run straight into some farmer's gun—you leave everyone in that house at his mercy. If you hadn't been so strong the other day, that maid would have died."

Philip blinked. "I suppose . . ."

"We'll turn his curse against him! Maybe we can break it. At least we'll have tried."

He straightened. "You're right." His eyes shone. "Can you really mean that you still love me, even after seeing what's living inside me?"

"I love you all the more for seeing you overcome it."

He drew me into a rib-crushing embrace. His heartbeat pounded fast and steady against my ear. He leaned down, and I inhaled slowly, remembering his last, passionate kisses. But he smiled and kissed me once, gently. "We'll overcome it together. I have one condition, though."

"You're putting conditions on promises of eternal love?"

He laughed then his eyes turned serious again. "Yes, I am. If I ever hurt you—if I ever come close—you get away from me. Make sure I can't hurt anyone, if you can, but get far away."

"I won't stop loving you."

"Nor I you, but I have to know you're safe."

"I agree, because I know you won't ever—"

"Lucy! Please take this seriously."

I took a deep breath, searching my heart. When I'd wondered what I'd be willing to do for love, I hadn't considered walking away, but if there ever came a time when it was the right thing, my love was strong enough to do it.

"Yes, Philip, I promise."

He pulled me again into the warm safety of his arms and smoothed back my stray locks. "Lucy." His breath sighed over my hair, and I closed my eyes.

"I love you, Philip." I couldn't imagine ever tiring of saying it, the words as reverent and powerful as a prayer, giving new hope and meaning to every moment.

"I love you too."

I grinned. "You were right."

"Of course I was," he said with forced lightness. "About what?"

"This place is like heaven."

"Getting much closer, anyway." He caressed my face, and I blushed again. "Let's stop Jason and break this curse, and then it will be perfect."

Chapter Twenty-Six

The house seemed dim despite its gaslights as we stepped in from the moonlit yard.

Nellie shuffled down the hall, peering inside vases and behind side tables. "Where did it go?"

"Can we help you find something?" Philip asked.

"Out of my way!" She pushed past us, muttering as she searched. "Lost! All is lost!"

"Oh, no." Cold wrapped around me, and I gripped Philip's arm. "Edmund said the same thing. It's Sir Jason. His influence is spreading." If the rats under his control died, what would happen to the people?

"The moon is waning. It doesn't rise now until after the sun has set, and the darkest part of night is when he's strongest," Philip whispered in my ear. "We have to find the moonstone before he does. We'll start at the top again."

We scoured our antechamber again for the moonstone. I opened the clock case, bathing us in the fragrance of raw mahogany, but only a dusty spiderweb hid beneath the lifeless brass pendulum and weights. Philip lifted the rug, slit the sofa cushions along their seams, and rapped a rhythmic pattern along the walls, looking for hollow spots. We combed through our bedrooms but came away shaking our heads.

I sank onto the torn sofa and buried my face in my hands. It was hopeless. How could we find one tiny stone in this huge house? Philip put his arm around me. I leaned against his shoulder.

"We're going to break the curse. Then we'll both be free," Philip whispered, his gentle tone a balm for my despair. "Let's backtrack to the library."

Miss Matthews and another maid walked down the hallway toward the stairs, their heads bent together in whispers and their gazes darting around the corridor.

"Mr. Ketley!" Miss Matthews straightened, her eyes wide. " 'Ave you 'ad any luck with the search?"

"The search?" Philip shifted back, giving me a concerned look.

I drew a deep breath, keeping my expression neutral. Was everyone in Sir Jason's thrall?

"Don't be coy," the other maid said. "We all know. Sir Edmund's nearly mad over it."

"I'm afraid I've been unwell," Philip said. "I'm sincerely baffled."

The two girls exchanged a skeptical glance, and Miss Matthews said, "Miss Ridgewell's gone missin'."

My chest tightened.

Philip's eyebrows rose. "Missing?"

"No one's seen 'er since the ball. The poor master's near mad over it. 'E 'asn't rested, out searchin' with the other men."

"I'll join them directly," Philip said, nearly crushing my hand as he pulled me past them. They gave us odd looks and continued to the stairs.

"Lucy?" he whispered. "Could I have—?"

I swallowed. "I didn't leave you during the full moon. Where did you . . . come to?"

"In my room."

"When?"

"Just as the sun came up."

"There was no time, then. You remember all of today?"

"I slept for a while." He gave me a look full of despair. "What if the beast took over? Or if Sir Jason did? I could hurt someone without even being aware. I'm dangerous to everyone." He leaned against the wall and rubbed his eyes. "I wanted to be strong enough to protect people from monsters, and I became one instead. I can't live with myself if I . . ." He shuddered.

I rested my hand on his shoulder. I wanted to say he would never hurt anyone, but with Sir Jason or the beast working through him, how could we know? "We'll break the curse," I said softly, glancing around for rats.

Philip straightened, his expression dark. "Yes, we're going to fight back," he whispered.

He strode down the hall, pulling a folded piece of paper from his pocket.

I ran after him. "What are you doing?"

"Banishing the spirits," he said in a low tone. "We may not be able to get rid of Sir Jason without the stone, but we can make him weaker."

"Do you think that's wise?"

"I won't let him hurt anyone else."

He banged the library door open. The room sat empty and quiet. Philip paced to the center, his face shadowy in the gloom.

"Please, Philip." I caught his sleeve. "You're frightening me. There must be another way. We could help with the search."

"Sir Edmund has everyone looking for her."

"Except the people under Sir Jason's influence."

"This will weaken him, maybe break his hold on the household." Philip looked at me, and his expression softened. "It's a simple spell, just words and willpower with no ritual symbols or anything unpleasant like that. I'll summon the spirits to me and then order them back into the abyss. I think you could argue this is white magic."

Was there such a thing? I shook my head. "There has to be something else we can do. Magic is no escape; it will only dig us in deeper."

"Lucy, I can't let him harm people if there's something I can do to fight him." Philip's expression was pleading.

Tears stung my eyes. Maybe there was no right answer. We needed to protect the people in the house. Fighting magic with magic still seemed like a dangerous idea, but I had no other suggestions to offer.

"Very well," I whispered, adding a silent prayer for forgiveness. "I understand."

He smiled wanly. "Thank you. It would have been better to do the spell at midnight but this will have to do."

We glanced at the library clock, but no one had restarted it. Its hands still pointed to eight.

I stepped back and bit my fingernail.

Philip straightened and began chanting, a mix of Latin and Greek. My stomach churned and I clutched the back of a chair. I'd expected some kind of fanfare or warning. Was it so easy to taint your soul? Of course, Philip had spent hours over the last week studying for this.

The walls rumbled, rattling the bookcases. A pair of rats raced toward Philip. I grabbed a wooden chair and herded them back.

A sick, inky feeling poured into the room. The rats shrieked and fled.

"Philip, stop," I whispered, but my words were lost in a torrent of ghostly voices.

Shadows oozed from the walls and the floor, moaning and hissing in a deep, aching pitch on the edges of my hearing. The forms melted into a dark cloud circling in the confines of the library.

Philip stepped forward, and his voice changed to a commanding tone. The black cloud drew tight around him. I clasped my hands together.

The shadows tensed then shot apart like shattered glass. Philip's eyes widened, and he stepped back, his voice faltering.

Shadows plunged into him like black blades. He roared and doubled over, clasping his head.

"Philip!"

His forehead glistened with sweat, and his eyes had a wild, animal gleam. His hair lengthened, and his shoulders stretched against his coat.

"No!" I threw my arms around him.

Some of the hovering shadows fled, but his face contorted with pain. He grasped for me, his fingers digging into my arms. I held him, praying he could fight the shadows, keep the beast trapped and sleeping. I buried my face against his shoulder, and my tears dripped onto his neck.

The tears flashed against his skin. He screamed. Dark mist rose from his back and rolled away. He collapsed to the rug, his eyes unfocused, his breathing ragged.

"Philip?" I touched his face, my fingers trembling against his stubbled cheek.

He blinked slowly and looked up at me, the sense returning to his eyes. He grabbed me with one arm and pulled me down to his chest. I huddled against him, listening to the fast beat of his heart.

"I'm sorry," he whispered at last. "You were right. That was a foolish thing to do, and Sir Jason's going to be angry."

"At least you're all right. That's all I care about right now."

He grunted. "Let's get outside. I can stand now, and it isn't safe in here."

We fled for the safety of the yard. Philip kept my arm through his as we walked across the moonlit grass. A cool breeze tugged at the edges of my skirt, sending chills over my skin.

"We have another problem," Philip said quietly. "I could . . . understand the shadows in the midst of the spell. When Sir Jason summoned them, he bound them to something, probably to help him draw strength from them, like he did to us. That's why my spell didn't work."

"He bound them to the stone?"

"It felt bigger than that, maybe the limits Sir Jason set on his power. I think we have to destroy those before we can send them away. No wonder you were concerned about boundaries. You knew we had to find them before we could do anything else."

I groaned and glanced at the word on my palm. "And we don't even have the stone."

"At least he doesn't either."

We meandered closer to the house and peered through a wide window. Nellie crawled along the floor, examining corners and mouse holes. She rose to run her fingers along the windowsill, and her eyes narrowed when she saw us. We leaned back, but she lunged at the glass, slamming her hands against it. Her face contorted with rage, and she screamed.

Philip pulled me from the circle of light pooled outside the window. Nellie shouted incoherently, her face red and spittle flying from her lips.

She stepped back with a smile. A small army of rats swarmed around her, clawing their way over her dress. I gasped and covered my mouth.

Philip swore and smashed the glass with his elbow, banging away the broken pieces, and jumped through the gaping frame. I grabbed the empty window frame, my knuckles white.

Nellie's smile faded, and she backed away, her face slack. The rats flowed from her to Philip, but he kicked at them and grabbed the maid. She writhed and screamed as he hauled her out the window.

She bit Philip. He dropped her to the grass with a shout. Her struggles stopped, but she stared trance-like at the dark sky.

"Come away!" Philip said to me.

A wrenching jerk in my arm stopped me. My hand stuck to the wooden window frame. I wiggled it, trying to break free, and it sank further. My heart skipped. Not again! The house moaned as if in pain but refused to release me.

"Philip! Help!"

"What happened?"

"My hand's trapped, like when the wall had me." The dense wood pinched my fingertips, sending shocks of pain up my arm.

Philip's eyes widened, and he grabbed my waist to pull me back. My arm throbbed. "You're tearing my hand off!"

He slammed his fist into the wood. I whimpered as the impact rattled through my bones. The house slowly sucked my hand deeper, though I braced myself and leaned away. Tears stung my eyes.

Philip swore. "Fight it. I'll be back."

He raced into the night. I gritted my teeth and twisted my arm. My shoulder throbbed, but I couldn't pull away. I wiped my tears with my free hand and tugged, muscles burning and joints aching.

Philip charged up to the window with an ax.

"Let her go!" he shouted and swung the ax deep into the wood. The blow jolted my arm and rang across the yard. Still no one came to check on the racket. Was everyone on the estate under Sir Jason's influence? Or had Springett Hall fallen so far that a woman's screams and the sounds of vandalism no longer roused any interest?

Philip struck again, and the wooden frame broke from the house. The pain in my fingers eased, and I yanked them free, flexing my hand. The tips of my fingers tingled like the pricks of pins and needles.

"If you hurt anyone else, Sir Jason, I swear I'll find the stone and smash it! I'll burn Springett Hall to the ground and spit on the ashes!" Philip hit the building once more, sparks flying from the ax as it chipped the bare stone.

"Philip, stop!"

He paused, chest heaving and teeth bared. His eyes flashed with animal rage in the light spilling from the house. A chill raised the hairs on the back of my neck, but he shook his head and tossed the ax aside to pull me close.

"Are you all right?"

"Yes," I breathed into his chest.

"What happened?"

"I don't know. My hand just slipped in like I wasn't solid anymore."

Philip caressed my face and clasped my arm, sending warmth pouring over my skin. "You seem solid enough now. It must have been part of Sir Jason's magic. We need to keep you out of that house."

"Then we need to find the stone."

"Yes." He looked back at the maid. She breathed a slow, steady cadence. Philip gently closed her eyelids, and her head sagged to the side. "I think she's asleep."

"That makes sense. It's when it's easiest for Sir Jason to get into people's minds. What if we woke her?"

"Farther from the house." He lifted Nellie, her limp arms swaying as he carried her across the lawn and gently lowered her to the grass. "You try. It'll be less of a shock."

I nodded and gave Nellie's shoulder a hard shake. She opened her eyes with a gasp.

"Where am I? What 'appened?"

I put a hand on her arm. "I think you were sleepwalking. You . . . came out of the house."

She blinked at the moonlit lawn. "I did?"

"Yes. Are you all right?"

"I don't know. I feel a bit . . . oily, like I need to scrub my 'ands." She rubbed her arms. "What are you doin' out 'ere?"

I glanced at Philip, and the maid gave us a dismissive gesture.

"Oh, nevermind. I won't pry into your affairs."

I blushed and cleared my throat. "There's been a disturbance at the house tonight—vandalism." It wasn't a lie, at least. "Do you know anyone in the village?"

"I 'ave some friends there."

"Perhaps you'd be better off sleeping somewhere else."

Nellie stared up at the dark stone walls looming behind us. Shadows moved behind the windows. She shuddered and looked away. "Yes, I think you're right."

"We can walk with you," Philip said.

"Thank you," she said. "I'll come tomorrow to give my notice. Most of the staff's already gone, and I'm startin' to think they're right."

We walked with her along the wooded path to the village and bid her farewell.

Philip sighed. "Sir Jason takes their minds before the moon comes up, and then he doesn't let go. We need to figure out a way to get everyone from the house, even if we can't find the stone."

"Do you think the house is the boundary he tied the spirits to?"

"I don't know. Sir Jason's influence is stronger inside, but he seems to be able to reach past the walls."

"Yes, I've felt his pull out on the estate. Could he have set the boundaries out here?"

"Possibly. It sounds as though he had to mark them somehow, though. I've walked the estate with the groundskeeper, and I never noticed any arcane symbols on the ground." He paused and stared up at the house. "We have to help find Miss Ridgewell. I don't want to know if I was involved, but . . ." he swallowed several times. "My senses are still very keen. It's the least I can do."

I squeezed his arm. "Yes, we should look." Poor Miss Ridgewell. I hoped we weren't too late.

Chapter Twenty-Seven

I disappeared from Philip's side as we hunted the estate for some sign of Miss Ridgewell. When I reappeared the next night, Philip was waiting for me. Lady Henrietta paced behind him, wringing her hands and keeping her gaze on the floor.

"Have they found her?" I asked, though the dark circles under Philip's eyes gave me little hope.

"No, not a trace. Everyone's combing the grounds now, but it's like she vanished."

"It that possible?" I asked. "Could this be magic?"

"Maybe. I haven't let myself sleep, though, just in case."

I squeezed his arm and whispered, "Lady Henrietta's here."

Philip's eyes narrowed. "Where?"

She glided closer and gestured toward the hall, her mouth moving rapidly.

"What's wrong?" I asked.

She beckoned for me to follow.

"She wants us to go with her," I said to Philip.

"We don't know we can trust her. What if she's helping Sir Jason? What if he controls her?"

Lady Henrietta shook her head and made a pleading gesture.

"What if she can help us?" I asked.

He set his jaw and looked away.

I put a hand on his arm. "This may be the fastest way to find Miss Ridgewell. If she's in danger, doesn't every moment count?"

Philip scowled. "Very well."

We hurried after Lady Henrietta. She guided us to the library. I slowed my pace. After the failed banishing spell, it seemed like the worst place to return.

"I don't like this, Lucy," Philip whispered. "Let me go first."

I nodded, and we followed Lady Henrietta to the back bookcase.

She gestured for Philip to open it. I stepped back, filled with foreboding.

"She wants us to go in the spell room," I whispered to Philip.

"That's not a good idea." Philip looked almost frightened as he stared at the bookcase.

Lady Henrietta pointed and clasped her hands. I hesitated. I didn't want to confront the shadows again either, but Lady Henrietta's fear and concern seemed sincere.

"What if Miss Ridgewell's in there?" I asked. "It would be a perfect place to hide her."

Philip glared at bookcase and took a deep breath. "Fine." He pushed the secret door, but it refused to budge.

"Lady Henrietta?" I asked.

She pointed to the room, her eyes wide. Shadows shifted along the walls of the library, circling closer to us. Perhaps it was a trap.

"You might be right," I whispered to Philip. "We can search elsewhere."

He closed his eyes. "No, I smell something. Someone."

"Not . . . a body?"

"I'm not sure. The spell room has never smelled pleasant anyway. Watch the door. This is going to be loud."

He pulled the books from the case hiding the secret door and tossed them onto a chair. Then he grabbed a large stone from Sir Jason's collection and pounded the back of the shelves. The noise resounded in the room, but the door held fast. I kept expecting someone to come check on the racket, but everyone still must have been searching outside.

Philip winced and flexed his hand. "Still not strong enough."

"Are you holding back?"

"I don't want to lose my temper." His voice dropped. "What if the beast comes out again? I can feel it right now, prowling under my skin."

"You can control it," I said firmly. "The moon is waning; its influence is getting weaker."

Cold, faded laughter rolled around us. Sir Jason or the spirits?

Maybe it didn't matter. Philip flipped out his folding knife and offered it to me. I shook my head.

"Just in case," he whispered.

I reluctantly reached for the handle, but my fingers closed without touching it. I pulled my hand back. "What just happened? It felt like my hand went through it."

Philip took my fingers in his and gently turned my hand over, warming my chilled skin. "You're fine, see? You just missed. Please, I need to know you're safe."

I nodded, and Philip placed the knife in my hand. He braced himself and closed his eyes then slammed the stone against the door. The crash exploded in my ears, but he did it again and again. His face hardened, his eyes narrowed, his muscles strained. Sweat trickled over his forehead. The shadowy voices grew stronger.

Tear free. Break your bonds. Murder! Murder!

I tightened my grip on the knife's hard wooden handle and prayed. Philip growled and smashed the stone into the wood, knocking away long splinters. He dropped the rock and leaned against the shelves, panting.

"Philip?" I asked.

"I'm all right," he said between deep, raspy breaths.

"You did it." I exhaled, and my hand relaxed.

"Yes." He wiped his hair back from his face and smiled weakly. "I'll take back that knife." Then he peered through the gap and swore.

"Philip?"

"She's in there."

I squeezed my eyes shut. "Is she . . . ?"

"I don't know."

He slammed the stone into the shelf until it cracked away and widened the gap. He tore away another chunk of wood.

"Can you fit through?" he asked.

I peeked in. A pastel gown almost glowed in the darkness against the black of the altar. Poor Miss Ridgewell. "Yes, I'll go." I squeezed through before Philip resumed his pounding.

Distant laughter whispered from the silver rings. My heart jumped, and I squinted at the faint points of darkness hovering above the altar like black stars in a dim sky. They bobbed and rippled in shallow waves, as if resting on an invisible sea. I swallowed, wondering how deep Sir Jason's portal pierced into forbidden planes. Each tiny black spot seemed like a perdition waiting to yawn open and swallow me or spew forth legions of angry shadows. So many ways things could go wrong, and the way to make it right eluded us.

The shadows in the circle quivered and darted about. One flitted over Miss Ridgewell, who lay bound and still on the cold, black slab. She moaned, and my heart skipped. She wasn't dead, but what would the spirits do to her? If I breached the circle, though, more of them could escape.

Philip shoved his way in and ran to the edge of the silver circle, his lips curled back in a snarl.

"The spirits are waiting," I said. "What do we do?"

"I'll jump across, so the circle's disrupted as little as possible."

"You'll be in there with them. They were goading the beast on."

"I don't see any other choice. We have to move her."

The spirits hovered over Miss Ridgewell, and she whimpered in fear or pain. I couldn't move her. It had to be Philip.

"Be quick!"

He leapt over the barrier. I bit my fingernail. The shadows hissed and whirled around him. He stumbled. They gathered over his back like a dark cloak. He clutched his head and screamed, a yell of animal rage and pain.

"No!" I darted over the line to Philip's side. The shadows fled for the far edge of the circle, their voices a low murmur of anger. Philip panted, heat radiating through his coat, and clung to me like a lifeline.

"Are you all right?" I asked.

He nodded and pulled me against his chest, resting his chin on my head. I leaned into his warmth. When his breathing steadied, he eased his grip on me and lifted Miss Ridgewell from the altar. Her eyelids fluttered but didn't open.

The house moaned, and the floor shook. We raced from the circle. A few muttering shadows darted out with us as we crossed the silver line—a small price to pay for rescuing Miss Ridgewell.

Philip stopped at the door and kicked it, but it stuck fast. He lowered Miss Ridgewell to the floor. "I have to widen the gap." The dim light gave his grimace a wolfish look. I shivered.

He scanned the room. The light from the splintered door flickered wickedly over the skull. Philip frowned and touched it, yanking his hand back with a snarl.

"What's wrong?" I asked.

"The skull," he said slowly. "I remember digging it up."

Chapter Twenty-Eight

"You dug it up?" My stomach rolled.

"With Sir Jason. He said he wanted to do an experiment. Then he . . . removed the skull and carved those symbols. I looked them up behind his back. It was a spell." Philip squeezed his eyes shut and whispered, "He used it to kill his brother, and I had helped him."

I swallowed, remembering all the notes in my handwriting. "I was the one who researched those spells on using cadavers . . ."

"And I helped execute them. He was clever that way. He didn't want us to put it together."

The points of darkness in the circle stirred. Shadows mumbled in the corners, and I thought I caught the word *murder*. We'd helped a murderer. We might not have known his intent, but the filthiness of it coated my hands, and I had no way to scour away the stain.

Philip stared across the dim room to his desk. "He'd gone too far. I searched his papers and found the will. Then I understood. That's when everything went wrong."

"Or when everything went right," I said quietly. "We finally turned away from his madness."

Philip shrugged, apparently comforted as little as I was by the thought.

I scooted away from the skull and huddled closer to Miss Ridgewell. "Killing his brother made Edmund his heir. The will showed he wanted you for that role."

"Maybe I was just one option. Sir Edmund would be his heir without the false will, and if things went wrong with Sir Edmund, John might be a possibility. Sir Jason could keep experimenting until he got it right, as long as his heir was young and susceptible to his influence."

We looked at each other in the gloom. Radiant darkness pulsed from the black points in the circle. Memories opened before me of standing at the threshold of my room, alarmed and embarrassed that Philip had woken me in the middle of the night, shocked as he told me of Sir Jason's plans. The full weight of our involvement had crashed around me, stripping away the façade of our innocent dabbling to reveal the horror we'd steeped ourselves in.

"We had to stop him," I whispered. "He was going to perform the spell to steal our bodies."

We'd disrupted it, stolen the stone, but too late. As Sir Jason chased us, the wave of magic we helped unleash rolled through the house, across the estate. It grated our souls open, jarring them loose. I remembered screaming, and so much pain that everything else became a desperate blur. Keeping the stone from Sir Jason was all that mattered—the only thought I could even remember through the agony.

Miss Ridgewell groaned, and I stroked her hair. "He intended her as my replacement. Lady Henrietta doesn't want this. She warned us."

"It took her a day to do it," Philip growled. "We're getting Miss Ridgewell out of here."

His kick cracked the frame of the hidden entrance, and he jerked the door open. I held it as he tore the cords from Miss Ridgewell and carried her through.

"Hide the damage," he said. "We don't want anyone stumbling through and letting more darkness out."

I did my best to cover up the hole with stacks of books. Miss Ridgewell's hands hung lifelessly, and her head lolled as Philip shifted her.

"What's wrong with her?" I asked.

"Maybe drugged, maybe under a spell. Where do we take her?"

"Outside. It's the only place she'll be safe."

"Make sure the way is clear. I don't want to be seen carrying an unconscious girl around."

I dashed to the servant's staircase, peering down the steep, dim path to the bottom. It was empty, so I ushered Philip on. The walls moaned. Our boots played a staccato rhythm on the wooden stairs, sending echoes flying in the tall corridor. Wavering shadows swam along the ceiling. They drew near, like a net closing around us. Philip winced and hunched over Miss Ridgewell. The shadows laughed and hissed but pulled back without touching him.

We stumbled to the bottom landing. The door jumped open of its own accord to smash my nose. I reeled back, eyes watering. The door slammed shut. Philip swore and kicked it until it splintered. It creaked open. The shadows rolled ahead of us, a dark escort.

Panting and shaking, we reached the back door. I yanked the brass knob, but it slipped from my sweating hands. The walls undulated, dumping over a wash basin and shooting shards of broken blue and white porcelain around us.

Shouts sounded from down the corridor. Shadows raced toward the noise. The angry human voices turned to screams. Were the other spirits just causing trouble wherever they could, or was this part of their war with Sir Jason?

I rattled the stubborn handle. If we were caught like this, we'd probably end up arrested. Unless Sir Jason had the rats or servants tear us apart.

Philip kicked the door. Miss Ridgewell's hair swung wildly at the motion. "I'll break it to pieces, Sir Jason, if you don't let us out!"

He banged it again, cracking the wood, and it groaned open. We raced into the darkness.

"What now?" I gasped for breath, learning to hate my corset all over again.

"We need to see if she remembers what happened then get her to a doctor. Maybe we can make it look like she wandered off and hurt herself."

"Where?"

"In the woods, near the garden."

I followed him to a secluded spot where the ground dipped low, sheltered by overhanging trees. We slid down the steep embankment, stirring up the rich scent of loamy forest earth.

Philip laid Miss Ridgewell gently on the ground, and she stirred.

"Can we wake her?" I asked, stroking back her hair.

"We should try. Whether it's magic or drugs, we need to bring her back."

"Sir Jason couldn't have done this himself. Someone tied her up."

"He could be controlling anyone at this point. I'm hoping Miss Ridgewell can give us some idea of what happened."

She stirred, and her eyelids fluttered open.

"Let me talk to her," I said.

Philip nodded and stepped out of sight.

"Miss Ridgewell?" I asked.

She murmured, and her head lolled to the side. I wished I could let her rest, but this unnatural sleep couldn't be healthy, especially with Sir Jason prowling everyone's minds.

"Miss Ridgewell?" I turned her face to me. "Can you hear me?"

She groaned again. "Where?"

"You're in the woods. At Springett Hall."

"Edmund?" she asked.

"He's not here, but he's searching for you. What happened? Do you remember?"

"No." Her voice was slurred and raspy. "I drank some tea, and then it's all dark."

Not much help there. She was probably drugged, but anyone could have gotten to her tea. I bit my lip and looked at Philip, who shrugged.

"Let's get her to a doctor," he whispered. "Stay with her. I'll raise the alarm and have someone bring a carriage around."

"Edmund will come. He'll see me."

"I'll pretend I don't and keep the others back. You can slip out of sight if more people arrive." He sighed. "One other thing. We need to make the injury plausible." He drew his folding knife and cut his finger, smearing some blood by her ear.

I sat with Miss Ridgewell in the nighttime stillness, cradling her head in my lap. She groaned and stirred from time to time, but remained insensible even when shouts and the rattle of a wagon approached the little hollow.

"She's down here," Philip called over the rustle of branches. "I didn't want to move her without the doctor."

"Of course, of course," Edmund pushed his way through the trees. "Good, clear thinking. I can't . . . think clearly. I've let my head get too muddled. How badly is she hurt?"

"I don't know. That's why I didn't move her."

"Of course. Oh, my fair Elise!"

Edmund scrambled down the embankment, Philip on his heels.

"Muse!" Edmund exclaimed in a whisper. "Excellent, angelic creature. You've been watching over her?"

I nodded and backed away before Edmund drew close enough to feel that I was substantial. Philip gave me a quick wink, but otherwise ignored my presence. Edmund cradled Miss Ridgewell, tears shining in his eyes. My heart ached for them. Like Philip and I, they would never have peace as long as Sir Jason haunted their lives.

"The doctor's here!" someone called from the trees above, and a stocky man with a trim beard appeared at the top of the embankment.

I scuttled into the shadows of a large rock, behind a stunted tree growing in a wild corkscrew shape. The doctor grunted as he half-slid down into the hollow. I peeked out to see him bending over Miss Ridgewell, checking her eyes and pulse.

"There's a little blood, but I don't see the injury. She's warm and has good color, and her eyes are normal. She may have just fainted and hit her head."

"Then she's all right?" Edmund choked out.

"I can't promise anything, but the signs are encouraging."

"I'll take her to her room," Edmund said.

Philip cleared his throat. "If she takes a bad turn, it would be better for her to be near the doctor."

"I'd like to take her to my surgery for observation," the doctor said with a nod. "That blood could have come from her ear."

"Oh!" Edmund exclaimed. "I can hardly bear to have her away from me, though."

"You could go with her," Philip said.

I nodded. That would keep Edmund safe too.

Edmund glanced back at the house, and his expression hardened. "No. I cannot leave. My work here is not finished. I won't allow anyone to separate me from my love again!"

Philip's jaw tightened, but he spoke gently. "At least let Miss Ridgewell go with the doctor. The separation will be temporary, and of course you'll prove your love, suffering for her benefit."

Edmund's expression relaxed. "Yes, very well. Let's carry her up. Give her the very best care, Dr. Sanford. I'll pay for whatever's necessary."

"Of course, Sir Edmund."

Together, Edmund and Dr. Sanford lifted her, and Philip guided them up the embankment. I sighed and sank against the cool rock. That was one person safe from Sir Jason. Now, we just had to worry about everyone else. Philip returned a few moments later.

"Do you need a hand up?"

"Probably. These skirts weren't meant for climbing."

He took my hands, half dragging me up the steep sides of the hollow.

"She's going to be all right, then?" I asked when we stood at the top, catching our breath.

"I believe so, as long as they keep her from the house. Sir Jason must think he's close to finding the stone, though. He'll need it to finish the spell. Unless we're making him desperate."

My stomach soured. "He'll try for someone else."

"Yes, he won't stop until he's accomplished his goal." Philip stared at the house. "There's something bothering me."

"What's that?"

"The spell twisted our hearts' desires into a curse, but what about Sir Jason?"

"He wanted his wife back."

"Yes, but I think he wanted more: to keep her here forever. He wanted permanency, remember."

"Is there such a thing?"

"Probably not. He wanted to break the rules—we all did—and the spell altered us. It transformed you and me into something . . . not quite belonging to this world anymore, but it didn't uproot us from our bodies completely, as he'd intended. So, what happened to him?"

"He's haunting the house," I said.

"Is he? His body died, but the spell was meant to move his spirit into a new vessel, probably something here, in the center of his power." Philip looked back at the dark windows. "What if he went into the house?"

"What?" My hands turned clammy.

"It makes sense. We think he set the boundary of his spells somewhere on the estate, focusing all of his power here, and he made sure he would retain control of Springett Hall. What would seem more permanent to him? Besides, we've seen him in mirrors and windows, but no other spirits. There are times it feels like the house is watching us, fighting us." He met my gaze. "He's not just haunting the house. He *is* the house."

My stomach turned. "Then that was him I sensed in the walls. Can't we just . . . chase everyone out and burn the house to the ground, like you threatened? Wouldn't that fix everything?"

"Probably not. The boundaries of Sir Jason's powers seem to extend beyond the house, so I don't think it would banish him. For all we know, it would set the spirits free. We have to send them back before we could try anything so drastic. Even then it would be safer if we knew it would get rid of Sir Jason and not just destroy answers we might need."

My shoulders sagged. "You're right."

"I'll go back when it's light and get our things out of the house. We won't go back in unless we have to."

"I don't think I have a choice."

"We'll figure out why you're locked to that room and break the connection." Philip brushed back my hair, and I shivered with delight. I could believe anything when he said it with such confidence.

"Is there any chance the moonstone's in the antechamber still?" Philip asked. "That might keep you coming back to it."

"It makes sense, but we've searched the room." I closed my eyes, trying to piece together the fragments of pain-shattered memories from those last few moments. "It may just be because that's where I was when the spell hit."

"Maybe." He wrapped an arm around me. "If it comes down to it, I'll find another spell to undo Sir Jason's curse."

"Please don't." I huddled into his warmth. "Don't waste our second chance by condemning yourself."

He raised an eyebrow. "You think this is some sort of divine opportunity?"

"I do, and don't you dare laugh about it."

"I wasn't going to. If that's the case, though, why us?"

I chewed my lip. "Maybe second chances are always there. We just had to be brave enough to take ours by standing up to Sir Jason. I may be trapped by that room until we finish what we started, but I don't think magic's the answer."

"Hmm. Then I'll leave it alone for now." He yawned.

I caressed his forehead, frowning at his bloodshot eyes. "You haven't been sleeping enough."

"With Sir Jason waiting to take over my mind? No, but I'll try sleeping in the clearing after you leave, as long as I can wake before sunset."

"Rest now, and I'll watch you."

He hesitated, then stretched out with his head on my lap. I guarded his sleep and dreamed of the future as dawn snuffed out the stars and the sun broke over the treetops, scattering bright patches over the grass.

Moonset tugged at my core. I grabbed Philip's arm. I wanted to tell him to be careful, that I loved him, but my jaw locked shut.

"Lucy?" Philip asked sleepily. "Oh. I'll see you about midnight, then."

He smiled, but the words filled me with foreboding. Sir Jason would be strong the next time I awoke.

Chapter Twenty-Nine

Moonlight summoned me to a new night. Half a dozen footmen and maids with snarling mouths and blank eyes gathered in the dimness of my chamber.

"Philip?" I called.

"Lucy!" he roared from the doorway over the thud of knuckles hitting flesh. "I'm coming!"

Rough hands grabbed and tugged at my dress. I twisted away, stumbling over the edge of the rug. I didn't want to hurt the entranced servants, even if I could, but they forced me nearer to the walls, where Sir Jason waited. He knew our weaknesses so well. What would happen if he captured me? I would be his hostage. Would Philip resist his demands? I didn't think I would be strong enough to if he captured Philip. I would return the stone, even sacrifice myself to save him.

Shadows billowed in the corners, whispering and laughing.

Three maids surged forward, their pale faces slack. I searched for a way to defend myself, but there was nothing within reach. The girls grasped for my arms. I cowered back. Their clawing fingers swiped through me as if I weren't there.

Philip charged toward me. The maids turned on him, pushing him back and scratching at his face. He shoved one of them into the others, and I ran to him.

"Clever, Lucy! How did you . . ." His hand slipped into my arm. "Lucy?"

"I don't know! Run!"

He nodded and fought his way past the footmen. I ran through them. Why could I run through them? I didn't have time to ponder it. They were on our heels.

We raced down the stairs for the front door. George, the butler, shambled into our path, reaching knobby fingers after us. Philip grabbed him by the lapel.

"Don't kill him!"

Philip gave me a withering look and pushed the old butler aside. The door rattled when Philip yanked the knob, but it refused to open. I clasped my hands. The small army of sleepwalking servants tromped down the stairs. George growled and snatched at the edges of my dress, but his fingers only caught air.

Philip snarled and picked up a chair, smashing it through a window. He knocked out the rest of the glass and leapt out. I jumped after him.

He grabbed for my hand, grimacing when it slipped through his grasp, and motioned for me to run. His feet crunched over the gravel drive, but mine made no sound, nor could I feel the moist night chill or smell the sweet grass as we raced for the shelter of the woods. I felt a tug, like the house calling me back, but I forced myself to outrace it.

Philip panted and leaned against the white trunk of a birch at the edge of our clearing.

"What happened?" we asked at the same time.

He shook his head. "I came to meet you, and the hall was full of servants. I hope I didn't hurt anyone, but all I could think about was what they might be doing to you." He reached for me. "What did you do?"

I held out my trembling hands. "I don't think I did anything. I don't understand."

"All right." He took a shaky breath. "Let's . . . let's stay calm. Are you calm?"

"Of course not! I'm frightened. What's happening to me?"

"You're all right. Concentrate on me. Try to touch my hand. I won't let you slip away from me again, Lucy." He met my gaze, sending me a lifeline of courage. "I love you."

"I love you too." I focused on the memory of his touch, the calluses on his palm, the strength of his hands. My fingers trembled, but I kept my eyes on Philip's. The warmth of his touch melted over my skin, and he sighed. Then the sensation was gone and my fingers passed into nothing. I gasped.

"No!" Philip whispered.

My eyes burned, but tears wouldn't come. "I don't want to fade again."

Philip stared at me, his eyes betraying his helplessness and fear. The moon broke from behind a cloud, and its light poured over us, spilling through me. He glanced at the sky then back at me and groaned.

"It's the moon, Lucy."

"What?"

"The moon. The fuller it got, the more substantial you became, but it's waning again. I've noticed my senses getting duller too."

I shook my head, thinking of the few brief days I'd been real. Was that all I was granted? A teasing reminder of the life I couldn't have, the things I could never enjoy? "No, that's not fair! I don't want to go back to being dead."

"You're not dead, Lucy. Listen to me!" He paced, moonlight playing over his hair. "You said it yourself. We're in between." His eyes lit with excitement. "No wonder I could see you when no one else could—we're not just under the same curse, we're a little out of alignment with everyone else. You're worse off than me, maybe because you were closer to the stone or the spell room—"

"I don't care why, Philip," I moaned. "I just want to fix it."

He bit his lip. "I know, but I think understanding might help us put things right. It's rather amazing. It's as if . . . you're a reflection of the moon, a vessel for its light. That's why when you cried, your tears were little beads of light. It's probably why the shadows fear you."

"I don't want to be trapped in between. I don't want to be a vessel for anything. I just want to stay near you."

"I want that too, Lucy." He stepped close and put his arms out as if to embrace me. "I'm not leaving you. At worst, we wait for the full moon to come around."

A fresh panic rose in my chest. "What about the new moon? Will we have to start over, not knowing what happened, or who we are, or what we mean to each other?"

"I don't think so." He loosened his cravat and paced. "I think the moon woke us when it began waxing, and now we just have to ride the lunar cycles. You become more human, the fuller it gets, and I get less. That means I'll be myself when the moon is new. When you come back, even if you forget, I'll be here to love you and remind you." He stopped and leaned against the tree trunk. "Besides, I don't believe we're going to forget again. If so, we'd be remembering less, not more. We're getting stronger as we recover from the spell, just like Sir Jason."

"He's growing stronger, but without the moonlight, we're weaker."

Philip stepped closer and bent his face near mine. "But we're free to move about and to act. We can still defeat him. In the meantime, we can decide what to do with the stone when we find it." His shoulders sagged. "I've made some progress on that score."

He motioned me to the flat rock and pulled books and documents out of a large trunk. "I'm afraid I don't have much in the way of good news. Our problem is that we're caught mid-spell. The dark magic took hold of us, but didn't have time to finish our transformations."

"If it had?"

"Sir Jason and Lady Henrietta were supposed to take our human forms. I suspect that would've left you as pure moonlight and I as some spectral beast. When we interrupted the spell, though, it trapped us halfway, stripping Sir Jason's soul from his body, dragging Lady Henrietta from her rest, and leaving our forms floating between the mortal and spirit planes." He shook his head. "No wonder we forgot who we were—our identities were nearly shattered."

"There must be a way to break the curse."

Philip closed his eyes. The pain and defeat in his expression filled my chest with heavy dread. When he spoke, his voice was weary and low. "Magic's like a stream. It only travels one way."

I gaped at him. "You mean we're stuck? That isn't fair!"

"That was my thought too, so I went back through Sir Jason's notes. We can't undo the curse, but we can bend the spell. From what I can tell, we have two choices."

I tried to inhale, missing the feel of air tickling my throat, filling my lungs. "Well?"

"The first option is to redirect the magic in a course similar to its original purpose. It would transform us and bind us to this plane like an anchor. We'd be solid, real—human, at least on the surface. Neither of us would change anymore, though. That could mean . . . at all. We might not grow or age. It's possible we wouldn't die, or if we did, we'd stay on as ghosts."

To never change? We'd still be trapped, but we'd be together. Perhaps this was our chance to choose life, to be free from our foolish choices. We'd have nothing to fear, not loneliness nor monsters nor shadows. It meant doing magic one more time, but it wasn't as if we were creating the spells, just fixing them. Maybe oblivion wouldn't be able to touch us.

"If that's the closest we can get to a normal life, I might be able to accept it," I said.

Philip sighed. "It would also bind Sir Jason, Lady Henrietta, and maybe the other ghosts to this plane. We're tied together through the stone. We could get away from them, but we'd leave them free to haunt this place."

"Oh." I sank onto the rock, wishing I could feel its rough, solid surface. Philip stared at the moon, giving me space to make my decision. What were we supposed to do?

If we used Philip's spell, the ghosts should still be trapped within Sir Jason's boundaries. Maybe I could convince Edmund to desert the estate. That would likely keep people safe. Unless someone else came along, Edmund's heirs or children from the village daring each other to visit the haunted mansion. We might have to stay and guard the estate forever. Our lives wouldn't ever move forward.

We wouldn't be the only ones trapped, either. Lady Henrietta was more a victim in this than we were, and she'd be caught in limbo for eternity. Sir Jason might not give up on finding a new vessel, and we didn't know how far his reach extended. Was our freedom—a stagnant future—worth endangering Lady Henrietta's peace, Miss Ridgewell's safety, or Edmund's sanity? No, if we were willing to sacrifice everyone else for our own happiness, we weren't really any different than Sir Jason. That wasn't who I wanted to be.

My eyes stung. "It's not really a choice, is it?"

"I didn't think so." He smiled wanly. "I'm glad you agree."

I nodded, but my chest burned with repressed sobs. I wrapped my arms around my knees. "What's our other option, then?"

Philip wet his lips. "If we destroy the stone, its magic will dissipate."

"Wouldn't that free us?" I didn't dare grasp at the hope.

"I don't think so. From what I can tell, we'd stay as we are now, caught between worlds, governed by the moon."

"Then what would be the point?"

"Sir Jason could never use it, and we wouldn't be tied to him anymore. We could send him and the other spirits back, once we find the boundary and destroy it." Philip stared at his hands. "I'm sorry I can't find an alternative that ends better for us."

The quiet nighttime rustle of the forest whispered behind our painful silence. Maybe we hadn't given ourselves the option for a happy ending. Philip wasn't even sure if his plan would work. We could still lose ourselves completely or end up alone in the darkness.

And what of everyone in the house who depended on our decision? If we failed—if I failed again—what would Sir Jason's magic do to them? Philip's plan might be the only chance to save them. It was the only chance I saw for Philip and me too, even if it only gave us a few days near the full moon to hold each other.

"We started down this path a long time ago, didn't we?" I asked. "Maybe we can make some good come of our mistakes."

"I envy your optimism," Philip said. "For now I'll have to borrow it, because I've used up all my own."

"All that's mine is yours," I said with a smile. Though I burned with grief for everything we'd lost, a spark of hope deep in my chest whispered that maybe there was still some light on the other side of the darkness, like dawn after a moonless, starless night.

"We have a better chance against Sir Jason if we wait for sunrise to go back to the house," Philip said.

I nodded. "Will you read to me while we wait?"

He hesitated then pulled out one of my books. We huddled by

the light of his little lamp. His deep voice filled the clearing and soothed away my sorrows and fears for a few hours. When dawn streaked the sky in shades of indigo, Philip yawned and closed the book.

"Time to look for the stone. I don't want you to wake up again in that house."

"We've searched everywhere, and so has Sir Jason. What's left?"

He rubbed his face. "Let's try to piece together the timeline. Maybe we've missed something. He was performing the spell in the hidden room. We ran in to stop him—"

My spine tingled. "At what time?"

"What?"

"You said midnight was the best time for spells."

"Yes, that's probably when he did it, but what does that tell us?"

I leaned forward, trying not to shake with excitement. "I wake up every day staring at a clock forever pointing at twelve. That can't be what time they found Sir Jason's body, because they stopped the clock in the library at eight, and it's just down the hall. And if the magic had stopped the clock, it would have stopped all of them at the same time."

Philip chewed his lip. "True, but we already checked the clock."

I laughed. "We checked the case, but we never looked behind the face, in the mechanism. If I jammed it up there—"

Philip's eyes lit. "It would have stopped the clock and stayed hidden from everyone. Lucy, that's ingenious! Let's check."

Chapter Thirty

I passed through the woods behind Philip, a silvery ghost with my black hair flowing behind me. We crept out of the trees to the sound of birds chirping in the early morning quiet. Draperies covered the broken windows. We skirted around to the cracked side door.

Philip stepped in first then motioned to me. "Can you scout ahead? Warn me if someone's coming."

The corridors were quiet except the occasional creak of Philip's steps. The lingering malaise kept me checking the corners for shadows, even in the daylight. I came to the top of the first flight of stairs. John walked toward me from the bedrooms. I jerked to stop, but he didn't see me.

"Watch out, Philip!" I hissed.

He was too close behind. John gave a start when they nearly bumped into each other on the stairs. "Oh! Mr. . . . Ketley, isn't it? You're still here?"

"Yes, sir." Philip straightened to attention.

"I must commend your loyalty. It seems the evil rumors about this place and the vandalism of the past few nights have driven nearly everyone away." John tilted his head. "You're the only servant I know of who worked for our uncle."

"Yes, sir." Philip shifted. "He had trouble keeping staff on too. This place has an unsavory reputation."

"Hmm. They're like frightened children. My uncle was just a bit eccentric."

A rat crept onto the landing, whiskers twitching as it watched them. I tried to shoo it away, but it ignored me. I bit my fingernail. Sir Jason probably wouldn't attack Philip until we found the stone, but what about John? He was one of the potential heirs, but that might not be enough to keep him safe.

"The stories don't bother you?" John asked.

More rats scurried behind the younger Springett, so quiet he didn't notice their approach. Nearly a dozen of them watched him with empty black eyes. Philip paled and gave me a worried glance.

"Leave him alone, Sir Jason!" I called. "We're looking!"

"I've seen too much of the truth to be scared by stories," Philip said, "and I have no tolerance for threats." Before John could puzzle out the statement, Philip added, "Besides, I have nowhere else to go, and I'm outside most times."

"Oh, of course. What were you doing in here?"

"I heard there were some repairs that needed doing, and I'm pretty handy."

"Well, there's certainly work enough for you if you're willing. Good lad. I won't keep you."

John trudged on down the stairs. I watched the rats, wondering if Sir Jason believed that we were cooperating. The rats all turned to look at me one last time then scampered back into the shadows. Philip rubbed his face and motioned for me to follow him up.

"Sir Jason's making his intentions clear," he whispered. "Mr. Springett didn't notice anything at all, though. I wonder if he even would have seen you when you were tangible?"

"I don't know. I didn't run into him then."

Philip shook his head. "I'm all for practicality, but that man is so locked in his here-and-now thinking, he's missing things that are right in front of him."

"All the better for us," I said, "and maybe for him. That might be why Sir Jason's influence doesn't seem to affect him."

Philip nodded, and we strolled to the antechamber, making a pretense of searching along the way. It took all my willpower not to rush to the clock as soon as we entered the room.

Philip slowly worked his way to the case, opening it to peer inside, and nonchalantly reached behind the clock's face. I clenched my fists, trying to hide my excitement. The hope in his eyes dulled, and he shook his head slightly. My eyes stung, and I clasped my hands to my chest. We were out of ideas, out of time.

Philip pressed his lips together and twisted to reach further. I bit my knuckle. His eyes widened. Relief gave fresh color to his weary face, and he pulled his fist out and shoved it in his coat pocket with a look of triumph. I covered my mouth to keep from shouting my happiness.

"Let's keep looking." His shoulders drooped in exaggerated disappointment. We'd need to have a talk later about his acting skills. Hopefully Sir Jason's awareness wasn't all that keen. I would rather have rushed outside, but Philip meandered around the room in a half-hearted search.

I wandered toward the doorway and glanced back. Would I ever wake up in this antechamber again? A strange sense of loss settled over me as I thought of our hidden rooms upstairs. We'd probably never remember everything, and it seemed like robbery to forget a part of our lives, even if it hadn't been an entirely pleasant one. There must have been bright moments, even in the darkest times. At least the experience gave us each other.

I turned into the corridor and nearly walked right through Edmund. I swallowed and faked a smile. What was he doing in this part of the house?

"Lucy!" he exclaimed. "My muse! How I've missed you." A gleam crept into his eyes that reminded me too much of Sir Jason. "What are you doing?"

"Edmund!" I said, hoping Philip heard and stayed back. Deep, purple circles hung under Edmund's eyes, and his hands moved constantly, yanking his sleeves, sweeping through his hair, adjusting his haphazard cravat. "I'm concerned about you."

His eyes softened again. "Of course you are, my muse. Of course. I haven't felt much myself lately. I can hardly write anything, and it mostly comes out in gibberish. I dream wild things—of carrying Elise to a dark altar so we can be together, yet it isn't her anymore. Of boys who become dark beasts, and of you. I'm seeking you. Seeking something. I can't find what."

My throat tightened. How much longer before he was just a shell with nothing left of himself, of his beautiful passions and talents?

"Edmund, I think the air here is unhealthy for you, and for Elise. Listen to me, please. You should close up the house and leave. Go stay by the sea. Take John too. You all need rest. Refreshment."

"I won't leave!" Edmund's voice boomed, not at all like his own. "Everything I've worked on for so long is here, within my grasp. I just have to find it." He pointed at me, and I took a step back. "You know where it is. You could tell me. If you won't, I'll squeeze it out of you."

"Edmund!" I squeaked. "Please, listen. It's at the sea. If you take John and Elise away with you, you'll have everything you need. There's nothing here but sad, old memories and ghosts. You can't write here. You need a new beginning."

He stepped back, pale, his breath haggard. He shook his head, and sense returned to his eyes. "Perhaps you're right. This place may not be healthy for me."

"If you've ever believed me about anything, Edmund, believe me about this."

"Will I see you again?" His gaze was sorrowful.

"I don't think so. Elise will be your muse now. You'll write poems that are fresh and hopeful again. If you spend time on your other responsibilities, you'll find your mind more clear."

"Other responsibilities?"

"Yes, Edmund. How can your inspiration come pure and clean when you're neglecting your duties? Don't stop writing, but remember what kind of man you're meant to be. For Elise, for your family, for your tenants."

Edmund looked chagrined. "You speak truth, as always, my muse. I'll consider what you say."

He glanced into the antechamber as he walked past, and I held my breath, but Philip was nowhere to be seen, and Edmund moved on. After a long moment, the door to our rooms creaked, and Philip trotted up next to me.

"You know, for a false muse, you don't do a bad job."

"Why, thank you," I said. "And you're not a bad counterfeit assistant gamekeeper."

We grinned at each other then burst out laughing, dissolving the tension lingering in my chest.

"Fair enough." Philip rested his hand on his coat pocket. "Let's go."

We headed downstairs to the front door, making aimless gestures of searching along the way. When we crossed the threshold of the house, the building gave a great shudder and a moan rolled down its corridors, becoming a roar.

Philip and I looked at each other with wide eyes.

Inside, a man screamed in terror. Philip whirled back.

"Wait!" I tried to grab his arm. "You can't let Sir Jason have the stone."

He paused at the threshold. "You want me to let Sir Jason hurt them?"

Another visceral scream echoed down the staircase.

"No," I whispered.

"I'm coming!" Philip shouted.

"Stand aside!" Edmund called.

He staggered down the stairs, carrying John over his shoulder. Philip ran to help, but Edmund brushed past him and raced outside. A dark mass of writhing, hissing rats scurried after. Philip slammed the door on them and followed Edmund to the grass beside the drive. Edmund lowered his brother to the ground, tears on his cheeks as he examined him.

I stifled a gasp. John's face and arms were gashed and bleeding. His eyes were open in a dazed stare. Edmund was injured too, his hands oozing blood. "I'm sorry," he whispered to his brother. "First Elise and now you, hurt by this cursed place because I was lost in a daydream."

John groaned.

Edmund glanced up. For a moment, his gaze rested on me, but he blinked rapidly and shook his head, turning to Philip.

"Ready my horse. I'm taking him to the doctor."

Philip nodded and ran to the stables. Edmund took off his cravat to stanch the worst of John's injuries, pausing once to glare at the house.

Philip hurried back, leading a sleek, chestnut brown mare. The poor creature rolled its eyes in terror and strained against the lead to stay as far from Philip as possible. He helped Edmund mount and hefted John, who whimpered at the movement. Together, they positioned the semi-conscious man in front of Edmund on the skittish horse.

Edmund got the mare under control and looked down at Philip. "The other servants have deserted Springett Hall. I'm appointing you temporary steward until I return." He glanced at the house. "Though that may not be for some time. I recommend staying away from the building. It's not a healthy place."

"Yes, sir," Philip said without a trace of disrespect.

Edmund gave him a nod and rode away. Though he had to steady his brother in the saddle, he sat with his shoulders straight and his gaze focused ahead. I silently wished him luck. I would miss him, but not too keenly.

"Will John Springett recover, do you think?" I asked Philip.

"I believe so. He's been through something traumatic, but none of the individual injuries looked serious." He scowled at the house. "Let's get away from here."

We hurried to the woods. In the cover of the trees, Philip threw back his head with a sigh of relief and yanked out the stone, smooth and luminescent in the morning light. Almost translucent. Rather like me.

"We did it!" I yearned to throw my arms around him but settled for smiling foolishly.

"You did. That was brilliant!" His grin faded. "I hate even touching it, though. I can feel the dark magic."

"We're almost through with it. As soon as we get somewhere safe, you can put it down and not touch it again until tonight."

"Right." He slipped the stone into his pocket. "I'll search for the boundaries, and maybe tonight, when the moon rises, we can end this for good."

I smiled and glanced back at the shadowed house as the moon touched the western horizon. We wouldn't be free of the curse, but at least we'd no longer be trapped in Sir Jason's grasp.

Chapter Thirty-One

I melted into being among a haze of midnight blacks and greens, illuminated only by the light of the rising moon. No walls surrounded me, no sofa or clock met my gaze. An owl flew overhead, a silent shadow crossing the silvery light. Springett Hall loomed behind me.

I was free! I hovered at the edge of the woods, near the place where we hid Miss Ridgewell. A moonstone globe sat on its pillar before me, strangely dim in the moonlight. A circle of dead grass and wilted plants surrounded it. I reached toward it, transfixed by its luminous beauty.

"Lucy?" Philip called from the trees.

I snatched my hand back. "Philip! I'm here!"

He crashed out of the shadows. "Lucy! I hoped you'd come to the clearing. The stone is there, after all. Is this where you appeared?"

"Yes, right by this pillar. The globe is moonstone like the others, and I almost feel as if it's pulling at me. I don't think it's a coincidence."

"Neither do I." He frowned and held up the small stone, comparing it to the white globe. A black spark jumped between them. We recoiled and stared at the stones.

"There's a connection," Philip said, frowning at the smaller one. His eyes narrowed. "I have an idea." He pulled a paper and pencil from his pocket and sketched a map of Springett Hall. "We know of four stones." He marked their locations, a trapezoid around the house: maze, mausoleum, garden, and woods. "They look pretty even, except it's a strange shape."

I remembered the candle sticks spaced evenly around the silver circle.

"If there was a fifth one . . ." I said.

"Yes! There might be." He tapped his pencil where the lake

sat in front of the house. "Right here. They would make a perfect pentagram, and you appeared by the point closest to where I had the small moonstone—the keystone. This is probably the boundary, Lucy! I was looking for arcane symbols on the ground. I never thought about anything like this. The moonstones are all tied together, along with us and the ghosts."

I edged away from the off-white globe. "If we're all bound together, why can we go past the pillars and he can't?"

"Hmm. Sir Jason's spirit is trapped in the shell of the house or he might be as free as we are. I think it's only because his magic reaches to the boundary stones that he has any influence outside of the house. His summoning spell tied the ghosts to the boundaries of his power too, so they're trapped with him. He only connected us to the stone, not to the boundaries."

"Do you think having something left of our physical forms gives us an advantage?"

"It probably does." Philip straightened and smiled. "Maybe it shields our raw spirits, gives us extra strength against Sir Jason's magic."

I glanced through my hand uncertainly. I didn't feel strong, but as a ghost I'd been able to stand up to the spirits, and having some semblance of a body made me feel more powerful. Sir Jason possessed the form of the house, though. Was that an advantage for him, or would he be more dangerous if released from his prison? I didn't want to find out. We just had to make certain he never escaped.

"What does this mean for undoing the spell?" I asked.

"If we've found the boundary, I think we're ready to banish Sir Jason. Let's make sure we're right about the fifth moonstone before we get our hopes up, though."

I nodded, and we hurried to the lake. It shimmered under the moonlight, rippling in the breeze like black silk.

Philip leaned forward, squinting into the blackness. I scanned the dark water, wishing for a moment I had his supernatural senses, though I didn't want the price that came with them. We strolled the shoreline. Philip glanced at his map from time to time, trying to pinpoint where the stone would have to be.

"There's nothing out there," I said.

"No, I think I see it!" Philip pointed to a spot in the middle of the wide lake. I saw a flash of white in the dark waves, just under the surface of the deep water.

Philip's grin was bright in the moonlight. "It's underwater. That'll be a trick to reach. Sir Jason obviously didn't want it found."

"Then we have what we need?" I shivered, not certain if what I felt was excitement or dread.

"I think so." Philip chuckled. "That was quite a promotion Sir Edmund gave me, but I'm about to fail miserably at the job. Let's go."

I followed him to the clearing. Philip had set up a lean-to shelter with our few possessions arranged inside. Not quite the cottage in the woods he'd promised, but still a place I wouldn't mind haunting. He lit his lamp and leafed through papers and books, mumbling to himself.

"All right. It looks like we have to place the keystone in the center of the pentagram then destroy the outer stones. The keystone we break last. That will banish the spirits. Jason should be trapped within the house, so if we burn it down after the stone is destroyed, I think it'll force his spirit to move on too."

"You think?" I asked.

He shrugged. "We're trying to dismantle a spell that was put together wrong from the start. I'm as sure as I can be."

Philip's tone was steady, and he gave me an earnest look. He wouldn't make such a claim lightly.

"Very well. Where's the center?" I asked, but I already knew what his map would show.

He tapped his pencil on the house, exactly over the library. "The spell room, of course."

"And we have to put the stone back there?"

"I would guess in the center of the circles, on the altar."

"Naturally." I sighed and squinted at the dark battlements looming behind the trees. "But not until the sun comes up."

"Yes, though it won't give us much time."

"Sir Jason will know what we're doing."

Philip smiled grimly. "It will make for an exciting morning."

I wrapped my arms around myself. "What do we do until then?"

He set the paper aside. "Want to take a walk?"

"A walk?"

"We might as well." The cheer in his voice sounded forced, and I saw the worry in his eyes.

I nodded. It might be our last chance to spend time together. We strolled down the lane to the sleeping village, where a couple of cottage windows glowed with candlelight. I wondered what kept the inhabitants up at an hour that belonged to ghosts and witchcraft. Tending the ill, worrying, fighting, loving?

"Do you envy them?" I asked.

Philip looked away from the stars sprinkled across the night sky. "Who?"

I shrugged. "Everyone."

He chuckled, then his voice grew serious. "I suppose in some ways. They don't have to carry this burden, this knowledge. They're not frightened of the hordes of Hell spilling out over the world, but they have their own fears, of being hungry or lonely or hurt. They might be able to spend every day with the one they love, but do they appreciate how precious it is? How often do they reach out just to feel how warm and real they are? They don't have to worry about turning into a beast, but they still carry their own demons, and maybe they're not even aware of it." His voice dropped to a whisper. "Like my father."

We stood in silence. Was it ever possible to appreciate something fully without facing the threat of losing it? Loss showed us how much—or how little—things really mattered, but its results were painfully final. I wondered about my family, who I remembered only in broken images. Did they miss me? Even without the specific memories, I ached at not having them to share my joys and fears.

"Would you want to see your father again?" I asked quietly.

Philip bit his lip. "I don't know. He wasn't always bad." He stared down the road. "I dream about it sometimes. He used to play with us or take us to watch the puppet shows on the street." He smiled. "Sometimes he'd even bring us home some little treat from the bakery, if he had a few extra pennies. When times got hard, it brought out the worst in him. I suppose my own beast found its way in as I watched him. Not that it's any excuse for my choices." His shoulders rose in a sigh. "I have an image in my mind—so clear I think it must be truth—of him a broken, gray little man all alone. The beast takes a terrible toll."

He looked down, and I stood close to him—all I could do to offer comfort.

"What about your family?" he asked.

"I can only imagine what they must think of me, running off." I shook my head. "I believe they wanted what they thought was best for me. They just didn't realize my dreams were different from theirs. Now that I know myself more, I wonder if things would be better with them. I may never have the chance to find out."

Philip's gaze traced my face. "I'm sorry your dreams didn't work out the way you hoped."

"I haven't given up hope, especially since I have you."

"Always," Philip said seriously. Then, he grinned. "As long as the moon shines, we'll have each other. It's so painfully romantic I may actually have to write a poem about it."

I laughed. "Then I'm happy, and I expect to see your poem."

The pale gray of dawn crept overhead, washing away the fainter stars. Philip stared up. "Shall we?"

I nodded, and we walked back through the woods as birds heralded the new day and the sun brought true colors back into the world. I tried to drink it in—perhaps the last dawn I would ever see—but I felt cut off from it all, as if I were already gone. In a way, I suppose I was. Philip's feet crunched over the paths and rustled through the undergrowth. I forgot to lift my skirts as they slipped through the bushes and brambles.

We reached the outer edges of the estate. Springett Hall cast a long shadow over the lawn. By moonset, I hoped to see it a smoldering ruin. As the sun highlighted its battlements and chiseled gray stones, I felt a twist of regret at destroying something so ancient and dignified. The artwork, the piano, the painstakingly embroidered tree offering its dilemma of knowledge versus life: all would be purged together. Dark shapes rippled from window to window. I shivered and stepped back. It had been beautiful, but now it was defiled.

Philip put his hand in the pocket that held the stone. "About an hour's work, and it'll all be done."

I bit my fingernail then pulled my hand away. Maybe if I left my nails alone, they'd grow back. My habits had ruled my existence, even as a ghost, but I could change them. This was going to be our new beginning. I wasn't running away anymore. I nodded at Philip, longing to hold his hand as we walked forward.

Chapter Thirty-Two

We stood in the grand entrance that had received the house's guests in centuries past. The staircase swept up in front of us, daring us to climb. Without the bustle of footmen and maids, the house had a crypt-like stillness. Dinginess hung over everything, a film dulling the gilded splendor and leaving it old, worn, tired. I sensed, for a moment, that it would welcome the funeral pyre we planned for it.

Sir Jason and the other ghosts wouldn't accept our interference so easily, though, and they might guess our plans. Could they act against us while the sun shone? I trembled for myself, and even more for Philip, who suddenly seemed vulnerable in his tangible frame.

His muffled footsteps were the only sound as we crept to the hidden chamber. The black altar reflected the hazy light from the window. Philip rubbed his face with a shaky hand, and my chest tightened. Was he less certain than he acted? If we made a mistake now, perhaps we'd end up more cursed than before, trapped in our non-human forms or banished forever to oblivion. We could be separated, never to see each other again.

I reached out to call Philip back, but he lunged across the circle and dropped the white stone on the altar. He scurried back to my side, eyes fixed on the moonstone.

Dark haze rolled across the stone's milky surface, and a roar shook the house. Bits of plaster rained onto Philip's dark hair. Voices hissed and whispered from every corner, angry and excited.

"I thought the shadows had to sleep during the day." My voice trembled.

"Maybe the magic is calling them forth." Philip motioned to the door. "Go!"

We raced back down the corridor. Lady Henrietta stood at the top of the stairs, watching us with an angry frown. I wanted to stop, tell her we were making things right, but Philip dashed past her, unseeing. I followed with an apologetic glance. We reached the grand staircase.

The house quaked, sending Philip reeling against the bannister. It creaked, threatening to give. I gasped and rushed for him, but he found his footing and bounded down the rest of the steps.

Darkness bled into the corners of the entrance hall. Rats dashed after us, claws clicking on the tile, as we raced for the front door. A few leapt onto Philip's clothes. He shouted and tried to shake them off as he ran. The door slammed shut.

Philip charged for the boarded-up window. He slammed into the boards, but they held. He staggered back, clutching his shoulder. I swatted helplessly at rats gnawing at his legs and back. Philip smashed his forearm into the boards until they splintered and tore them away to plunge outside. As soon as he did, the clinging rats dropped lifeless to the ground.

I hesitated at the window, then jumped out, trying not to touch the house. My skirts brushed through the broken window frame. I felt a jerk and tumbled to the ground next to Philip. He examined his bleeding legs. I muffled a gasp at the sight of the many gashes.

"None of them are deep," he said, his voice tired.

"Are you all right?"

"I will be." He glared at the house. "It's begun."

He wiped the blood from his hands on a wrinkled handkerchief and led me to a shed, where he pulled out an ax to check its edge.

"Will that break the stones?" I asked.

"They're not that hard." He hefted the ax. "Which one first?"

Morning shadows reached across the estate. "The most difficult ones first, in case Sir Jason can do something to stop us."

"The one in the lake?"

We jogged to the edge of the water. Waves stirred the murky surface and lapped at our boots.

Philip frowned. "I can take a boat out, but it's going to be hard to find the right spot once I'm on the water. Could you walk across the surface?"

"Walk on water? Really, Philip, isn't that a bit sacrilegious?"

He laughed. "I don't think so. Saint Peter did it too, and those little water bugs. Besides, you're made of moonlight. It doesn't sink. Give it a try."

I took a deep breath and placed my boot on the water, willing myself to feel the surface. It was only habit telling me I couldn't do it. My foot held. I quickly placed the other in front of it, whirling my arms to keep my balance. Philip cheered, but I didn't dare look back, focused on convincing myself that the dark, shifting water could hold me. I took a few more steps and straightened with a grin.

Philip pushed out one of the rowboats beached on the shore. The oars splashed in a steady rhythm to mark his progress.

I squinted through the blinding flashes of sun bouncing off the water. The moonstone globe shimmered below the lake's surface, supported by an underwater pedestal.

He maneuvered the boat near me and laughed. "You're making me look like an idiot, rowing this thing around while you stroll beside me."

I smirked and held out my hand. "Do you want to get out and walk with me?"

"I wish I could."

Philip set the oars down. They clacked against the side as the boat rose and dipped. He lifted the ax. The waves hissed—an angry, almost human sound—and they rolled higher, bucking the boat. Philip grabbed the side. The ax slipped from his grasp with a loud plunk. We stared into the murky depths as it glided down, stirring up a brown cloud of silt when it hit bottom.

"There's no other way." Philip sighed and stripped off his boots, coat, waistcoat, and shirt. I blushed and glanced away, but not before admiring his muscular chest.

He jumped over the edge of the boat and bobbed up to slick back his dark hair. With a halfhearted smile, he drew a deep breath and slipped into the grasp of the turbid water.

His form wavered beneath me, and more plumes of silt muddied the water as he searched. Finally, he shot for the surface, the ax clutched in his hand. He sucked in a deep breath when he broke free. Then he hefted the ax, nodded to himself, and slammed it into the stone.

A painful jolt cracked through my core as if I'd been shocked. I winced, and Philip gasped. Waves lashed across the lake, and the boat pitched and skittered away on rising swells. Clutching the ax, Philip darted after it.

The waves roared, and I thought I heard an echo of Sir Jason's voice in the sound. They surged higher, rushing through me, waist high. I flailed to keep upright. They battered Philip beneath the surface. I shouted and searched for him in the cloudy water. He splashed free, gasping for breath. I cried out in relief. Wiping his eyes with his free hand, he turned the wrong way.

"Philip! Over here!"

He pushed toward me. Dark waves shoved him back, forcing him toward the deep, churning water in the center. I struggled to follow the boat. If only he could reach it! He gritted his teeth and swung his arms in long strokes until he reached the madly spinning vessel. He tossed the ax in and tried to pull himself after it. The lake flung the boat up, nearly capsizing it.

Philip grasped the side of the tiny vessel and panted. "This will keep me afloat, at least. Can you guide me back? I can't see the shore over the waves."

"Of course."

I pushed across the roiling lake, sinking lower into the dim water. Murky waves thrashed me. I clenched my trembling hands. I didn't have to obey the waves. They couldn't even dampen my dress. Onward.

The waves fought to tear the boat from Philip, but he clung to its side, hauling it in the direction I pointed.

Finally, we got close enough for him to stand. He staggered forward against the pounding waves. Lifting the ax and soaked clothes from the boat, he stumbled to shore and collapsed on the grass, gasping in long, shaking breaths.

I pressed ahead, but the water pulled at me, dragging me into the darkness. I stumbled. I could almost hear Sir Jason's angry whispers in the ceaseless beat of the waves. *Foolish, incompetent girl.* My torso sunk, half submerged, until I could hardly move.

I gritted my teeth and pushed forward, each step bringing me closer to the shore but deeper into the inky water, until it swallowed me to my shoulders.

"Lucy!" Philip called, staggering up from the ground.

It was like walking through a deep mire, but I kept my eyes on him. I found the shallows, and the water's grip on me loosened. I stumbled into Philip. He tried to catch me and clutched his fists in frustration.

"Are you all right?" he asked.

"I think so." My hands shook, and I dug my fingers into my skirts.

"You were right. If we'd waited to do that one last, I never would have made it."

I squeezed my eyes shut. Sir Jason was still so strong, and now he'd be ready for us. "The tomb next, then?"

"Yes, before Sir Jason has more time to react."

He pulled on his socks, boots, and damp shirt and tossed aside his drenched coat and waistcoat. Shivering in the morning cool, he hefted the ax over his shoulder and pressed on to the mausoleum with a faltering jog.

Chapter Thirty-Three

Philip heaved the mausoleum door ajar and brought a rock from the woods to brace it.

We stepped into the gloom. When Philip reached the caskets, the ground jolted. Philip caught his balance against Sir Jason's sarcophagus. The door slammed shut. Philip swore and pounded it with the ax handle. I hovered at his side. I could go through, but Sir Jason might be able to catch me here as he had in the house.

A glimmer flickered over the walls, driving back the deep shadows. My back prickled, and I turned. Lady Henrietta watched us from the corner.

"Philip!" I hissed. "It's Lady Henrietta."

He jumped. "Where?"

"In the corner."

"You're awfully calm for someone trapped in a tomb with a ghost," he said to me, his voice tight. The faint glow cast a green pallor over his face. "Just because she can't hurt you . . ."

"She's not trying to harm us," I said, but a glance at her angry face made me wonder. I swallowed. "*Are* you?"

She folded her arms, her expression guilty.

I clutched my chest. "Why? We want to help you. Don't you want to be free?"

She stared at me for a long moment before nodding once.

"Then why?"

She pointed to her sarcophagus, jabbing at the words *Beloved wife.*

Of course, Sir Jason and Lady Henrietta had truly loved each other. She didn't want to see him hurt, even if she didn't like the things he'd done. I couldn't know Sir Jason as he'd been, but I could believe that, once, he hadn't been such a monster.

"I'm sorry," I whispered. "Maybe if we send you both back, you'll be together again."

Her eyes filled with tears, and she shook her head. She pointed to herself and up, then gestured at Sir Jason's sarcophagus and pointed down.

I shuddered. Had Sir Jason's attempts to bring Lady Henrietta back doomed them to be apart forever? I believed he'd have a price to pay, but I felt a stirring of sympathy for his foolishness, especially since I'd made some unwise choices myself. "Is there any hope, on the other side? Everyone has some good and some bad, don't they?"

She shrugged and tapped her head.

"You don't remember." At least it wasn't a no, and Philip and I were trying to make the most of our second chance. How terrible it must be, though, to fear for the welfare of someone you loved, not certain what horrors might await them. "Where there's love, there must be hope."

She covered her face, shoulders trembling.

"I know you still love him," I said softly, "but he opened a rift between the planes. We have to send the spirits back before they hurt more people. Fixing his mistakes—keeping him from making more—is probably the best way to help him."

She covered her mouth.

"Will you help us?" I asked.

She shook her head.

I pressed my lips together. "Then, will you at least stay out of our way?"

Her teary gaze found mine, and she nodded. Then her airy figure faded, leaving me blinking at the dark.

"Well?" Philip asked.

I rubbed my eyes. "I think she's decided not to interfere. Can you see?"

"A little, from your glow."

I saw only perfect darkness, but Philip's eyes were sharper than mine. Perhaps they were even attuned to moonlight. His boots echoed on the floor as he walked toward the second moonstone. He grunted, and a crack rang through the tiny space when he shattered the white globe. I gritted my teeth at the flash of pain.

"That's done, at least." He sighed. "If I don't starve before the next full moon, I guess we'll find out if this is an effective cage."

"Philip!"

He forced a chuckle. "You should go, try to find help."

"I'm not certain I can get out if Sir Jason's reach extends this far. Besides, no one's left on the estate, and not many people are able to see me." My throat tightened, and I lowered my voice. "Even if they could, it's dangerous to bring anyone here. He could take control of them, and the moonstone's in the house." I rubbed my forehead. Had we played into Sir Jason's schemes after all?

"What's your plan, then?" Philip asked.

I bit my lip. We had the ax, but the stone walls were thick, and so was the door. Philip was strong but exhausted. I shivered as a possible solution presented itself.

"Moonlight makes you stronger?" I asked in a hushed tone.

"It seems to, but the moon is waning."

"You said I'm a vessel for moonlight, so maybe I can help. Hold out your hand."

I stretched my fingers for him in the darkness. If this didn't work, it could be days or weeks before Philip escaped. Even if I were outside, there was nothing I could do to protect the moonstone. Sir Jason might still be able to use it, and Philip and I could lose each other, become mindless specters—moonlight and beast—and Sir Jason would go on hurting people.

"My hand's over yours," Philip said. "Do you feel any different?"

"No," I whispered. My shoulders sagged. "Do you?"

"Maybe. It could just be wishful thinking, but I feel like I have more energy. Is it uncomfortable for you to pass through someone else?"

"I don't feel anything. It's only strange because I know it *should* be." Could it hurt me, if Philip drew away my strength? Even if it did, this might be our only chance. "Let's try."

I followed his voice until he said I was standing inside his space. It seemed like it should have been awkward, or even intimate, but I couldn't see or feel. The screech of metal on metal made me jump and set my teeth on edge. I braced myself. I had to stay with Philip.

I winced as each sharp clang echoed in the gloom. He paused, panting for breath. My lungs ached in sympathy, and I tried to breathe with him. He grunted and slammed the door again. It bowed along the edge. A sliver of light pierced the darkness.

Philip's face was cheek-to-cheek with mine, his skin flushed red. He clenched his teeth and struck at the weak spot. The deformed door groaned and bent under his blows. I blinked at the bright light and stepped to the side.

"It worked!" Philip rested his hands on his knees and gasped for breath, his head hanging down. "It didn't hurt you, did it?"

"No." I glanced at my hands. Did they look a little less substantial than before? Maybe it was just my imagination. Either way, it was too late to worry about it now. "I think I'm fine."

"That's a useful trick." Philip wiped his forehead and forced a smile. "Where now?"

"The rest should be easy, right?" My voice sounded more pleading than I liked.

"I hope so. We'll just go around the circle."

I nodded, and we headed for the moonstone on the edge of the woods. I looked at it closely before Philip hoisted the ax up.

"It looks different," I said. The sun struck it full on, but shadows swam deep in its shimmering blues and yellows.

"Yes," Philip said. "The other markers are reflecting the keystone."

I shuddered. "At least we know for certain they're connected."

He nodded and splintered the stone apart. I cringed and turned away.

We ran to the gardens. Buds swelled on glossy green bushes, revealing glimpses of pink and red. I concentrated on them as Philip raised the ax. Pain flashed through my body when he smashed the ax down.

Philip rubbed his face. "One more, then on to the house."

We walked to the maze, its tall hedges as imposing as fortress walls. The deep shadows seemed to be waiting for us. I shrank back.

"You don't have to come," Philip said.

"I want to." I glanced at him, taking in the set of his jaw, the weary slump of his shoulders. I wouldn't let him go alone.

He nodded, and we stepped into the deep shade. Philip jogged through the narrow maze, skidding to a stop at a dead end.

I stared at the tight-knit branches, their tiny, spoon-shaped leaves bristling upright. "I thought you knew the way."

"I do," he said slowly, back-tracking to take a different path.

"Are you certain?"

We came to another dead end. Something rustled behind us. We looked back. A dark green wall blocked us in.

"Yes," Philip said. "I'm certain."

"Sir Jason trapped us," I whispered.

Philip sighed. "I have an ax."

He hefted the weapon and searched for a thick branch. He swung, and the ax lodged deep in the wood. Branches whipped and clawed his face. He clenched his jaw and jerked at the ax, but the greenery vined around his arms. I gasped. He recoiled, and the branches ripped his sleeve, raking bloody gashes into his arms.

The handle of the ax protruded from the hedge. Philip lunged for it, but it disappeared under the slithering branches. The dark wall of green rustled, tightening around us. I whimpered and stood arm to arm with Philip, my form melting into his.

"Run," Philip said.

"I'm not leaving you." My voice trembled.

"You're going to stand here and watch me get choked to death, then?"

"No." Never that. I'd fight with everything I had to protect him. I jumped forward and pushed my hands into the hedge. They stuck fast. I gritted my teeth and strained back. My arms sank further.

"Lucy?"

"I can't get out," I whispered.

Philip tried to grab my waist as he had before, but his hand slipped through. "Lucy! No!"

"Look!" I struggled to keep my voice steady. "The other branches stopped moving. He can't fight both of us out here, in the daylight. Go! Please!"

Philip snarled and shoved through the hedge toward the center. The bush pulled me in. I twisted to slow the draw. I jerked my shoulders as my face neared the dark branches. If only I had enough substance to dig my heels into the ground.

Thick, cloying silence smothered everything in the maze. Had Philip made it through, or had I sacrificed myself just to let him get trapped at the next dead end? I gritted my teeth and squirmed against the pressure constricting my arms. If Sir Jason consumed us both, would we be together or forever kept apart? The more I fought Sir Jason, the better chance Philip had.

A jolt surged through my body. The branches went slack, and I tumbled back.

"Philip?" I called.

He pushed his way through hedges, his face bleeding from several scratches. "You're free!" He grinned and wiped the sweat from his forehead. "I broke the stone—shoved it off the pedestal."

"I think that's when the branches let go."

"Let's get away from here."

We fled the confines of the maze.

"Just one to go," Philip said, picking leaves out of his hair.

We turned to stare at the house. Its dark windows glared back.

Chapter Thirty-Four

Everything looked just as we'd left it, but the brooding silence sharpened when we stepped through the front doors. We tiptoed across the dim entrance hall and started up the stairs. The ground rumbled, and the staircase pitched. Philip swore and ran up two steps at a time. I raced after.

The stairs groaned. A section in front of us crumpled as if a giant had squeezed it. Philip jumped back against the bannister. It cracked, and a rail clattered to the floor far below. Philip swayed on the edge of the one-story precipice then leapt for the broken landing above. His boot slipped on the ragged edge. I clasped my hands. He threw himself forward, digging his fingers into the carpet and kicking the open air. He swung a leg up and rolled away from the gaping hole.

I stared at the chasm separating us.

"Come on!" Philip called.

What would happen if I fell? I wasn't quite alive, but I still might be able to destroy myself, and oblivion waited for me. Feeling very mortal, I gathered my skirts and jumped for the landing where Philip waited. I stumbled past him and looked back at the yawning hole. My vision blurred at the height, and I swayed. Philip beckoned me onward, up the second flight of stairs.

The staircase twisted, snapping the steps, but Philip clutched the bannister and climbed up with me gliding after. Walls rumbled and doors slammed open around us in the corridor. We clung to the center of the hall. The floors rolled, forcing Philip into a drunken stumble.

In the library, books tumbled off trembling shelves, smacking Philip's hunched shoulders. He smashed open the splintered door to the spell room. The moonstone sat on the black altar in the center of the circle, darkness seeping across its pale surface like black blood.

Dark, clawed hands reached from the floor and the walls, but they recoiled from my presence, clearing a path. Philip grabbed a paperweight from my desk and glanced at me. One last question passed between us, a moment of uncertainty. There was no turning back after this. I nodded once. His face twisted into a snarl, and he slammed the weight onto the stone.

The crack echoed through my soul, piercing my chest and burning through my limbs. Pulses of black flashed across my vision. Philip screamed and doubled over, clutching his head. I stumbled back, falling through Sir Jason's desk before I caught my balance. The house rumbled and groaned as if it would fly apart.

Something tugged at me. A storm of shadows clouded the ceiling and walls, howling and hissing. I covered my ears and cowered as the clawing forms pulled into a funnel over the altar. The grasping hands vanished into the swirling darkness. It circled tighter and tighter, breaking into black points that blinked out like snuffed candles.

The maelstrom faded as the last of the darkness dissipated. Philip and I straightened. Lady Henrietta hovered in front of me, her eyes full of sorrow. I wanted to reach out, tell her I was sorry for Sir Jason, but she raised her hand in a farewell and stepped into the circle, disappearing in a flash of light.

The groaning stopped, and everything sagged into stillness.

"I think the spirits are gone," I whispered.

A howl of rage shook the walls. Philip scrambled to his feet, but the ground jolted under him. He staggered into the library, shielding his head from the books tumbling over him. The cases exploded, showering glass over the room. Tiny shards glimmered in Philip's hair. He shook himself off in the hallway. The floor pitched and cracked. Splintered timbers burst from the floor.

Philip dodged the jutting spears of wood and raced for the staircase. More of it had collapsed, leaving gaps too wide to jump. Philip looked back down the hall toward the servant's staircase.

I nodded, and we fled down the rumbling corridor. The door at the end jammed shut. Philip slammed his shoulder into it until it cracked apart. The staircase yawned below us like the gullet of a hungry demon.

"Are you certain it's safe?"

"No," Philip said. "The only other choice is to jump out a window, and this seems a bit better." He gave the hallway a speculative look.

"What?"

"You'll be able to get out, regardless of what happens, but you can't light the fire. I could start it now, up here, and then we'll find our way out."

"But if something goes wrong . . ."

He refused to meet my eyes. "We have to get the job done. This way we make sure." He glanced up with a weak grin. "It'll be good motivation to keep moving."

Caught between laughing and crying, I squeezed my eyes shut. We hadn't come this far to fail, but I couldn't lose Philip. "It's too dangerous."

"Don't worry, Lucy," he said, his tone gentle. "One way or another, things will work out. Maybe I'll get my chance to haunt you."

My stomach twisted. "Don't say that! We're both going to make it!"

The floor lurched, and Philip stumbled. He grimaced. "Lucy, I want nothing more in the world than to hold you again. I'll do everything I can to make that happen, but we have to stop Sir Jason."

He was right. If Sir Jason won, we'd lose each other anyway. I nodded. "Very well. Do it."

Philip raced back for a lamp and slammed it against the wall. The paraffin painted a dripping stain over the wallpaper. He struck a match. The fire flickered, threatening to die, but he held it steady until it burned brightly. He tossed the blazing match into the oil pooling on the floor, and watched the fire spring to life.

"Go!" We dashed for the servant's staircase.

The house screamed as the flames licked up the wall. Tendrils of smoke rolled to the ceiling.

We fled down the rocking stairs. The house shuddered and wailed like a dying beast. Philip stumbled and braced himself on the shaking wall. A whoosh of flame exploded out the door above us, accompanied by the sounds of shattering glass. The gaslights!

The stairway pitched, and Philip tumbled down, smacking his head against the edge of the steps. He slammed onto the landing, his head at an uncomfortable angle and his arm outstretched.

"Philip!" I screamed.

He moaned but stayed still.

"Philip! You have to wake up!"

Black smoke trickled down around us. Blood from Philip's head darkened the floor. I covered my mouth. My eyes stung. No, no, not like this! We were so close!

"Please wake up." My hands passed through him as I tried to shake him awake. "I love you. Don't leave me!"

His eyes fluttered, but didn't open.

"You can't leave me! Wake up!" My useless fingers trembled over his head. I couldn't stop the blood. I couldn't do anything.

Smoke rolled through the stairwell, every bit as terrible as the shadows had been.

The beast! The inhuman, maybe immortal, part of Philip. The shadows had roused it, but it was moonlight that gave it strength. I'd given it strength, and now Philip needed it again.

Flames climbed down the walls. Another explosion rocked the stairwell.

I knelt to whisper in Philip's ear. "Don't let Sir Jason win, Philip. If you stay here, Sir Jason will kill you." I gritted my teeth, hating what I was about to do, but the beast was stronger when he was angry. "Don't let him hurt you like your father did."

Philip's eyes rolled, and I trailed my hands through his chest, searching for the beast awakened by moonlight, feeding it my strength.

His eyes snapped open, dark and animal. He growled at me and jerked up. Blood matted his hair to the back of his head, but he seemed unaware of the pain. He snarled at the staircase and started up, smoke billowing around him.

"Philip, no!" Had I only awakened the beast: pure anger and vengeance without any rational thought? I'd been able to hold it back last time, but that was with Philip fighting it. I threw myself in front of him. "Philip! We have to go! Wake up! Please!" I held out my hands. "It's me, Lucy. Please, remember."

His snarl relaxed, and he blinked at me. "Lucy?" He clutched his head, grimaced at the blood on his fingers. The floor jerked again, and he caught himself, looking pale. "What happened?"

I wanted to cry in relief, but we weren't safe. "You fell. The fire's spreading. We have to get out."

He nodded and followed me down the last flight of stairs. The whole house had become a crackling nightmare of flame and smoke. Philip coughed and hid his face in his sleeve. The heat burnished his face red.

He crouched down to crawl under the smoke toward the back door. A snap echoed above the crackle of fire, and a smoldering timber crashed in front of us. Philip winced back from the fire. We had to go out through the front. I forged ahead, making certain the path was clear, and Philip struggled behind until we reached the entrance hall.

The flames before us surged up and swirled together into a human form. Or rather, the absence of one. It was like a solar eclipse, the light of the fire spilling around the edges of the incredible blackness looming in our path.

The shape had no mouth, but it laughed over the snap and hiss of the fire. Sir Jason's laugh. Philip recoiled as though burned. I couldn't feel any heat, but the form shimmered like searing charcoal.

The burning figure lurched forward. Philip scrambled back, coughing and choking on the noxious air. I shrank back too. I didn't know what might happen if the darkness touched me. I could vanish in the blackness or burn away. What would happen to Philip? Unlike me, he didn't have the hope of waking up with the next moonrise.

"Lucy!" Philip gasped as he stumbled farther away.

The fire raged behind him. There was no going back. There never had been. Forward had always been the only way out.

"Run, Lucy! The fire won't hurt you!"

I thought of the next moonrise finding me alone in the woods, with Philip gone somewhere far beyond my reach.

"I'm staying with you. If I touched you, would it give you strength?"

"I can't fight a burning shadow. Not even if I were a beast."

No, the only thing that drove away shadows was light.

Moonlight.

Against Sir Jason's darkness, faint veins of luminescence threaded through my hand into my fingers, shimmering like the moonstone. I was no longer a creature of blood, but a vessel of light. Even the reflected light of the moon was stronger than darkness and shadow. I'd slowed Sir Jason in the maze, and now the shell of the house no longer sheltered the raw blackness of his soul. I stepped forward and thrust my hands into Sir Jason's shadowy chest.

We screamed together as light and dark flared between us like arcs of lightning. The searing pain, deeper than muscle, nerves, or bone, threatened to rip me apart, snuff out my existence. I couldn't jerk free. Flecks of light drifted from my skin like white ash and blinked out. Black haze clouded my vision. My knees buckled, and I threw myself forward into Sir Jason.

His shriek loosed a shower of burning embers from the ceiling. The darkness spearing me withdrew. I caught my balance. A soft light pulsed from my hands, much fainter than before. My throat tightened. What happened to a vessel when it was empty?

Sir Jason's monstrous black form shuddered and shrank back, moaning like the flaming timbers cracking and collapsing around us. He shook himself and roared, lurching forward.

"Get out, Philip," I whispered.

"Lucy?"

"I can do this!"

"I know. I was just going to say I love you."

We shared a smile. Then, I pressed forward, grabbing Sir Jason's wavering form. My scream echoed Sir Jason's. The floor above cracked and disgorged a roaring avalanche of sparks and cinders. I caught a glimpse of Philip in the yard beyond, coughing and gasping the fresh air. Safe.

The front of the building sloughed down in a curtain of flame. Philip stumbled farther from the house, shouting and beckoning. I edged toward him.

When I released Sir Jason, his form grew, gathering a pillar of darkness and flame that lanced the collapsing roof. If he escaped, no one would ever be free. He'd stalk every nightmare, haunt the dark corners of the world, seeking his immortality in shattered lives and dreams.

I couldn't fail at my task this time, even if it destroyed me. He wanted me to think myself incompetent, but I saw both of us now in our true forms, and knowledge was strength. Knowledge was life. Death could hold no terror for me, nor the blackness of oblivion. I was light, and shadows fled before me.

I rushed Sir Jason, grasping his burning torso. I froze, unable to scream. Pain, like needles drawing threads of ice and fire, pierced my insubstantial flesh. The flames fell over us with a deafening rush, and light and darkness whirled together in a blinding firestorm that consumed everything.

Chapter Thirty-Five

I hadn't expected the moon to shine in heaven, but it illuminated the darkness with a silver glow, revealing a clearing full of purple flowers. I gasped and looked around.

"Lucy!" Philip leapt from the flat rock by the stream and stumbled to a stop before me. His clothes were blackened and ragged, his face streaked with soot, and his hair singed away in patches, but I'd never seen anyone so handsome. He radiated life. We'd survived! I wanted to cry and shout for joy, fall into his arms, but all I could do was grin.

He reached for me. "I need to know you're real. I was afraid you wouldn't come back!"

"What happened? I remember the fire and darkness."

"The house collapsed. I kept waiting to see you come gliding out of the wreckage, but you didn't. I tried to go back—"

"You burned your hair and clothes. It looks frightful and dashing at the same time."

He choked out a laugh and shook his head. "As the flames died down, I picked through the timbers. I was terrified that we'd somehow broken the curse after all. Can you imagine? I was praying that we were still cursed, because if not . . . It was so hot, I didn't know if there would even be a body to find. Some people from the village came to help. They thought I was mad, but I didn't stop searching until it was too dark to see. My only hope was that the moon would bring you back."

He rubbed his eyes. Scratches and burns marked his knuckles. I reached to comfort him, and my fingers slipped through.

"I'm sorry, Philip."

He straightened. "No, don't be. You're here. That's all I prayed for. I debated waiting for moonrise by the house or the broken stones, but somehow it felt right, that you'd find your way here. To the place you love."

"To the person I love." I smiled at him. "I think no matter where you'd waited, that's where I would've appeared. Where I'll always appear."

He grinned, his teeth bright against his soot-stained face. I lifted my hand, longing to sooth his burns, and saw a flash of something white in his singed hair.

"What's that?" I asked.

He ran his fingers gently over his head and found a shard of moonstone. "It must have gotten tangled there when I smashed the stones."

I shuddered. "Throw it away . . . unless it's what's keeping me here?"

"Its power is gone. It has no hold on us anymore," he said gently. "We've been given a second chance, remember?"

"You're right." I watched the wisps of smoke still drifting over the landscape from the ruins of the house. "We're still cursed, but it's almost like we have a gift too."

"Maybe we made it into a gift by what we chose to do with it." A thoughtful glint lit his eyes.

I folded my arms and smiled. "What are you scheming?"

"Nothing specific." He gazed at the night sky. "We're creatures of the moon now, aren't we?"

"Creatures of light," I said.

"Yes. We're going to have to find a way to control the beast when it comes out, but the rest of the time I can use its strength. I can help people who are helpless like I was. And you . . ."

I held up my hands and looked at the moonlight falling through them. "This isn't quite the same type of gift as being strong."

"There are different kinds of strength," Philip said softly, "and the physical sort only gets you so far."

"I suppose I can go places other people can't. If there are shadows, I can stand against them."

"You really did make a pretty good muse. Maybe sometimes what people need most is an encouraging whisper in their ear. As long as you promise to be my muse too." He winked.

"Always." I smiled. "In fact, we're going to run away and get properly married as soon as the priest can see me."

"I have no objections to that plan."

I looked down at my translucent hands. "We might have trouble building a normal life, though."

"Who cares about normal? We're together. We're free. We can go anywhere the moon shines."

We glanced up at the silver orb casting its protective light over the clearing. Here beyond the edge of darkness, hope shone all around us.

"That's a splendid idea, Mr. Ketley."

"Why, thank you, Miss Tregarrick. If you'll be so kind as to turn your back, I'll get properly attired, and we'll start off immediately."

"Right now?" I asked, turning.

"Is there a better time?"

I smiled at the moon. "No. Right now is perfect."

Discussion Questions

1 How did Lucy's habits affect who she was and what she did? To what extent do people's habits influence them for better or worse?

2 Lucy felt useless and helpless when she didn't have a physical body. Have you ever had an injury or illness that made you feel less capable? In what ways do a person's physical limitations affect their interactions with the people around them?

3 Lucy sold herself short in the past and ended up in a dangerous situation because she didn't understand her own worth. How can knowing who we are and what we're capable of help us to be strong in the face of challenges and negative influences?

4 How did Lucy turn her weaknesses into strengths? In what ways can real-life weaknesses also be strengths?

5 Would Lucy and Philip's futures have been better or worse if they had found a magical cure for their conditions? Why?

Acknowledgments

This book exists because of the encouragement, support, and insight of many wonderful people.

The manuscript benefitted immensely from the tough love and thoughtful feedback of my critique groups: current and former members of UPSSEFW—Sherrie Lynn Clarke, Dustin Earl, Lauren Makena, and Finley Svendsen—and the Cache Valley chapter of the League of Utah Writers. I'm afraid to try to name all of you who gave input on this story for fear of missing someone, but thanks especially to Tim Keller and Eric Bishop for their ongoing encouragement.

I also owe a huge debt of gratitude to my beta readers: Karen Brooksby, Karen Chrystostom, Justin Clarke, Rosario Gil, Arielle Hadfield, Danette Hansen, Sarah Isert, Jocelyn McDaniel, and Karena Potter. Thanks for helping me sift the wheat from the chaff.

The encouragement and advice of the online writing community, especially the Neurotic Writers Support Group, helped me navigate the labyrinthine path to getting published. Thanks also to Brenda Drake, L.L. McKinney, and everyone involved in their online pitch contests, which helped me refine the story, as well as to Molly Elizabeth Lee, who chose me as her Pitch Wars alternate and was a fantastic mentor. And a shout out to National Novel Writing Month, the impetus to getting this story on paper.

I'm very grateful to the team at Cedar Fort for bringing this book to life: to Emma Parker for getting excited about Lucy's story, and to Angela Decker, Justin Greer, Kelly Martinez, Michelle May, and everyone else who did an incredible amount of work behind the scenes.

Most important, thanks to my family: to my parents who read me stories as a child, and to my usually patient children and my eternally patient husband, Dan, for making it possible for me to chase my dreams.

About the Author

E. B. Wheeler grew up in Georgia and California. She attended BYU, majoring in history with an English minor, and earned graduate degrees in history and landscape architecture from Utah State University. She taught and wrote about history and historic preservation before venturing into fiction. *The Haunting of Springett Hall* is her first novel. She lives in the mountains of Utah with her husband, daughters, various pets, and garden full of antique roses.